Praise for *A*

"It is precisely style and atmosphere that give *An Honest Living* so much electricity and dimension. Like the best noir practitioners, Murphy uses the mystery as scaffolding to assemble a world of fallen dreams and doom-bitten characters. . . . Murphy's hard-boiled rendering of the city is nothing short of exquisite. . . . For anyone who wants a portrait of this New York, few recent books have conjured it so vividly. For those who demand a straight-forward mystery without any humor, romance and ambience, well, forget it, Jake, it's *literature*."
—*The New York Times Book Review* (Editors' Choice)

"Set amid New York's rare-book trade, this slow-burning debut crime novel is also an atmospheric homage to the film *Chinatown*."
—*The New Yorker* (Best Books of 2022)

"Murphy's engrossing debut is a book made for summer reading. It's a smart, leisurely read, richly layered with movie references and philosophical reflections."
—*Star Tribune*

"[Murphy] knows not just where the bodies are buried but how readers want them to be discovered."
—*The Boston Globe*

"This territory-marking debut is seductively steeped in motifs reminiscent of the golden age of noir. Fans of the genre will likely be nodding appreciatively from the introduction of a mysterious woman out to get her husband, which launches this story, to the concluding shot of a vintage car."
—*Shelf Awareness*

"A rain-spattered love letter to a bygone New York, a wry homage to a classic of the genre, and a delightfully meta work of

neo-noir . . . Brilliantly assured . . . The mystery is beautifully constructed, the writing crackles on every page, and Murphy's portrait of early 2000s New York City is nothing short of exquisite. If you're looking to lose yourself inside a smart, atmospheric literary crime novel, *An Honest Living* will not disappoint."
—*Lit Hub* (Favorite Books of the Year)

"A lyrical valentine to New York City and literature."
—Oline Cogdill, *South Florida Sun-Sentinel*

"Quietly brilliant . . . The novel explores the ways in which we're nothing without our curiosities—even if those curiosities, in the end, undo us."
—*Los Angeles Review of Books*

"A smart and stylish ode to literature lovers everywhere."
—*Chicago Review of Books*

"An excellent mystery novel . . . if you're interested in a smart mystery, in a page-turner of a book that's 'meta' in a good way, you won't do wrong to pick up Dwyer Murphy's *An Honest Living*."
—*Mystery Tribune*

"*An Honest Living* is a novel about ambition and obsession, shadow and light, smoke and mirrors—a shimmering, often surprising, exploration of how fact and fiction reflect one another until the boundaries disappear."
—BookTrib.com

"If Cara Black's Aimee Leduc smoked pot, or if Michael Connelly was from Paris, their books might read a little something like Dwyer Murphy's absurdly entertaining and extremely literary debut."
—*CrimeReads* (Most Anticipated Crime Books of 2022)

"*An Honest Living* is an electrically good time meted out in fine, sharp, crackling prose that somehow manages to be an homage, a send-up, and a reinvention all at once."

—Téa Obreht, author of *The Tiger's Wife* and *Inland*

"A witty, observant debut that's as much a love letter to New York as it is a slick noir."

—Andrea Bartz, author of *We Were Never Here*

"Dwyer Murphy's *An Honest Living* is a deliciously smart PI novel set in New York's antiquarian book world that channels Chandler and *Chinatown* to take us into a recent past that already feels like a bygone era. A brisk, funny, and fabulous debut."

—Adrian McKinty, author of *The Island*

"Dwyer Murphy's *An Honest Living* is the lawyer-book-collector noir you never knew you craved. Evocative and suspenseful, the book hums along in an unusual space somewhere in the constellation of Roberto Bolaño, Julio Cortázar, and the Coen Brothers—an ontological puzzle nested inside a shaggy dog story, or the reverse."

—Jonathan Lethem, author of *Motherless Brooklyn*

"A terrific book." —Don Winslow, author of *City on Fire*

"Dwyer Murphy beautifully intertwines a noir mystery with the lore of New York. A captivating, beguiling novel right up to its shocking conclusion."

—Samantha Downing, author of *My Lovely Wife*

"*An Honest Living* feels like an instant classic—a polished gem of a PI novel that's wonderfully atmospheric and full of wit. Fast-paced as this book is, it's also a smart read you'll want to savor."

—Alison Gaylin, author of *The Collective*

"*An Honest Living* is a sublimely literate, literary, and crafty novel—
an homage to PI fiction that transcends the genre with style and
inspiration to spare. Lovers of crime fiction and lovers of books
of all types (as well as those of us who miss the old Brooklyn)
will be equally transported."

—Ivy Pochoda, author of *These Women*

"A many-layered, fascinating novel about the collisions that come
with city living, of people devoted to old books and those de-
termined to construct new buildings. In this swift-moving noir
debut, Dwyer Murphy has conjured a fantastically vivid homage
to New York."   —Idra Novey, author of *Those Who Knew*

"*An Honest Living* is a superb debut novel by a supremely gifted
writer. It's as if Roberto Bolaño and Lawrence Osborne got together to reimagine *Chinatown*. I was as gripped by the mystery
at the heart of this book as I was by Dwyer Murphy's perfect
prose."   —Jonathan Lee, author of *The Great Mistake*

"The best kind of private eye novel—one that feels wholly modern but timeless. Dwyer Murphy evokes the greats like Elmore
Leonard and George V. Higgins without losing his own sharp
voice. A stylish, memorable debut."

—Alex Segura, author of *Secret Identity*

Dwyer Murphy is the author of *The Stolen Coast* and the editor in chief of *CrimeReads*, *Literary Hub*'s crime fiction vertical and the world's most popular destination for thriller readers. He practiced law at Debevoise & Plimpton in New York City, where he was a litigator, and served as editor of the *Columbia Law Review*. He was previously an Emerging Writer Fellow at the Center for Fiction. *An Honest Living* is his debut novel.

AN HONEST LIVING

Dwyer Murphy

PENGUIN BOOKS

For Carolina and Eloisa

VIKING
An imprint of Penguin Random House LLC
penguinrandomhouse.com

First published in the United States of America by Viking,
an imprint of Penguin Random House LLC, 2022
Published in Penguin Books 2023

ISBN 9780593489260 (paperback)

THE LIBRARY OF CONGRESS HAS CATALOGED THE
HARDCOVER EDITION AS FOLLOWS:
Names: Murphy, Dwyer, author.
Title: An honest living / Dwyer Murphy.
Description: New York : Viking, [2022]
Identifiers: LCCN 2021054807 (print) |
LCCN 2021054808 (ebook) | ISBN 9780593489246 (hardcover) |
ISBN 9780593489253 (ebook)
Subjects: LCGFT: Noir fiction. | Novels.
Classification: LCC PS3613.U7284 H66 2022 (print) |
LCC PS3613.U7284 (ebook) |
DDC 813/.6—dc23/eng/20211222
LC record available at https://lccn.loc.gov/2021054807
LC ebook record available at https://lccn.loc.gov/2021054808

Printed in the United States of America
1st Printing

Designed by Amanda Dewey

Part I

THE DECORATION
OF HOUSES

1.

The first time I saw Newton Reddick he was drunk outside the Poquelin Society building on East Forty-Seventh Street. He was leaning against a cart filled with dollar paperbacks, looking pretty jaunty and not at all minding the cold. The Poquelin was a private library that had been started during the Gilded Age by a gang of bank clerks who believed reading during their lunch hours would make them into Rockefellers and Carnegies. It was still a private library in 2005 and also a scholarly society dedicated to the art, science, and preservation of the book, whatever that meant. Its membership rolls included a lot of academics, rare-book dealers, and a few unfashionable, old-money eccentrics who came down from the East Seventies on the chance of finding a literary evening. Newton Reddick was one of the book dealers, or had been anyway. I was told he was mainly a collector now. "Collector" seemed to me an overly polite term but at least it conveyed the fact he wasn't making any money at it. He was living off his wife, a much younger woman with inherited wealth to whom he'd been married just under ten years. That earned him a certain pride of place among the library's members, it appeared. He was holding court outside the Poquelin, leaning against that paperback cart and waving a cigarette around in his free hand while a trio of red-faced old-timers hugged themselves against the cold and seemed to hang on his every word. His voice, a crisp tenor, bounced off the skyscrapers and carried across the street to where I was standing with a coffee from the bodega on the corner of Fifth and Forty-Seventh.

He was talking about somebody named Richardson. "The problem with Richardson," he was explaining to the others, "is the man has no sense of history, no feeling of a higher purpose. He thinks a Pulitzer makes a book worthy."

The error of that kind of thinking was obvious to the little assembly outside the Poquelin, and before stubbing out their cigarettes and going back inside, they had a few more choice words for the Richardsons of the world, the ones who can't see the forest for the trees, who wouldn't know greatness if it walked up and punched them square in the nose. They were a lively bunch, those old bookmen. On another night, under different circumstances, I might have enjoyed listening to their fool talk. It was a Tuesday in November, just before Thanksgiving. All over the city people were drinking more than they should and visiting friends. It was the season for parties and parades and little flings that didn't mean anything.

Normally I kept away from divorce work, but the case had come to me on referral. A woman calling herself Anna Reddick had shown up at my apartment the previous week, on Thursday evening, saying that she had met my friend Ulises

Lima at a party. Ulises was a Venezuelan poet who sent me a lot of work. He thought it was awfully funny that I was a lawyer, not an artist or a writer or a poet like everyone else. He thought it was even funnier that I refused to work any longer at one of the big law firms in Midtown and was trying to make a go of it on my own in a careless and not very profitable way. He had sent around a good number of prospective clients for consultations. There were always people in his world who needed help and hadn't any ideas where to begin looking for it. Some had money and others would try to pay me with paintings or meals. Sometimes I took them up on it, though I didn't have an eye for that kind of thing, the visual arts, and I would have to ask someone, Ulises or another friend, to come by and appraise the thing for me. It was an endless cycle of imaginary economies, small profits, and favors done impulsively or not at all. That was fine so long as your rent was controlled. Anna Reddick came with cash in hand—ten thousand dollars. She had the bills neatly stacked and facing the same direction, the way a waitress arranges her tips at the end of a shift.

"Catch him at it," she said, "and you'll get a bonus, paid out in cash, check, wire, money order, however you'd like, your choice." It had been a lean few months, and I was in no position to turn her down. Something about the case bothered me from the start. Whatever it was, I managed to put it out of mind.

The job, as I understood it, was essentially a controlled buy, just as you might have bought some weed on the street or a box of Motorolas that had fallen from the back of a truck

or a hundred other things whose provenance and ultimate
destination you couldn't be sure of. Only in this case the
weed was books. I had a list of five titles written for me on
a note card. Any one of them would do, she said, and I didn't
need to worry about actually buying them, so long as I received an offer of sale from her husband, the one she was
about to divorce, and would swear to it in an affidavit. She
believed he was trying to sell the books, which belonged to
her. They had been passed down by her family. Her attorneys
said she would need some proof to back her claim and advised
her to get another lawyer involved, in order to cloak the job
in privilege. That was just the kind of thing a divorce attorney would think of. Layering the secrecy until the truth was
almost meaningless, so thoroughly and finally obscured you
could hardly find your way back to daylight. The titles of the
books were unusual. Long, ornate, and grisly. *The Last Con-
fessions of Tom Mansfield Who Corrupted and Murdered His Ser-
vant. Notes on the Investigation of Charles Mandell and of the Final
Killing of Luke M. Johnston.* They were legal volumes, apparently.

On the surface, it was all very sensible. A lawyer in need
of books. It happens all the time.

I followed Reddick and his disciples inside and went up a
narrow staircase to the third floor, where there was a banquet
hall decorated with chandeliers and threadbare rugs thrown
over the hardwood floors. It was debate night at the Poquelin
and open to the public, though from the looks of it I was the
only one who had taken them up on the offer. Seventeen old
men in shirts buttoned to their chins. A few paintings on the

walls and books on display. The speeches had already been delivered and the members had moved on to the drinking portion of the evening. I kept an eye on Reddick from across the room. He was long and slim and made an effort to hold himself up, propping his hands on the small of his back the way a pregnant woman does. He was sixty-three years old. His wife was in her early thirties. I suppose a part of me was bristling and judging him harshly, thinking meanly that if a man that age had been lucky enough going on ten years to hold on to a young woman of independent means, a really quite attractive woman in her own peculiar way, he ought at least to be modest and civilized about it when she finally came to her senses. He shouldn't go around selling her family's books. There was nothing worse than a shameless cuckold. Anyhow, that was the train of my thoughts as I carried a drink around the banquet hall and told the old men my story, which was meant to lure in Newton Reddick and eventually did. The story was more or less true: I told them I was a lawyer, an IP litigator. I was interested in the history of the Poquelin Society, but more immediately I was interested in buying a few books to decorate my office, preferably legal books, historical, rare.

Reddick came over with two drinks, one for each of us, and introduced himself.

"I understand you're just starting out," he said.

He gave me the drink and we touched glasses. His grip was unsteady and his smile looked like the smile of a man who naturally trusts the strangers he meets and their intentions. There was a guilelessness about him, that is, or else the whiskey had stripped him of whatever he had. We spoke for a while, in general terms, about the Poquelin and about the city. He wanted to tell me how it had changed. In those years you often found yourself in conversations like that, and what the other person was really trying to say was that they had been there, in New York, a long time, longer than you quite possibly, and that was supposed to mean something. I didn't feel that from Newton Reddick. He was telling me about the city, but his memories seemed innocent somehow, the way you might talk about a childhood home that had long since been sold. In that way we came back around to the subject of books and the collection I was considering acquiring.

"It's an exciting moment," he said. "I remember my firsts. I was sniffing around Book Row—you wouldn't know the shops, this was before your time. I worked in the back office of an insurance company but after hours I often found myself wandering downtown, toward Fourth Avenue, without really knowing why. I owned books, of course. Club editions. Boxes of dog-eared paperbacks. I had never given any thought to building a real collection, a library of my own."

He had an odd glint in his eye. If I had been feeling mean I would have said it was greed, but the conversation had softened me, and I felt it was more generous than that, his memory.

"What was the book?" I asked.

"*The Decoration of Houses*," he said. "Edith Wharton and Ogden Codman, 1919 edition."

"Was it very valuable?"

"Not especially. But it set me on a course." He smiled

sadly and ran his hands down the curve of his back. "You remember the books you lose more than those you keep. Steel yourself."

I took a slow sip from the whiskey he'd brought and pretended to be steeling myself for a long, melancholy future of book acquisition and loss. It didn't seem so dire to me. His library of late had been paid for with his wife's money and now that he had lost it, or was about to lose it to the divorce attorneys, at least he had his scholarly society to go to and they would treat him well and listen to his stories. All over New York, across the world, old men were suffering worse fates than that, disease and penury and loneliness, and they didn't have any book societies to go to.

That's what I told myself, though the truth is I liked him. He had an odd, upright quality.

"Do you care for Edith Wharton?" he asked.

"I like her fiction. The rest, I haven't read."

"Most people your age don't know anything about her. I'm told she's unfashionable these days. Not modern enough. I can't imagine how that figures. The only book of hers anyone wants to collect now is *The Age of Innocence*, and then they only want it because it won her the Pulitzer. They collect sets. Pulitzers, Bookers, Nobel laureates. A man was here last month who said that he owned every nonfiction Pulitzer finalist with a blue dust jacket. Can you imagine it?"

I couldn't. I didn't try to. After a while I said something vague about *The House of Mirth*. It was a book I had read many times at another stage in my life, when I first arrived in New York and was living by the Brooklyn Museum, above a jerk chicken shop that sold dinners on flatware through the window. You would bring back the clean dish the next day if you wanted more. It was a long subway ride to law school on 116th Street and I used to read all kinds of books over and over again. Edith Wharton was the best of them. Sometimes you would miss your connection to the local, reading books like that, and you would have to backtrack or walk from Harlem.

For some reason, I wanted to tell Newton Reddick about all that, but decided not to.

"Lily Bart," he said, "is an admirable figure. Forceful. So for you, a literary collection?"

"Sure, why not?"

"So long as it doesn't hew to the prizes. Nothing vulgar."

"No, nothing vulgar."

I checked my watch. It was nearly midnight.

"I'm also interested in legal documents," I said.

He was looking down into his glass, thinking still about Edith Wharton, maybe, or about the young people who declined to read her and all the people who would never know her thoughts on decorating houses. It took him a moment to regain himself. I wondered how many sales he had lost over the years drifting off that way into reveries and private disappointments.

"Legal documents," he said. "Yes, of course. There I can be of service to you."

"What would you recommend?"

"There's a fine tradition in the area of legal documents. And of course lawyers themselves have been great book collectors over the years. There was Pforzheimer at Yale, Walter Jr., not Carl. Allyn Peck and the rest of them at Harvard. It all depends on what area of the law captivates you."

"I'm thinking about something more particular than a few Blackstones."

"More particular?"

"Curious. Something readable would be nice."

It took him a moment but when the idea arrived, he smiled a kind, distant smile. I got the impression he had spent a lot of time and suffered some heartache looking for curious things. Tallied up, he had probably spent a good portion of his life stooped over in bookshops.

"I'd like to show you something," he said. "Will you come with me?"

He was good and drunk by then. His eyes were glass, like a lake at morning.

I followed him down a hall and through a series of reading rooms, each outfitted with armchairs and inlaid shelves filled with books. None of the rooms were occupied and I got the feeling, a strange feeling that I didn't quite know how to articulate or reckon, that the floors we were walking belonged to the books, everything in that building did, and it didn't matter whose name was on the deed or who joined the society or didn't join it, the books would be there regardless and there would always be old men to shuffle through the rooms and look after them.

Finally, we came to the place Reddick wanted me to see. It was a room like all the others we had passed, small and confidential, decorated in the handsome style of Edith Wharton's

New York. Reddick held out his arms. He seemed to think its glory was manifest.

"The legal collection," he said.

It smelled like an autumn rot. There were no windows and only a dim light.

He took a book off one of the shelves and handed it to me. It was cheaply bound, cheaply made, flimsy even, nothing I would ever think to collect or to display on the shelves of my office, the imaginary office I had come to the Poquelin Society in order to begin decorating. The title of the book was *The Life and Crimes of Mordechai Hewitt, Murderer Late of New York.* It was a trial pamphlet. The top shelf was filled with them. That was the source of the rotting smell.

I pretended to flip through the pamphlet, to admire it. Reddick was watching me closely.

"It's just the thing," I said. "It's perfect."

"Isn't it?" he said. "Like holding on to time itself."

Something had come over him since we'd entered the room. A quickening of the blood. He seemed twenty years younger, which reminded me again of the wife he was losing. Even shedding those couple of decades, he had no real business with her. That was the unavoidable truth.

"Could you sell me something like this?" I asked.

"Yes," he said, solemnly. "Not these, but there are others. Plenty of others."

"As many as you can give up."

"I'm glad you appreciate them. Truly."

Without having to be asked again, he found a notepad and pen on a reading lectern in the corner of the room and began to write. When he was done, he ripped the sheet from the pad and handed it to me. There were ten titles there and next to each one an annotation with the name of a publisher and the year, presumably, that the book was printed, and finally a column for the price. The numbers were dashed off very faint, like he was embarrassed at having to do it, embarrassed for the both of us at being vulgar. They were awfully expensive pamphlets.

"Those books would make a fine start to a specialized collection," he said. "Take this home with you. Study the volumes, consider the figures. Reflect. Then call me. We'll see to it."

"See to what?" I asked, a little stupidly.

"Your library," he said. "This is only the beginning."

I asked him if he wouldn't mind signing his name to the sheet. As a keepsake.

He did it gladly, without question or suspicion. We were on the cusp of a great journey, he and I. Of course we would gather souvenirs.

I thanked him and put the sheet in my pocket. It was evidence now.

Before I left, he wanted to shake hands, but I found a way around it without being rude.

2.

It seemed at the time like the easiest money a person could make. The next day I typed a declaration and affidavit, attached Reddick's handwritten, signed offer sheet as exhibit A, and emailed the documents to Shannon Rebholz at Rebholz and Kahn, Anna Reddick's attorney for the divorce. The next week, a courier showed up at my door with a sealed manila envelope. Inside was some fine stationery and another roll of hundred-dollar bills, fifty of them. Together with the retainer, that made fifteen thousand dollars. Not a bad haul for a few hours of work. I put most of it under the mattress and promised myself I would look into the bond market straightaway. With what was left, I treated Ulises Lima to a steak dinner at Peter Luger. I wanted to thank him for sending me such a brief, surprisingly lucrative case. He ordered the porterhouse with a baked potato and toward the end of the meal, after we'd both drunk a good deal, he was hell-bent on making a toast. It started out as a toast about loyalty and friendship and ended with him talking about Jorge Luis Borges and his early poetry, how truly awful it was, so awful it must have been part of a long con the great man was playing on the Argentines. We spent the rest of the meal trying to figure out what the con could have been, whether it involved a fake encyclopedia like the *Codex Seraphinianus* or a pack of gauchos. It was one of those nights. We were happy and well fed. The work had come easily, without either of us having to search for it.

Ulises was probably my closest friend in the city at that point, but if you had asked me how we first met, I couldn't have told you. He claimed it was in a bookshop on the Lower East Side, a place that sold paperback mysteries and anarchist literature, but he couldn't remember the name. He had me confused with somebody else. New York was full of small, dying shops then and it could have just as easily been a record store or a luncheonette or a news kiosk. Ulises had a good, sharp mind that was always misremembering things. That was what made him a poet, he would tell you. If he had wanted to recall things in the order they occurred he would have become a detective or a lab assistant. Memories were speculative. That was his theory, anyway, and it all tied back to Borges's poetry in a roundabout way and to some of the lesser-read works of Roberto Bolaño, another writer Ulises admired. Bolaño died two years before, in Barcelona somewhere, supposedly of liver failure. Since then he had become fairly popular and you would sometimes see people on the subway trying to read one of his books in the original Spanish, especially *2666*, the novel he wrote while waiting on a new liver that never arrived. It was all pretty inconvenient for Ulises, who had named himself after one of Bolaño's characters. He had done it back when he first arrived in New York and had been counting on the reference remaining obscure for a long while, possibly forever. His real name was Juan Andres Henriquez Houry. Everyone called him Ulises. He had friends all over the city, a lot of unusual, interesting people.

After the steaks we went to Fortaleza Café and kept on talking about work. The regular crowd was there. Some of them Ulises knew and others were people I had done jobs for in the past, acquaintances and neighbors and the woman who ran the bakery on Graham Avenue, who the summer before had wanted to trademark a drawing of the blue stove her grandmother passed down to her, a simple case that only required a filing with the Patent and Trademark Office and earned me a lot of free muffins for a time. Warm, unruly muffins overflowing with berries. She was wearing a baggy sweater and dancing with another woman. I thought I recognized the other woman. Possibly she was a colleague from the bakery. The ends of her sleeves, around the wrists, were dusted with confectioners' sugar. It was just after eleven and Fortaleza brought in music during the week. They didn't charge anything at the door, they only passed around a hat. You could ignore the hat if you wanted, but Miss Daniela, who owned and managed the café and who may or may not have come from Fortaleza—I never checked—would be sitting at the bar, watching who contributed and who didn't. Plenty didn't, but I never saw them there again.

"You two are always working," Miss Daniela said, when Ulises and I were sitting at the bar. She was three stools down, watching the band, which was a guitar, a drum, and a singer performing samba. Whenever a train passed overhead, crossing the Williamsburg Bridge, the band would speed up the tempo and play louder as the rattling of the tracks and the bridge's undergirding tried to drown them out but never managed to. It was all done very naturally. They played there every Thursday night, the same band, from around nine o'clock until midnight.

Miss Daniela changed stools to get a little closer. Closer to Ulises and to the band.

Ulises told her what we were discussing. The Newton Reddick case. Borges. Divorce. She hadn't really thought we were working—it was all a joke. She liked to tease Ulises. They were neighbors, she used to say, her from Brazil and him from Venezuela, they shared a border, why not a bed now and again, for laughs, for fun, for exercise? She wore her hair in great, old-fashioned hives wrapped with silk scarves. In the prior year she had been fined twice for violating the city's cabaret laws. The cabaret laws in New York were like nowhere else in the country, maybe in the world. You could only dance in a few places around town, in clubs and in the old discos, several of which were still hanging on thanks to the dancing. The fines weren't too exorbitant, but they added up for a small place like Fortaleza, which had only ten tables, the barstools, and a kitchen out back with four burners. The city used to send plainclothes officers around on weeknights looking for violators. The cabaret laws had been designed to keep Latin and Black neighborhoods under thumb. It was enough to make a businesswoman paranoid, especially one who brought in music, samba no less. But Miss Daniela couldn't bear to have her place any other way. I told her the next time she was fined I would fight it out for her, pro bono. She asked if Ulises would come along for the fight, pro bono, and he said that he would try, he would be honored to do it, but you can't fight city hall. That was something he had heard once.

"You know, I've divorced five men," Miss Daniela said. "Two in Brazil, three here. Every one a class act. Didn't take anything that was mine. Didn't hire lawyers. Just signed the papers when I brought them by. If I saw them on Sundays at church, they all tipped their hats."

"You chose good men to divorce," I said.

"You have to. You have to think about how it's going to end."

"You should have been a litigator. That's the same thing they teach us."

"Lawyers don't dance," she said. "No music, no dancing. Just fines, tickets, divorces."

She had us all figured out. Even still, she asked if I wanted to dance with her.

"What about the fines?" I asked.

"I got my lawyer right here," she said.

She was patting Ulises on the shoulder, flirting, though he wasn't listening to us anymore. He was talking to the waitress, a woman he knew who was a few decades younger than Miss Daniela, but what did she know about starting a marriage or carrying through a divorce? We went down to the end of the bar, Miss Daniela and I, where there was just enough space to dance between the service area and where the band was set up. The J train passed overhead and the rhythm quickened and I had no hope of keeping pace, though I worked up a good sweat trying. Miss Daniela moved gracefully. In the air you could smell the cheese balls they were always cooking and pushing out to accompany the sugary drinks. Afterward I dropped a twenty in the hat. It was a lot more than I was used to tipping, but we were celebrating the end of a good case. That was my reasoning as I dropped the bill in and watched the hat disappear.

"Twenty bucks," Miss Daniela said. "You think I'm getting fined tonight?"

I told her I didn't know. Nobody could know a thing like that.

"We got any police here?" she asked. "What do you see?"

"No," I said. "They're all at the policeman's ball."

"What's that?"

"The Benevolent Brothers' Christmas Ball. They have it every December."

"And none of them dancing? That's some party."

Maybe they did dance. I didn't know anything about it. I hardly knew any police. Lawyers are meant to cultivate friends in the department but I could never quite bring myself to do it. I knew some FBI people, task-force lawyers, but none of them danced, not that I ever saw. I was making up the policeman's ball, inventing it, though it sounded like something they would do, carpooling in from Staten Island and Long Island with their wives, then driving home plastered, running into deer, and the next day, in the morning,

seeing blood on their fenders or the edges of their windshields
and wondering what they'd done, asking their wives, who
didn't know, calling their union reps to make sure it could
be kept quiet and that nobody had reported any accidents.
No, I had never seen the point of hanging around police
stations trying to make a lot of friends.

"No more divorces for you," Miss Daniela said. "You're
not cut out for that, okay?"

I agreed with her though probably we had different reasons for thinking so.

Ulises and I stayed until close and walked the waitress
home, the woman he knew who was covering all ten tables
by herself, working like mad, bringing around all the drinks
and also the cheese balls, which were called pão de queijo.
Her name was Gloria Almeida and she lived on North Eleventh, by the brewery, nearly half a mile out of the way but
it didn't matter, we wanted to see her home. There was snow
in the forecast that night, but it hadn't started falling.

3.

It was another week, a quiet Wednesday, and I wanted to get out to see the city decorated for Christmas, so I walked over the bridge and headed north toward the Sotheby's auction house on York Avenue on the Upper East Side, just shy of the river. Sotheby's was a good place to pass the time. They were always changing the art on display but there was a great deal of order to the place and the order never seemed to change too much. On the first and second floors were the impressionists, modernists, and Pacific sculptures. Above those were the contemporary paintings, and then as you made your way upstairs you saw the illustrations and selections from private sales and, somewhere in a room I had never found, the gemstones. An escalator ran straight through the guts of the building. If you got all the way to ten, there was a coffee bar where they made good bitter espresso and gave it away for free. It wasn't at all a bad place to spend the afternoon, and now and again I would pick up a job there. I knew a woman in the watch department. She ran the watch department, in fact, and had thrown me an interesting case the year before: a shipment of watches needed to clear customs, but they wouldn't say whom the watches belonged to, only where they were headed—Sotheby's in New York—and where they had come from—Morocco by way of Lausanne. I thought she might like to get lunch, but I took my time getting to the seventh floor to ask her. They had some nautical drawings on display in the section for private sales. Not the heroic British imperial pomp, but nautical drawings from northern India and the plains of Central Asia, places where there was no water around, so the drawings were only the dreams of people who had seen the ocean once or twice in the distant past. By the time I got to the seventh floor, it was nearly two o'clock.

Katya, the woman I knew in the watch department, said she couldn't leave. She had four or five machines spread out around her desk, performing inscrutable tasks. The whole office was a clamor of activity. "That's all right," I told her. "Next time I'll call first or come ready to bid."

She must have heard something in my voice. A catch. She was used to listening to watches, with all their intricate workings and little hitches and flutters that told you what you needed to know. She asked how Xiomara was doing. She hadn't seen her around lately.

"She's doing fine," I said. "There's a show coming up in Paris."

"What show?"

I told her about the exhibition. In English it was billed as the "Young Voices of Latin America"—there were different names for it in Spanish and French. A prominent event, the kind that would be cataloged and covered in the art press and maybe beyond that, with write-ups in the culture sections of newspapers in France and elsewhere. A good number of reputations would be made, Xiomara's included. They were holding it at the Centre Pompidou. For some reason, talking with Katya and telling her what I knew about the show, I feigned having an opinion about the building, the Centre Pompidou, which I had never visited or even seen. That was the kind of thing Xiomara would have laughed at. She believed that was the heart of a lawyer's job, feigning opinions about events and people never seen, and in that way we weren't such a poor match, she and I. Our occupations were adjacent.

"She must be thrilled," Katya said.

I agreed. She must be. She was. I was happy for her. There was nothing else to be. Everywhere I went that winter people asked me about Xiomara. She was something for them to talk about, like the weather or delays on the subway. She had been gone just over a month and at home, in the apartment, I would still find her sculptures in odd places sometimes, miniature busts of nudes in classical positions, throes of rapture or torture or something in between, all carved from the most refined materials she could scrounge, including whalebone she sourced from a retired galley cook who was living in the seafarers' wing of the Prospect Park YMCA. From the neck down they were stark, classical depictions but above that they wore death masks. The masks were colorful and terrifying. I used to find them in between the sofa cushions or in the kitchen, stuck behind a drawer that wouldn't close all the way no matter how hard you pushed it.

"Listen," I said to Katya, "aren't any of the watches in your auction stolen?"

"They better not be."

"But if they are."

"You'll be my second call," she said. "Third at the very most."

The prospect of a long, damp afternoon was stretching out before me. I didn't have any work at home. Nobody wanted to start a lawsuit with Christmas coming. By the weekend everyone would be drinking in anticipation of the holidays and a few of them would get arrested and that would be something to do, but on a Wednesday in December there's less hope in the air and less desperation. You had only the Sotheby's auction house to cheer you up, and the windows of department stores.

Katya told me there wasn't much going on in the building—everyone was getting ready for the big seasonal shows. But if I was really hard up for distraction, somewhere in the building they were previewing a book auction. She said it like it was just about the dullest thing she could imagine. Compared to watches, I guess it all seemed pretty dreary.

"Look me up in a few weeks," she said. "We'll have all the lunches you can pay for."

I would, I told her. "I'll call you after New Year's."

"January I'm going to Miami," she said.

"What for?"

"They're crazy about watches there. And I hate January in New York. It never snows."

She liked to leave you on cryptic notes like that, something to keep you wondering what she meant. She was an interesting woman. I was disappointed not to be having lunch with her, though the truth was, I wasn't hungry. I had filled up on espresso from the tenth floor.

The book preview was way the hell downstairs in the subbasement. They had done a nice job decorating the room with old-fashioned touches that made me think about Newton Reddick and the Edith Wharton book he had described to me, the one she had written on the decoration of houses, the first book that had lit a fire under him about collecting. Probably he was on my mind, too, because it was a book auction, and it looked like just about every book dealer in New York was there at the preview and all of them were wearing tweed of one kind or another. Tweed jackets, tweed pants, there were even a few vests. It was all rather festive, and you could see that the auction was a big event in their world and that everyone was glad to be there. It occurred to me that Reddick might be there and probably he wouldn't be very happy to see me, not if his lawyers had received the new filing in his divorce, which likely they had. It had been a couple of weeks and divorce attorneys weren't known for their restraint. I checked around the room and didn't see him anywhere. Mostly the crowd was made up of dealers and booksellers, it seemed. There weren't any lawyers, none that I could pick out, so I handed around my business card, thinking there might be an opportunity there, I might carve out a new specialty tracking down rare books and the drunks and divorcées who occasionally stole them. I liked books. Ulises used to say that Balzac had never cost a man so much money as he had cost me. It was true: I did like reading that kind of thing, and not only Balzac but a lot of other authors with outsize, inchoate, and somewhat ridiculous ambitions. Probably those books had filled me with a lot of strange ideas about what I should and shouldn't do with my life and in that way some money had been lost in the form of salary, which was still quite high at the corporate law firms in those days, and in other benefits, but I didn't mind. Solo practice suited me. You could read what you liked and when there was nothing else to do you could walk to Sotheby's and find new worlds opening before you. The books on auction were from American authors and publishing houses. It was a Christmas tradition, apparently. The Sotheby's fine books, prints, and Americana auction.

There were some wonderful books on display and several others I had never heard of though the reserve prices were high, almost comically so, except that it was Sotheby's and Christmas was coming up and you never knew what people were going to buy on the Upper East Side. My favorite was a first edition of Mark Twain's *The Celebrated Jumping Frog of Calaveras County.* The first had been a special edition with a handsome green cloth cover and in the lower left corner was a frog embossed in gold, starting into his jump, looking like an animal on a crest, rampant. It was Twain's first book, apparently, but he was already famous by that time because the story had run in a newspaper, the *New York Saturday Press,* under the title "Jim Smiley and His Jumping Frog," and people had read it and were clamoring to buy it in a more durable format. The woman who was responsible for the Twain books told me all that, and she said that it was unusual to find first editions from that era with such special care paid to the book's printing, since typically the author's historical importance wasn't recognized until well after his or her death.

"Take Melville," she said. "He was popular for a time but nobody was gilding his edges."

I said I guessed that was true for nearly all of us, and she smiled and asked if there was anything else I'd like to see, but I told her no, I'd already taken up too much of her time. There were real buyers waiting to talk about Twain and his unusual legacy. I didn't want to keep her from them. On my way out the door, one of the dealers stopped me. He was wearing tweed like all the others. A sport coat. Otherwise, he seemed young for that crowd. Forty or forty-five.

"This is you," he said. He was holding one of my business cards.

I offered my hand, but he didn't appear to notice. He was caught up in some kind of internal debate. For a moment, I thought he was going to make a confession. He had that glazed, slightly constipated look that sometimes precedes an unburdening. In movies and even in books lawyers are always warning people not to confess to them but in real life it doesn't work that way. In real life you want to hear everything you can and later on you'll make whatever compromises you have to, or you won't. That's the essence of the job, making that decision quickly and then living with the consequences. I was curious and wanted to hear him out.

"You were admiring the Twain books," he said.

I told him I had especially admired *The Celebrated Jumping Frog*, which I called by some other name, *The Incredible Jumping Frog* or something else that was close but not quite correct. It didn't seem to matter. He wasn't listening carefully. The debate was still raging in his mind.

"Well, I was over here," he said. "And I guess I was just wondering to myself about how you sleep at night. I was thinking that's some profession you have. That's one way to make a living."

He was looking down at my card like the stationery was what made the living for me.

"I think you're mistaken," I said.

"You're one of the lawyers. A shyster. I know who you are."

I thought he might take a swing at me. His hands were shaking badly.

In the breast pocket of his jacket was a folded newspaper. He took it out and tried showing it to the man who was standing beside him, another dealer in tweed, an older man who shook his head and kept on staring across the room. He wanted no part of whatever was happening between us. I felt about the same. It would have been easier if it had been a confession or a case of mistaken identity. On any given day, there were about a hundred decent reasons for a stranger to wag his finger in your face and most of them could be handled swiftly, without perpetuating confusion. That was something they tried teaching you from the first day of law school, how to cut through the finger-wagging. It never worked too well, but after years of practice you might get the knack.

"Go ahead," he said. "Read it for yourself."

He handed it over. It was a cheaply made broadsheet called *The Rare Bookseller*, a newspaper of some kind that was laid out to appear slightly more august than it was, with a lot of old-fashioned fonts and a few photographs of sturdy-looking men posing grimly beside their books. You had to wonder where the money came from for an operation like that. Could they support it on advertising? Classifieds? Maybe they had a large and devoted subscriber base of pensioners or a benefactor. There was money all over the city and people who found crazy ways to spend it.

It was open to a page marked News and Notices, with a section for Reported Thefts. Under the heading was Newton Reddick's name. It said that he was suspected of stealing five books, legal pamphlets. They were five books I had itemized in the affidavit, the one I had sworn out and sent along to Anna Reddick's divorce attorney. The titles were printed in bold and underlined. There was no mistaking them, and beneath all that was my phone number and name, esquired for good effect. It said that anyone with relevant information should contact me.

"I'm sorry," I said. "But it's true."

"The hell it is. Newton's no thief. You'll ruin him. Do you realize how serious this is?"

I didn't, but I didn't see how that was any of his business either.

"He ruined himself," I said. "It happens all the time."

"How can you believe a thing like that?"

"Dishonesty doesn't materialize all at once. It's a rising tide."

"What are you talking about? A shyster like you. You wanted the advertising."

I hadn't thought of that, but he was right. I needed it. Free advertising, no less. I was in no position to turn a thing like that down. Just like I was in no position to decline the case in the first place. That's how it had felt. In winter the bills were always adding up.

I opened the man's jacket and tucked the newspaper back into his breast pocket. I was sure that if he had known how to hit a man he would have done it then. I felt a little sorry for him. A confrontation at Sotheby's must have been an important moment for him. He would be playing the thing over in his mind for weeks, thinking of better things to say than calling me a shyster.

"Go to hell," he said, but I'd already turned my back on him.

Walking home, I played the thing out once or twice myself, but soon got on to other subjects. I kept thinking about the Mark Twain book, *The Celebrated Jumping Frog,* and what the Sotheby's woman had said about it, how very few authors ever get that kind of white-glove treatment while they're still alive. Not from that era, and not Melville anyway. On the corner of Fifty-Fifth and Third Avenue, I passed my old law firm, the one I had quit. There was a long gauntlet of firms in that part of Midtown, and it seemed like all the associates were outside of them smoking and talking loudly about the things they were going to do after they were done paying off loans. Probably if I had looked closer I would have recognized a few faces, but instead I hustled along and out of the wind. Outside Grand Central they were ringing silver bells for the Salvation Army. I dropped a ten into the bucket and said a wish for Newton Reddick, that he would get what he deserved, luck or exotic books or a quick, painless divorce served up with white gloves.

4.

There's a strange satisfaction in quitting a job you shouldn't. It's a fleeting satisfaction and when the bills come due it feels like none at all, or worse still, but for a little while you're an aristocrat, a man with nothing to do all day but look into shop windows, or like one of the lesser deities in Bulfinch. That's how I had felt, anyway. I was just about three years into solo practice. The firm I quit was called Beauvois & Plimpton. Plimpton was the father of the writer, who was still alive at the time I joined, collecting annuities, presumably, or benefiting from some kind of trust. He died a few years later and there was a memorial in one of the conference rooms. I had read his boxing book and the football one, too, and imagined for a time that was part of the firm's allure. At Columbia I had won a prize for legal writing, and there was an idea once I joined up that I should be passed between litigation partners and used to revise briefs written by other associates who had been hired for other reasons, because of their dogged work ethic or because of the people they were related to in the business world, people who didn't care whether they could write clearly or how hard they worked so long as they kept on attending the same schools generation after generation and traveling to Maine in the summer. In New York there were golfing firms and tennis firms, and Beauvois was a tennis firm. Somebody told me that once and I never quite understood what it meant or implied, but it seemed true enough. Revising briefs was fine work. I didn't mind it, just the contrary. What I resented, if resentment was the word to describe what I was feeling in a time during which I was paid well—better than anybody else I knew, even the junior bankers—was having to believe in the rightness of the side we were arguing. In corporate litigation there always came a point in time when you were seated across a long, lacquered table from the client's executives and general counsel and they wanted to hear that you believed they should win, that they had been in the right all along. It was an absurd, childish thing to want but that's what they were paying for, and by and large they got it. There was a whole floor of the skyscraper dedicated to conference rooms, one after another like gurneys lining the hallways of a giant, gleaming hospital, and in each one of the rooms they were serving warmed-over meals on silver trays and telling clients all day long how right they were. The litigators there hardly ever lost a case. Their instincts were too sharp. They knew when it was headed that way and made sure to settle before, so that everyone could carry on being right.

I practiced at Beauvois for four years before quitting. I had been assigned to the intellectual property group, which brought in a great deal of money for the firm in those days. They had me policing our clients' trademarks, which was just a way of racking up billable hours and meant that I spent part of every day flipping through magazines and binders of advertisement clippings. The other part I spent writing expert reports. The reports were supposed to have been authored by outside experts in the field—washed-up trademark commissioners, professors, and retired judges—but they were only guns for hire and would sign whatever you put in front of them, so I wrote the reports and bent them to our purposes. It took up quite a bit of my time. Everyone was busy in that building, or trying to be. They expected you to bill around twenty-five hundred hours annually, and it was easier to do if you had a lot of small tasks to switch between throughout the day. Magazines to flip through, experts to embody. The woman in the office next to mine had only one client, an oil-rich autonomous region somewhere that wanted to declare independence. I was never told where the region was—that was confidential even within the litigation department—but I used to hear her late at night, on the phone, always speaking in short bursts so that the translator could convey things clearly, and then at midnight I would see her downstairs talking with the guys in the dispatch office, eating her dinner, always the same takeout from a Persian restaurant called Ravagh Grill. The firm represented a lot of hedge funds and charitable foundations, too, but the international disputes group always struck me as having a special kind of melancholy. For starters they had to navigate all those time zones, which disrupted their sleep.

The last case I worked was for a credit card company. They

wanted to trademark the color black, another ridiculous idea, but we agreed to do it for them and in the end were fairly successful at it. To thank us, they arranged a private dinner at Et Vir, a restaurant people were eager to eat at back then. On the upper level there were private dining rooms wrapped in dark wallpaper. The wallpaper looked black or midnight blue but when you got up close you could see dragons embossed there in gold. Between the company's officers and our sorry pile of litigators the dinner must have cost roughly what a paralegal made in a year, though the paralegals weren't invited, only the lawyers. It was a tasting menu, nine or ten courses or more—I lost track after a while. Oysters and pearls to start, foie gras, a striped bass served beside roast duck that was made to look like lamb chops. Dishes that were fine or better but were the product of an overexcited imagination and a manager somewhere who understood what drove people to spend that kind of money. Between the fifth and sixth courses the company's general counsel made a toast and gave us presents. I'm sure it was quite a speech though I don't remember what was said. It was about the case, most likely, the work we had done, the long nights. It had been a coup, trademarking a color of all things. The partners had already received their gifts, mostly in the form of those extravagant fees, and since I was the lead associate on the matter, they wanted to give me something special and had decided on a baseball bat. A Louisville Slugger made of ash, black like the color we had trademarked for them. I suppose they wanted to show us they could do with the color anything they liked, even put it on a baseball bat. There was a card with the gift that said

"Thanks for knocking it out of the park." On the fattest part
of the bat, the sweet spot, they engraved into the wood the
docket number of the case we had won and my name, or
what they thought was my name. Dwight Murphy. They
were only off by a few letters. I thanked them for the meal
and for the bat and told one of the partners at my firm, a man
I liked named Solloway, that I was done, I quit.

"All right," he said, "sure thing, understood."

Maybe he thought I was talking about the meal, the tasting menu, that I couldn't eat anymore. I didn't much care
what he thought. I took the bat and went downstairs to the
bar. It was too expensive a place for me to be drinking in,
but I could put the whiskey on the tab upstairs and they
would pay for it, so that's what I did. The bartender was a
kindhearted woman who flirted with me some. I was holding
on to the bat. I had it resting against my shoulder like you
see in old photographs of contact hitters, second basemen and
right fielders with long, narrow bats they never let out of their
hands except to take the field. The bartender didn't believe
me when I told her I had been upstairs quitting my job. She
said nobody quits at a goddamn restaurant during a tasting
menu. I figured she should know but I felt I had quit all the
same. The next day was a Thursday and I told her I wouldn't
go into the office, I wouldn't pick up my phone, I was done.
She didn't think I would go through with it. She believed
that I would go away for the weekend, lick my wounds, then
show up at the office on Monday and they would give me a
lecture and some more money. I wouldn't, I told her. I was
finished, resolved. I thought she was only being kind because

of how sorry I looked holding on to the bat and because it was an expensive place, but then she said she would go home with me. She lived in Greenpoint, not too far from my apartment, and her shift was nearly over. There was a town car outside, paid for by the client or by the partners—I didn't care anymore, it wasn't my business how they divided up the bills. On the ride home she told me that waiters and busboys didn't get tips or overtime when they served tasting menus. I couldn't get that out of my mind. It was the most expensive thing a customer could order. How could they stiff them on the service? It didn't make any sense.

"Nothing in the restaurant industry makes sense," she said. "Better not to dwell on it."

We made out for a few minutes and when we got to Brooklyn she said she had an early shift the next day and had better get going, she needed some sleep. A morning shift seemed odd for a bartender but for all I knew she had other jobs, two or three of them, and was always looking out for rides where she could find them, along with a bit of friendly conversation. I was feeling good and free and hanging on to the bat still. I had an idea that I was going to bring a class-action case on behalf of the fine-dining waiters and busboys someday and get them their back pay. I didn't know anything about labor law or the restaurant industry or class actions, but I could learn, there was time. I never saw the bartender again. I didn't file the class-action suit, either, though I kept it in the back of my mind and every now and again I would come across a labor lawyer hanging around the coffee stand at the federal courthouse on Worth Street and think about proposing

to him or her that we team up for a case. It was always a
good idea to have prospects in mind for an uncertain future.

Mostly I took on odd jobs and small matters. Neighborhood cases, petty disputes, contract work on the occasional
document review whenever I needed to pay for something
quickly. You could always glom onto a document review and
the hours weren't terrible and you listened to the radio while
you were doing it. Most of the work was being done by teams
in India but they needed someone with an American bar
admission to make the calls on privileged material. Besides
the reviews, new cases were always popping up. My landlord,
a licensed plumber and cruise ship singer who had grown up
in the building, wanted to sue one of the other cruise ship
lines for ripping off his crooner act. I looked into it and wrote
a few letters and got him a licensing fee of twenty dollars per
live offshore performance. Eventually I picked up a few criminal matters. For a while I hoped a murder case might come
along. I wanted something I could sink my teeth into and
bill extravagantly and then plea out. But the people I knew
never seemed to kill anyone. Artists and poets, they didn't
have the nerve for that kind of thing. Every now and again
one of them would come across a benefactor or make a sale
and would need to pull together articles of incorporation.
If I was lucky, I could persuade them to trademark their
names. That was good, reliable work and I never minded
doing it. I didn't mind making a quick appearance on a possession charge, either, or poking around for holes in a trust
fund or filling out the paperwork for an O-1 visa, which
supposedly was reserved for artists of extraordinary gifts but

really they would give to just about anyone in those days. "Extraordinary gifts" was a euphemism, and nobody wanted to get to the bottom of what it meant.

The second Monday of every month I worked a clinic out of a school cafeteria on Bushwick Avenue. There were two or three other lawyers who worked it with me. Consultations were free and lasted fifteen minutes. There were chess timers on the tables to keep things moving. Working for yourself, you learned all kinds of tricks like that. They weren't so different from the tricks the big firms used, only in this case the money was little and it went into your pocket instead of somebody else's. Or it would, if the consultations turned into something halfway billable. The clinic rarely produced much business, but it satisfied my community service as far as the state bar was concerned and occasionally I met interesting people, oftentimes directed to the clinic by Ulises, who told them to ask for me and nobody else, like it was a secret what we were doing. I always knew when Ulises had sent the clients because they would have my name wrong. Dwight, Don, Darren, Wyatt, and a few other staples. He thought that was pretty funny.

The clinic was where I met Xiomara. Ulises had told her to go see me for help with her taxes when they were overdue by eleven months. She was making too much money free-lancing in graphic design to need the clinic on Bushwick Avenue, which is what I was about to tell her when she said that she was working jobs using her cousin's Social Security number. She didn't sound too concerned about it. Ulises might have explained to her that I was trustworthy, although

it wasn't like him to explain much. He just sent people to you
and let fate do the rest.

"I don't want to put you in an uncomfortable position,"
she said. "If you'd rather not help me file knowing it's a fraud
on the government, that's fine, I'll find another lawyer, but
it seems to me a pretty insignificant crime in the grand
scheme of things. I'm just trying to pay my fucking taxes like
a good worker bee."

She had an accent, a faint one. She was from Mexico City
and had studied at an international school. She had watched
a great number of American sitcoms and in doing so had
refined her English, as well as her sense of comedic timing.
All that I'd learn about later, in bits and pieces, the way anybody learns something in a relationship. I told her I wasn't
uncomfortable, I would help her out in any way that I could,
I committed petty crimes every day, that's what being a lawyer is all about. She had all the paperwork with her, everything she needed, color coded and ready to be filed. Her
cousin's Social Security card looked like it had been run
through the wash.

She agreed to wait around until the clinic was finished. I'd
asked her to a drink. She said no, she didn't drink, but she
would go for a walk. We walked west on Broadway toward
the river. I was a lost cause from the beginning, I suppose,
because I was the one filling in the silences and getting spooked
whenever the J train rattled overhead. Walking beneath the
tracks at that hour, in the afternoon, there were these jagged
shards of sunshine. One moment they were blinding you and
the next you were in the shadows. I told her it was the same

street where they filmed the famous scene in *The French Connection*, where Popeye Doyle chases the man from Marseille and then shoots him in the back from the bottom of the subway stairs.

"It wasn't Broadway," she said. "It was Stillwell Avenue, and Popeye Doyle was a racist and a coward." She was looking at me with what seemed to be genuine concern. I had probably mentioned that scene, that piece of inane trivia, to twenty or thirty or forty people over the years. Nobody had ever corrected me in all that time.

When she moved into my place a month later, there was an understanding. She had already been accepted to the show in Paris, the Young Voices of Latin America at the Centre Pompidou. She would move there at the start of November to keep an eye on the installation. It was something she had been dreaming about and working toward for years. Her debut. Our arrangement, our relationship, was temporary. That was fine. I always told her it was fine and tried to mean it too. She was good at making plans and following through on them. She was never late showing up anywhere, not even by five minutes. Everybody in New York was late and would blame it on the subways or crosstown traffic, but not Xiomara. One afternoon in October we met up in Coney Island on a cold day when hardly anyone was there and only a handful of games were operating. We'd agreed to meet outside the train station at six. I thought for sure she would be late or maybe early. She was coming all the way from Manhattan, the length of the F train, whereas I'd had an appointment down the road in Brighton Beach. Just as my watch ticked over on the hour she was there, wrapped in three different scarves against the cold blowing off the water. She wanted two hot dogs and a basket of crinkle fries from Nathan's. I had a bottle of vodka gifted to me from the Russians I'd met on Beaumont Street but we didn't drink it, not even to stave off the cold. After dinner we looked around for games to play but nothing was open. The roller coasters were closed, too, so we walked the beach. You had to be careful of glass in the sand but anyhow it was too cold to take off your shoes and the sand was packed hard near the boardwalk. The city felt very far away. We talked about moving to the outskirts, possibly to Rockaway, into a little beach shack with lousy insulation and sand on the floorboards that you could never get rid of. It was a strange thing to talk about. She was leaving. She wasn't moving to Coney Island or the Rockaways or any other part of New York. We kept talking about it, though, and the thing I hung on to was how she'd arrived at the hot dog stand exactly on time, down to the minute, ready to order, knowing exactly what she wanted to eat. About a month before she left for Paris, I had drawn up some paperwork—a limited liability company based in Panama called Xiomara Fuentes Inc. I figured she could use it once she was abroad and selling her art and working in her own name again instead of her cousin's, the one with the Social Security number. It was a going-away gift—a gesture. She liked gestures, and if they were a little crass or sentimental, all the better. There was a seal at the top of the charter and it all looked very official and serious. She wanted to get me something in return and finally settled on a plaque for the door, made of copper and polished to a sheen. She had done the engraving work herself. The plaque had my name carved into it, with an LLP at the end. She nailed it up and I told her there was no LLP, no limited liability, no partners, there was only me, but she just laughed about it and said people ought to know who they were dealing with. It was just about the last thing she did before getting a taxi to the airport.

The Reddick case was the first one I had worked under the new auspices, the limited liability partnership, which the state of New York agreed to ordain without asking too many questions or making me wait very long after I filed the paperwork and paid some fees that didn't amount to all that much. It seemed like a good case to start on. I even thought about calling Xiomara to tell her about it. I thought she would have liked hearing about the Poquelin Society and all the old men puttering around the banquet room.

5.

It was a Monday afternoon, the day after Christmas, and I was coming back from the movies with Ulises. They were showing *Touch of Evil* at the Sunshine on Houston Street and we had walked home by the bridge. Along the way we smoked a joint and talked about the movie, not one of my favorites although Ulises liked it a great deal: the way nothing that happened in it was done naturally and all the characters seemed to know they were in a movie only there was nothing they could do about it. Plus, you had Charlton Heston playing a Mexican character, another odd feature. It was a good movie for a blustery Monday and it got me wondering what would happen next in my life. I was living off the Anna Reddick cash and could manage awhile longer, several months if need be, but I was also feeling my age and the winter chill. I was thirty-one, entering the prime of what some people might call a career. Seven years of lawyering, what did I have to show? My law school debts were paid off, at least.

In any case we were walking back from the movie, Ulises

and I, talking about our plans, such as they were, both of us careful not to mention certain things, such as Paris or Xiomara. She would call him from bars on public phones just about every week. I didn't know who paid the bills, maybe neither of them did. Maybe the barmen of Paris had taken up a collection. I hadn't spoken to her since she left town. That was the way she wanted it and we had agreed that it would be the best, most practical thing. Once I tried calling her apartment but another woman picked up—a roommate, maybe. She spoke halting English and wanted to tell me a story about something that had happened to her that day. She had been walking through the park—which park she didn't say but I got the impression it was one of the big parks, Luxembourg or the Tuileries—and there was a student there who had collapsed in the dirt. He was there on the ground, in between the flower beds, holding his chest, gasping, when she passed by and noticed what was happening. She turned him over and called for an ambulance. She rode along to the hospital and in the end he was fine, he lived. They pumped his stomach. But now she couldn't remember his name. In the excitement she had forgotten what it was. She thought I might be him, the student who had tried killing himself, that I had found her name somehow, or Xiomara's, and had managed to track her down to say thank you. She sounded pretty disappointed to find out who I was. It was an odd conversation and went on a long time, twenty minutes or more, just about all the time I had left on that calling card. When you were down to thirty seconds, a voice came on explaining that your time was up. That's what I thought it was saying, anyway.

The voice was speaking Arabic. Ulises used the same calling cards and told me once that he had a friend translate for him, and the friend said the final message was a prayer. It had something to do with travelers and the beauty of invention, supposedly.

As we were coming over the bridge the wind worked its way under my jacket and into my bones. It was that cold, restless time of year when it feels like anything could happen and you wish that it would. It didn't seem so odd to find a stranger, a woman, waiting outside my building. She was sitting on the stoop and looking across the street at the playground, which was nothing much, just a jungle gym, a chain-link fence, and a stretch of grass where the Russian and Ukrainian men slept at night on cardboard sheets and talked about the old country. They hadn't arrived yet, the men, and there were no kids on the jungle gym, it was too cold. The woman on my stoop was staring over there intently. She looked like she could have gone on watching that empty playground forever. I wondered if she were a new neighbor. People were always moving in and out. The man who owned the building, the cruise ship singer, liked young people and once or twice a year, when he was on shore leave, he would perform his crooner show in the banquet room behind Carmine's pizzeria, and he would leave free tickets for all his tenants. We would go together and sit there at a table. The tickets cost forty dollars each and he packed the room, which held up to a hundred. Each ticket got you a bottle of Chianti along with the show. Seeing the woman, I was thinking she might be new to the building and had locked herself out or was waiting on movers, but then Ulises looked closer and said that he recognized her. It was A. M. Byrne. When I didn't respond straightaway, he repeated the name very deliberately.

"She's the goddamn best novelist in America under the age of fifty," he said.

I knew who A. M. Byrne was. By reputation anyway. By name. What I didn't know was what she was doing on my stoop.

"You're the book lawyer," he said. "Better go ask the woman."

She hadn't seen us yet, or maybe she had but the empty park still had her enthralled.

Ulises went over and said hello first, asked how she was, what was she up to, how was the work? She seemed to recognize him, though just barely, and it was her amusement more than anything that kept the conversation going. Ulises could be pretty amusing when he wanted to turn it on, and besides that he was a handsome guy, not especially kempt but he looked the way you wanted a Venezuelan poet to, with all that hair, and he was fairly tall, six feet two in shoes.

She didn't tell him anything about her work, I noticed. He asked her twice, in an offhand way, and both times she deflected the question without being too obvious about it. She was content to talk about practically anything else, it seemed. She told him she was thinking about taking a class, an extension course, the kind they offered for adults. She wanted a practical skill, something she could do with her hands. Maybe she would build a house one day or get into

aquatic engineering. She loved the idea of studying the move-
ment of water, its courses and tendencies.

That was just the kind of thing Ulises might have said,
but she had beat him to it.

Finally, he asked what she was doing on the stoop, was
she there to see the lawyer?

"That's right," she said. "You know him?"

I reached into the back pocket of my jeans and came out
with a business card.

After studying the card, she said, "We better go upstairs."

There was a great resolve about her, a sense of finality.

I agreed, we should go upstairs, and turned to say goodbye
to Ulises, but he was already gone. That's how it was in those
days. You were always running into people and then somebody else would be gone, maybe around the corner to pick
up cigarettes or juice from the bodega, or they would be gone
forever. There were buses and trains leaving the city just
about every minute of every day. It was hard to keep track
of your friends but easy to pick up new business.

I was probably a little stoned. We had smoked that joint
coming across the bridge.

Heading upstairs I was feeling good and optimistic and
curious. It was always like that at the beginning of a new
case. A. M. Byrne was, as Ulises had said, one of the most
prominent novelists in the country, an author whose books
were taught in college courses though apparently she was in
her early thirties, thirty-five at the most, younger than she
looked on the backflap of her book jackets, which I had come
across once or twice at the Dockside Bookstore on Fulton

Street but had never bought or read, not knowing that one day she would turn up on my stoop. The hallway lights were out and it took a few tries to get the keys in the lock. The door was stuck, but finally gave way. The doorjambs always swelled up with moisture after a night of rain.

The apartment wasn't much, but I was occasionally vain about it. There's an art involved in living in a railroad setup, with one room spilling into the next and no real doors to speak of. It requires a special discipline, and you have to try to hide the bed behind something to avoid awkward situations. Mine was behind a bookcase. There were a lot of bookcases in there. They had been built and installed by a former client who had gotten into a fight outside the Loco Burrito shop on Graham Avenue and accidentally fell backward through a plate glass window. He was a painter and a woodworker, a pretty sensitive guy who felt bad about the situation with the window, and in the end the judge threw out the disorderly charge and let him work off the damage by building a new counter for the burrito shop and helping them fix the window frame where it had splintered. The bookcases he built me overwhelmed the apartment, which was only about seven or eight hundred square feet, but I didn't mind, something had to overwhelm it. Most of the decorations had come into the house that same way—bartered for services. In any case, the place was all mine. I didn't have roommates. I had been living there for several years.

"You like Conrad," she said when we were inside. She was making herself at home. She had taken off her coat and hung it on the doorknob and helped herself to a highball glass from the drying rack beside the sink and filled it with tap water. From the kitchen to the nearest bookshelf was a distance of ten feet or more but she was standing there reading the names of authors off the worn spines. Conrad and others. Her eyes were green, the same dark forest shade as her jacket.

"Vanity plays lurid tricks with our memory," she said, quoting Conrad's Marlow.

"Tell me," I said. "How can I help?"

"Help?" She looked bewildered, like she had never needed any before, or had never had to ask.

"Is this a social visit?"

"Not exactly," she said. "I came for guidance."

"Legal guidance?"

"That's right."

"I'd be glad to help."

"Guide," she said again. "I'm careful about words, if you don't mind. Professional hazard."

I poured myself a glass of water and drank it slowly while she watched. "So, you're an author," I said.

She shook her head. "I hate that word."

"What do you prefer?"

"Let's just talk."

I kept quiet and let her consider what it was she wanted to talk about.

"I went to law school once," she said.

"You like it?"

"All that brutal reasoning, boys in chinos, professors running a cold hand up your leg."

"They call it the Socratic method."

"Well, I made it all of two weeks. I wasn't cut out for it."

"I'm not sure I was either."

"And yet here we are, with me rambling on. I'm a little nervous."

She didn't strike me as nervous or like she was rambling. She seemed to be enjoying herself. I was glad. Confused, but glad. After all, she was my guest and maybe she would come to be my client. That was what I liked about solo practice. You never knew where your next case would come from. So long as your debts were paid off and your rent was controlled, it was an agreeable way to live, or that's how it appeared to me as A. M. Byrne, the best American novelist under the age of fifty, drank my water and perused my shelves with green eyes that could see titles from across the room. She asked me something about Pushkin and I stumbled over an answer, something about superstition and Russians, then she said it was time we came around to it.

"I'm wondering about libel," she said. "Is it a specialty of yours?"

"It was," I said. "It used to be. I'm a general practitioner now."

"Is it libel," she asked, "not slander, I mean, if it's written?"

"Defamation, if you want to speak more broadly."

"Good, then. What are the pleading requirements for a defamation case in New York?"

"Publication of a defamatory statement unprotected by privilege plus actual damages."

"Christ, did they make you memorize that?"

She was looking at me the way you might look at a

precocious child who had recited the state capitals, or maybe that was just how I was feeling with my glass of water and my lousy copies of Pushkin. I could have used some coffee but there wasn't any left, not that I could find.

"Miss Byrne," I said, "it would be better if we spoke in particulars."

"I'm coming around to those."

"Well, if you're thinking of bringing a case, don't."

"Why not? Aren't you a litigator? You're supposed to be ready for a fight."

"A defamation lawsuit brings attention to the thing you wish hadn't been written."

"Maybe I don't care about that."

"In the end you'll lose the case, and you might wind up paying a critic's legal fees."

"What makes you think it was a critic?"

"I'm deducing. From your line of work."

"My prickliness, you mean? My sensitivity?"

"Maybe that too. I don't know you all that well."

She shrugged and picked another book from the shelf, Edith Wharton this time. It was a paperback copy of *The Age of Innocence* and she didn't say anything but took her time flipping through the pages in search of something. When she found it, she read quietly to herself without looking up from the book or excusing herself and without shifting her weight from one foot to the other or touching her face, as almost anybody else would have in that situation. She had a notable comfort about her, like she was in her own living room, in her home.

After she was done, she told me she had been reading up in her spare time on defamation law and did I know about the substantial truth doctrine, sometimes called the gist privilege? She thought it was an awfully strange doctrine. There was truth and there were lies and why should there be a doctrine for those who couldn't hit the mark? I told her the common law arrives at all kinds of strange rulings and outcomes. I meant to relay a few of them to her, but just then none were coming to mind. I was feeling out of sorts and still looking around for any kind of coffee.

"One thing I'm stuck on is intent," she said, "whether you have to prove it."

"It depends on the defendant," I said, "and whether they're a public or a private figure."

"For public figures, people can say anything they want and it's okay. Is that it?"

"More or less."

"Well, then, here's the question: Am I a public figure?"

"Come again?"

"Am I a public figure?"

The color had rushed into her cheeks. It was an unusual blush, like an orange left in the sun. I had a strange feeling, one I didn't quite know how to articulate just then. I felt as though we were acting out the parts in a movie, as though *Touch of Evil* had carried on playing and I had been dropped into it, or rather she and I had been dropped into it together. It wasn't an altogether unpleasant sensation. Disorienting, but then so was the film, especially the tracking shot that opened it, trawling through all those streets and alleyways and cars and conversations in Tijuana.

"Probably," I said. "You must have known that already."

"Yes," she said. "But what about my real identity?"

"Your real identity?"

"A. M. Byrne is a pen name. They're used all the time. George Sand was Amantine Lucile Aurore Dupin. John le Carré is David John Moore Cornwell. A charming man, you should meet him sometime. Your Conrad was Józef Teodor Konrad Korzeniowski. Although that's more of an abbreviation, isn't it? You get the idea, I'm sure. So, is my pen name a public figure? Or am I?"

She paused a moment and waited for a response. I didn't have one.

It was a good question, worthy of a law school final.

"I don't believe we've met," she said. "Privately, that is. My name is Anna Reddick."

Her hand was extended. Without exactly meaning to, I shook it.

"I should have introduced myself earlier," she said. "You understand."

She picked up my glass, filled it from the sink, then took two ice cubes from a tray in the freezer and dropped them into the glass and drank the water down in a gulp. Her own glass was on the table, still full. She was wearing perfume. It was a lavender scent. I hadn't noticed it before but now lavender seemed to fill the room, clouding in on me like a fine ocean mist in autumn, or a nerve toxin. From her wallet, she took a license, a health insurance card, and two credit cards.

Each one read Anna Moore Reddick. The picture on the license was a match.

"I've got a dozen more," she said, "or you can just tell me when you've seen enough."

"Yes," I said, then realized she hadn't asked that kind of question.

"Since we've never met nor spoken nor coordinated through proxy," she said, "I imagine you'll agree I didn't hire you to bring any kind of legal action against my husband, Newton Reddick. And as you're evidently knowledgeable on matters of defamation, and without a doubt you have other pleading requirements soldered onto some woebegone corner of your brain, you'll also be so kind as to agree that telling people I hired you to accuse my husband of being a thief in various publications, including *The Rare Bookseller*, a tedious newspaper he reads with the utmost fervor, amounts to a defamatory statement. The only question is whether I'm a private or a public figure. If I'm a public figure, I'd allow from the dumbfounded look on your face you might have been unaware of what you were doing, and you might be able to throw yourself on the mercy of the court, claiming you never acted with malice. But if I'm a private figure, your negligence won't be an excuse, will it? In any event I imagine the state bar will be interested in hearing about it. Do you have the address around? I haven't written anything all day. It makes me anxious not to write something. A letter would do me good. I've been thinking that all afternoon."

She went over to my rolltop desk and took out a pen and pad. Her tongue poked out the corner of her mouth as she wrote. When she was done, she ripped the top sheet from the pad and brought it over for me to read. The apartment seemed to be drowning in her lavender perfume.

On the paper she had written "Fuck off. Yours, A. M. Byrne."

"You'll mail that for me," she said.

Her jacket was on and she was out the door.

6.

That week I finally got on the list to be assigned indigent defendants at 100 Centre Street. It had taken a lot of paper-work and asking around to get my name on it, with a few chits bartered and called in. The night court defense roll wasn't a particularly prestigious post, just the opposite, but it was something I had been thinking about for a long while and I didn't mind the hours. I liked staying up late and hav-ing somewhere to be, something to do, even if it was only once or twice a month. My first stint was on a Wednesday night, two days after *Touch of Evil* had shown at the Sunshine, after that strange encounter at my apartment. I had done some preparation for the new work. Criminal law, in its more tra-ditional jailhouse form, was never my specialty. I was trained as a corporate lawyer, one of the more useless types unless you were desperate. Studying kept me busy that week and my mind distracted. When I arrived at the courthouse the guy working the metal detectors nodded and called me chief like we had known each other for a long time, like we were colleagues. He had a bag on the chair next to him and inside the bag was a small dog that didn't seem to know him. Maybe he had confiscated it from someone, or one of the judges had asked him to look after it. In those days every courthouse had its own idiosyncrasies and together they added up to something like a culture. The only things the different courthouses had in common that I ever noticed were an antiseptic tinge in the air and the news kiosks, which were run by blind people. There was a law about that, giving priority to blind vendors, and the guys at the register would have little tricks and strategies for figuring out what kind of bill you handed them, or they would just ask and hope you were being honest.

The arraignments came in quickly in the night session, not at the relaxed pace you might expect from a court that hit its stride at two in the morning. Everyone who worked there seemed to me very efficient and professional and nobody was cracking jokes or talking about where to get breakfast afterward, which diners they liked or didn't like. If there were any office romances or intrigues underway, they were kept discreet. I worked through two possession charges and pled out a breaking and entering with a no contest and a stern lecture from the judge, who told the guy, my client, that he couldn't go into his mother's apartment on Avenue B anymore—it didn't matter that the apartment was empty or that he knew the super. His mother was gone, dead, and nothing would bring her back. Sentimentality was no defense. That was what the judge told him. He was a pretty good judge, and I wondered what kind of offense or insult or grievances had landed him in night court in downtown Manhattan on a Wednesday in winter, or whether he enjoyed the hours and wanted the work, the same as I did. It was nine in the morning when we finished. The day crew came in looking rested and arrogant and nobody seemed to mind. I had made some money that night. Not much, but enough. It felt like good solid work and about as far away from corporate law as you could get, short of becoming a magistrate in a national park or taking one of the other far-flung jobs you sometimes heard about.

I spent the rest of the morning chasing down pay, courtesy of the State of New York, which required showing up like a courtier and flattering a lot of clerks in obscure buildings all over town and persuading each of them to punch my card so that I could move onto the next and eventually get something close to a respectable wage. It was one of those warm days after a week of snow when everyone comes out of their office buildings surprised to see pavement and you notice people all over town leaping off sidewalks like frogs to keep from stepping in puddles.

After lunch I caught a movie. *Roman Holiday* at the Angelika. They always used to show it during the holiday season, although even after seeing the three o'clock show I couldn't have told you what it had to do with Christmas. Still, it did me good to watch a movie about mistaken and secret identities and all kinds of treachery treated lightly. In the end, things worked out fine for just about everyone, even Princess Ann who returned to her duties but with a newfound lust for life or something else. I must have been thinking about Newton Reddick and Anna Reddick and the mess I'd caused for them. I had never been sued before, not even when I was at the firm and there was real money backing me. Negligence comes to bear just about every day in a lawyer's life, but you muddle along the best you can and hope the insurers won't jam you on the premiums.

After the movie I went back to the clerk's circuit, chasing up paperwork. Toward the end of the day, I was having some luck at an office in Hell's Kitchen and decided to ask the woman whether she wouldn't mind looking up another of my cases, a new one I'd just taken on and couldn't keep track of the details. She didn't seem to believe my story but then again she didn't care. Clerks and night court attorneys were in it together. That was the message I took from the soulful look in her eyes as she handed over the printout with Newton Reddick's address. There was a temporary restraining order in place. It came from a divorce action. That part of the story I'd been fed was true, anyway. The Reddicks had been separated and were headed toward an uncontested divorce. Anna was the one who put in the action. The clerk handed over the file and let me look through it for a few minutes, taking notes.

"So that's your guy?" she asked.

"That's him," I said. "Not much of a case."

She shrugged. All cases were the same to her. All crimes, a kind of divorce.

"Better go check on him," she said. "You don't want to get stiffed on your fees."

I wanted to apologize. Some people will tell you never to apologize—it's practically an admission of guilt—but in my

experience it sometimes does the trick and saves everyone involved a lot of time and expense and the inevitable heartache
of litigation. I wanted to talk to the man, Newton Reddick,
and I was already wearing a suit and looking professionally
sorry, so I took the train uptown and walked three blocks
north from the Seventy-Second Street station, the old needle
park, and turned east. At that point I was going on about
thirty-six hours without sleep and feeling good and optimistic about the city and the snow that was melting from
the sidewalks and about my powers of persuasion. 33 West
Seventy-Fifth Street was a classic four-story brownstone halfway down one of the prettiest blocks in Manhattan, or at least
that's how it looked at five thirty on a mild December evening with a crystalline dampness in the air and Central Park
another half block over letting you know it was there in case
you ever needed somewhere to disappear or flee or sleep. The
stoop went up a story and a half at a near suicide pitch, with
flower baskets on both rails. Going up, I passed a well-dressed
couple, a man and a woman. The man muttered something,
maybe to me, about being careful inside that house, it was a
melee. The woman told him to shut up and find a taxi. Just
as she said it, a cab parked at the end of the block turned on
its lights. Behind them, the door was open, so I knocked
gently and showed myself in and saw there was a party going.
It wasn't a raging bacchanal but a party all the same, with
some music and thirty or forty people standing around drinking and carrying on a variation of the same conversation happening in about a hundred other living rooms and parlors

across the city on a given night, especially in between the holidays. I looked around for Newton Reddick but didn't see him.

The interior of the house was polished wood all over with some paintings in elegant frames and family portraits along the mantel, but even with the decorations and all those people it seemed somehow empty, and it took me a few minutes to put my finger on why that was: the bookcases were empty. There were inlaid shelves across the first floor, and except for a few photographs and knickknacks and stacks of old magazines and a spare volume here and there, they were bare. There were no books at all. I wondered if I had the right address.

After taking another lap around and pouring myself a drink so that I would have something to hold, I noticed somebody across the room, a man looking pointedly in my direction, and saw that it was Jim Albee, a man who had dated someone I knew. He was a failed novelist—that's what he always told people. He was working as an editor somewhere, a publishing house I could never remember the name of, although it was meant to be one of the proud old houses people imagine when they think of New York. Like just about everyone, I figured the internet or something else was going to kill the publishing industry, but it hadn't died yet and Albee always seemed to be in high spirits, maybe because he had failed at one profession and found another and it had given him a false sense of security, believing he could do it again when the time came. The city was full of secure young men like him in those days. The banks and law firms were spilling over with them. They had even penetrated the publishing houses. They all wore the same button-down shirts tucked into their slacks and never complained about the broker's fees on apartment rentals. You'd see them on the subway, leaning against the poles, checking their BlackBerrys for a signal.

I didn't much like Albee, although he wasn't the worst person to run into at a party when you didn't know anyone else. He seemed like he'd had a good deal to drink, or else he wanted you to think that he had. It was vodka that he was drinking. He told me that it wasn't Newton Reddick's party—he had never heard of any Newton Reddick before. We were in A. M. Byrne's goddamn house, he said, which launched him off into a kind of reverie or dream, talking about what an enormous talent she was and what it would do for his own career if he could only get her away from her publisher, and how the president of his own company would start to look at him differently and would know that he was somebody who ought to be taken seriously.

"She hasn't written anything lately," I said.

"How do you know that?" he asked. He looked alarmed, or worse. "Hell," he said, "it doesn't matter anyway. She'd never give it to me. A writer like that doesn't ever go anywhere. Inertia takes over and you can't even sway them with money. Jesus, they're an ungodly bunch, authors."

He had more to say about her, but I got the impression as he was talking that he didn't actually know her. It was the way he was glancing around the room, like he didn't want to be overheard, caught, and he wasn't sure who might be listening or what she looked like. Albee was the kind who was always going one place then tagging along to another and hoping the women at the second stop would like him better. It was entirely possible he'd ended up at that party by pure chance. But then again, they were in the same field, in a way. They might have been close friends.

Finally, I found someone, a woman in a sweater dress, who said Anna was upstairs.

It was a narrow staircase, the kind that creaked and threatened to buckle under every step, which some people found charming though you took your life in your hands every time you used one. On the second floor there were more empty bookcases and at the end of a long, dark hallway a solitary light shining from beneath a door. For some reason I had the feeling it was a child's bedroom. I knocked and heard a voice on the other side telling me to quit shuffling my feet and come in already. There was a lacquered card table in there, a few hardback chairs, and in one corner of the room, Anna Reddick, A. M. Byrne, sprawled on a settee with a notepad on her lap.

"Hullo," she said. "Did somebody bring you to the party?"

It took me a moment to remember what was happening downstairs. It felt very far away.

"No," I said. "I came on my own. I was looking for your husband."

"You wanted to apologize to him?"

"I was thinking I owed him that much."

"Well, forget about it. He's not here, and you don't owe him anything as far as I'm concerned. I'm sorry if I put a scare into you the other day. That wasn't too kind. I was feeling neurotic, maybe. I get a little trapped in my head sometimes and the only way to get out again is to do something, if that makes any sense, so that's what I did. Something. I came here, too, thinking I would see him, maybe ball him out a little, but he wasn't around. He still isn't, as far as I know."

"Where is he?" I asked, not really sure that we were talking about the same person.

She shrugged. There were the empty chairs next to her, but she didn't invite me to sit. To keep from shuffling I looked at the photographs on the wall. They were of Newton Reddick posing by various storefronts. The bookshops he had opened and closed over the years. I had been reading about them earlier that day or that week, the kind of diligence best performed at the outset of a case, before throwing yourself headlong into a marital dispute, although there was nothing to be done about the timing of it now. You can't beat yourself up over mistakes like that. In any case I'd spent seven dollars in Lexis charges on the Reddicks and in the process had learned a few things about them and in particular about his book business. He had spent a lifetime in the trade, opening and closing shops, unloading his inventory, auctioning things off, collecting, and then starting over again. It struck me as an erratic business but that's how most of them look from the outside and it seemed like he was pretty well respected in the field, which sometimes makes up for the money. She was more interesting. I knew the basics already, that she was a novelist, an abundantly well-known one who had won a National Book Award and been named a finalist for a fiction Pulitzer. That was when she was twenty-four. She had gone on to publish two more novels in the time since. The rest I gleaned from articles. From a profile in *The New Yorker* and a five-thousand-word interview in *The Paris Review*. From the semiannual spotting on Page Six and the endless stream of posts on a website called Gawker. She came from one of the older families in New York. A Dutch name, Van Alstyne. Her mother died when she was a teenager, possibly of an overdose. Her father was a minor real estate player and occasional philanthropist. None of the gossip items or profiles or interviews ever mentioned a husband, which made me feel better, knowing I wasn't the only one in the dark about her marital status. About her husband, Newton Reddick, the book dealer. In the photographs framed on the wall, he always had that same stooped posture, even when he was posing.

I asked her about the room. "Is this what he uses for an office?"

"I'm using it just now," she said. "You don't mind, do you?"

"It's just that I thought he lived here. This is the address they gave me."

"He does. But I own it. Newton is a respectable caretaker, whatever else you want to say about the man. I thought I'd get some writing done here. That's why there's the party happening. A failed experiment. I always think it'll be nice to have people around, close at hand."

"Isn't it?"

"No, never. Only you have to try."

She smiled a little sadly. She seemed to me very different from the woman who had come into my apartment only a few days before, talking about lawsuits and pen names and writing pithy notes about fucking off. I couldn't tell which version was authentic but then figured that wasn't the point, it wasn't my business. She was the aggrieved, I was the offender, and if she wanted to throw parties and go upstairs to write novels, that was her decision and nothing for me to judge or try to evaluate. She watched me curiously, then put down her notebook.

"What do you think of the house?" she asked.

I stammered a response, something about solidity and the color of its stone.

"I can't stand it here," she said. "This is where I grew up. My mother had a building across the park, but she thought the West Side was bohemian so they bought this one as well. I met Newton here too. He was called in to appraise the books, if you can believe it. Insurers sent him, or somebody did, I wasn't paying close attention. I was writing then. Not like now. I wish he would just keep the thing, but he says that's inappropriate. Says it belongs in my family, like it's an ancestral home or Howards End, for Christ's sake. If he would just agree to take it, the whole thing would be simpler."

"You could sell it," I said. "He might take the cash."

"That's an idea," she said, then seemed to be thinking it over carefully. I kept quiet and glanced again at the photographs. They looked old, even the ones that weren't. It had something to do with the way they'd been exposed to the light or the sun, or else it was their subject matter.

"What kind of lawyer reads Conrad?" Anna asked. "That was you, wasn't it? *Lord Jim.*"

"That was my apartment. Is that what you mean?"

"Newton would have liked that. He liked going places and seeing what was on the shelves. Got thrown out of a party once for berating the hosts over color coding. That's how they had them arranged, all the books by the color of their jackets and spines. They didn't care what the books were about or who had written them so long as the bookcase looked like a rainbow. Newton thought that was the most deranged thing he had ever seen. He was drunk, and that didn't help. He could summon up outrage when it came to books, though. Not bad."

"What happened to the books here?" I asked. "There aren't any."

She gave me a quick, sharp glance, and immediately I regretted asking.

"I had them packed and sent away," she said. "That was ages ago. Fucking mean of me too. I'm not sure he ever quite forgave me for that. Sent the movers over with the keys one fine summer morning and they were done by dinner. Regular movers, some guys I hired from the neighborhood. They weren't book specialists, that was the part that wounded Newton. I knew it would."

The room went quiet again and you could hear the music playing downstairs. It was rattling through the walls. Outside, those brownstones look like nothing could ever unsteady them. Inside, you feel how old and narrow they are, built for a different time, prone to leaks and drafts, and in the winter, mice come in from the street to nibble on the warm wiring behind the old walls. Still, they could have sold it for a lot of money if they'd wanted. Enough for five or six divorces.

"Would you do me a favor?" she asked.

"What is it?"

"Could you get rid of those people? Christ, it was a dumb idea. I don't know why I did it. An experiment, like I said. And really, don't worry about Newton. He's got a thick skin and he knows how to drink. If you want to find him, try that bar on the corner or look around the park. He takes his worries on tour, brings them all over town to see who might be interested in buying."

"Sure," I said. "Thanks for your time, Ms. Byrne."

"Anna," she said. "Anna would be simpler after everything."

On my way downstairs, she came into the hall and leaned over the railing.

"I'm working on something new," she said. "I'm thinking about it, anyhow."

Her hair was hanging loose and seemed to form a shroud around her face. It made me dizzy looking up at her and I reached out for the banister to balance.

"It might have a lawyer in it," she said. "What I'm writing. Could I call you sometime?"

"Call me?"

"For legal questions. Questions about what a lawyer would do. If they come up."

"Sure."

"You could bill me."

"I wouldn't."

"All right. If they come up, I'll call you."

Downstairs the party was still going, but it only took a few minutes to clear everyone out. Flickering the lights five or six times and announcing there were taxis outside did the trick. I emptied the ice into the sink and put some glasses into the dishwasher and turned off the lights on the Christmas tree, which I hadn't noticed before but was there in the front window, the one that faced the street. It was decorated with lights and tinsel and looked like it hadn't been watered in a long time. After locking up I went to the bar on the corner and asked about Newton Reddick, but the bartender said he hadn't seen him around lately. I wished him a happy holiday.

7.

She didn't call, not that week or in the weeks after, and eventually I began to forget about the Reddicks—about their divorce and their Christmas tree and why they had been married in the first place, another thing that had bothered me until I decided not to let it anymore. How does a person like that—an artist, a woman of independent means who throws parties in the other room while she lies down on a couch to write novels—end up marrying a sexagenarian antique hound? Sure, Reddick was in his fifties when she married him, but she must have known where it was headed. I wished I had asked while I had the chance. Anyway, I didn't think about either of them all that much and it was a good, productive stretch, one month to the next through that dark, clean spell of winter. I took on some new cases, a few of which paid out squarely while the others kept me busy. None of them involved marriages or divorces, not in any direct way. There were companies to form, another trademark case, and a neighbor down the block who was being evicted. I could have helped him stave off the order and stay in his apartment but what he wanted was a settlement and in the end he got it. Two thousand dollars to leave with. He had a daughter on Long Island with a basement suite who would take him in. It was nice out there, he said. There were beaches and the schools were well funded. He kept telling me about the schools like he thought I had kids or was planning on getting some. Xiomara had always liked him, that neighbor. He used to strip down and sprawl himself across the stoop and drink iced tea all afternoon while the sun painted his chest. He would do that nine months out of the year, until it was so cold he would have been putting himself in real danger. He worked nights, he told her once, and he needed the sunlight, gallons of it, or he would have gone crazy working that job. He was a night watchman at the Frick. He told her that you could get by, communing alone with all those paintings, night after night, but you couldn't get sunlight, not the real stuff. She liked that he had called it the real stuff. I always remembered that, too, and thought of him fondly. I was glad that he had his daughter on Long Island and those good public schools.

Every couple of weeks that winter I would show up to 100 Centre Street for night court and put in my hours and spend the next day hustling around the city trying to get paid. There was a lot to learn and you met interesting people and others who were less interesting but provocative all the same, although at a certain point you would pause, at the end of a day while you were lying in bed, or else on the subway when you'd forgotten to bring something to read, and you would think about how much longer you wanted to keep it up, whether this is what you had in mind when you went to law school and took on that debt and spent years working a lousy, cruel job to pay it off, then struck out on your own and fought like hell to get your name on a few lists in the old courthouses. You would think, also, about the people you had known in that time, the ones who were still around and the ones who were gone. Vanished, like it was an everyday occurrence, or like they were getting away with something. Maybe you would run into them again, years down the line, and neither of you would recognize the other; only later it would come to you, reach you like an echo, and you would have to think about everything that had changed in that time and everything that hadn't. It was never easy getting through a winter in the city, not with the sun going down behind the buildings at about four in the afternoon and all the doormen looking warm and distrustful on the other side of the glass. Keeping busy with work was the only way to manage it, or the only way I knew about.

Soon enough, spring came in. There's very little of it in New York, but what there is the city takes seriously. The cherry blossoms blushed along Eastern Parkway and great clusters of salty rain swept off the ocean and reminded you that New York is a port town. I started running, jogging all over Brooklyn and occasionally over the bridges and into Manhattan. Exercise, especially running, was something I always turned to in moments of transition, if not crisis. That spring I got to know the best routes and developed a lot of outsize affections for odd sections of the city, like the gentle slope that ran from Williamsburg down to Flushing Avenue, through the heart of Hasidic Brooklyn, or the cemeteries in the borderland between Brooklyn and Queens, which always had a breeze and felt like just about the greenest places on earth when the gravestones were coated in pollen. You got a new perspective on the city that way, running and putting in those miles in unfamiliar neighborhoods. A new perspective on yourself and how you fit into it all.

It was time to develop a specialty. That was the answer to the question that had been dogging me throughout the winter and those long dry nights: What comes next? At least it seemed like an answer when I was on the Williamsburg Bridge looking at the Midtown skyline and at the old navy yard and at the housing projects that ran beside the highway and at the helipads in the East Thirties, along the water. My twenties were over. It was time to stick with something, to see it through to the end. A specialty was just the thing. Art law was my first thought, but I figured I should put some time into learning about probate and possibly estates too. Art would come and go but people were always going to die—there was no way around it. That's what I was thinking during those runs and on that day, which was toward the end of May—not a naturally pensive time of year. Although certain notions had a subtle way of trailing behind and then finally overtaking you when your guard was down—when you were crossing a long bridge or having a meal or checking out new books from the library and sorting out your late fees.

Since I didn't have anywhere in mind to go and had already committed to the descent into Manhattan, I let momentum carry me across Delancey and then north through

SoHo and into Chelsea. I wanted to check in on some galleries. You could always count on the people working the doors and phones at galleries for a little conversation. They were so bored, boredom being a part of the job, an integral piece of the affectation that kept the galleries in business and occasionally got them into trouble, since the truth was none of them knew what they were doing. The prices were all made up—they had no connection to reality. It was an industry built on illusions and ignorance and occasionally I would find work that way, or I would run into somebody I knew or somebody Ulises knew who was having legal problems. Just a few weeks before, I had helped out a woman with a gallery on Nineteenth Street who was being hassled by the FBI Art Crime Team, a law enforcement unit I had never heard of before that spring. It turned out to be real, not an elaborate Russian or Nigerian scam like I was thinking when the gallery woman first called me to talk. The squad mostly focused on the restoration of paintings stolen by Nazis, the ones they sent all over the world through secretive channels like the old ratlines they had used to get themselves to New York and South America with the help of the church. It was a pretty good unit, the Art Crime Team, but in this case they had the wrong woman, the wrong Nina Schulberg. It took three or four days of filing papers and responding to interrogatories to convince them of it, but in the end we did convince them and they were fairly decent about it. One of the agents even turned up at the Schulberg Gallery for an opening party and told some charming stories about her work with the FBI—how it wasn't what you expected, not exactly, and what life was like in the training academy in the Virginia woods, with all those obstacle courses and shooting ranges and the occasional seminar about Nazi looting, and how they made the women wear pantyhose on training exercises. She was drinking a lot of white wine and had some thoughts regarding her employer, the bureau. Anyway, I liked going by the galleries and talking to people, but there wasn't any work around, not on that morning in May. Since I was already in Manhattan and feeling the strain of new blisters that were forming, I decided to stop in for something to eat at a coffee shop on West Sixteenth, the Golden Hound. That was another place I always liked looking in on.

It was still early in the day and Marcel Gonscalves was seated at one of the corner tables with five or six different newspapers spread out in front of him, one of them in English, *The Wall Street Journal*, and the rest in other languages, Greek and Turkish and Portuguese. When I was first starting out in solo practice, I received some advice from a jailhouse lawyer that I'd been hanging onto ever since. He said that I should always be kind to the fences, for they would inherit the earth and then unload it for a 50 percent markup. I never knew exactly what that meant but like many useless sayings it had the ring of good advice. Marcel was the only fence I knew well, and I tried always to keep that piece of wisdom nearby whenever I dealt with him. We first met at Columbia, in law school. He dropped out before the first semester's bill came due and went to JPMorgan to trade currencies instead, then dropped that after a few years and in a roundabout way had gone into business for himself, selling antiques at the

Chelsea flea markets, a cash business that covered up his other activities as far as the IRS was concerned. He had put together some seed money in those years on the trading desk, and I helped him set up his first shell company. Fencing was a good business, or else he was just the kind of person who would excel at anything he turned his attention to. Eventually he decided that he wanted to register shell companies in offshore tax havens. He was from Cyprus originally, a good place for offshore accounts, but he wanted his first company to be based in the Caribbean, so that's where we had done it, in Grand Cayman. Now he spent mornings at the Golden Hound in Chelsea, a café two steps below street level whose regulars played on a softball team in the summer. When he saw me, he pulled out a chair and asked one of the busboys to bring me a coffee, light. There were no waiters or waitresses at the Golden Hound but the busboys liked looking after Marcel. He was gallant, you would have to say. Polished, like the sideboards and escritoires he sold at the flea markets.

"You have that look," he said. "A dog with a bone, thinking someone might take it from you."

"That doesn't sound too pleasant."

"Pleased," he said. "But anxious about how it's all going to end."

He always did have a sharp eye. You needed one, in his line. I told him about what was on my mind, what I had decided on the Williamsburg Bridge, that I needed a specialty and was thinking of art law or maybe trusts and estates, something where the workflow was steady and I could bill my

time efficiently and wear a suit to court now and again, but
not too often. I was thinking he might have some ideas for
me. Marcel knew a lot of people around town, interesting
people who had money and were always getting into minor
calamities. He was a good listener, too, and somehow or another I got onto other subjects, other worries active and dormant, and told him about what had happened back in
November, how I had been hired to implicate an old man I
didn't know in the theft of some rare books that belonged to
his wife, how it was all a joke, a setup, and I'd been made to
look like a fool or worse. While I carried on, Marcel nodded
a few times in that knowing, infinitely tolerant way fences
have, the way that allows them to do what they do for a
living without making anyone overly anxious or sentimental.

"You should have come to me," he said. "I would have
warned you against this business." He always pronounced
words carefully. His accent was faint, almost a whisper.

"I didn't know that I was being set up," I said. "That, and
it wasn't a true theft."

"No," he said, "it wasn't. A mere change of status. That's
quite different."

"A legal matter."

"Still, I would have warned you against this line of legal
work."

He was smiling and had his hands folded on the table. He
had deep reserves of composure. That's how he always seemed
to me, like a desert road.

"Books are too specialized an item to move," he said. "Thefts are exceedingly rare. The collectors know the world too intimately for true theft. They study the catalogs and know one another's libraries backward and forward. Any man who knows a book's worth knows its provenance. That makes it difficult to market the product. There isn't any room for mischief."

There were paintings hanging around us on the brick walls. The Golden Hound consigned them for local artists, and Marcel was their best customer. He liked to always have a lot of paintings around in his storage units, so that when truly valuable things came through nobody noticed. He had a good network in place for movable art. A community, he called it. He had lots of different communities, for paintings, sketches, sculpture, stones, metals, electronics. I envied him all that community sometimes, but then you knew that it was difficult work maintaining it all.

"With paintings," he said, "there's more subjectivity, less scholarship. Mischief, you see?"

"Yes," I said, although I wasn't sure I that did.

"Any man can hang a painting in his dining room," he said. "He can show it to his friends, tell them how much he paid for it, how much he can sell the thing for in Geneva or London. They look at his painting and agree it's interesting. With a book, your pleasures are private. Private pleasures are not much in vogue these days. What's the point of being privately rich?"

I thought about that for a while.

One of the busboys came over to check on us. He was young, in his early twenties.

"We're entirely fine," Marcel said. "Wonderful. Two blueberry muffins would be heaven."

The muffins came out a few moments later, still warm from the oven. Marcel was very slow and precise taking the top off his muffin and spreading butter beneath it. The blueberries were broken and spilled onto the plate and he picked up each of the skins with the tip of his knife and then dropped them back into place. It seemed to me there was something on his mind.

"Is it obvious?" he asked. "I've met someone. It's fairly serious, as far as things go."

"That sounds like good news."

"It's not that simple. You see, he's older. Retired from Madison Avenue, all of it."

"He doesn't know about your work?"

"Oh no, nothing like that. I've taken him into my confidence. We met here, at the coffee shop."

He looked around the room like the man, his boyfriend, might be there.

Two busboys hurried over with pots of coffee and competed to refill our mugs. Marcel thanked them each by name and then turned back and told me the rest of the story. James came to the coffee shop once or twice a week in the mornings to read the paper. Marcel had sensed that James was watching him from across the room but didn't think he was police. There were never police at the Golden Hound—it would have been a red flag on their personnel files. The NYPD was still very homophobic in those days. In any case, James was watching Marcel in a different way than police would have, and eventually he came over to speak. There was nothing suave about the way he did it, and that was what Marcel liked about him. For a retired executive, a former accounts man, he was shockingly unrefined, naive even, or maybe in other parts of his life he was plenty elegant but not in the way he came on that day at the Golden Hound. He said that Marcel looked like somebody he had known, exactly like him.

"That's how we got started," Marcel said.

"A resemblance?"

"It was more than that. An affinity, a recognition, you understand?"

I thought that I did. We both sat with the idea for a little while. A resemblance.

"Then," Marcel said, "a few weeks pass. Things move quickly. I spend a lot of time at his place. He has this fantastic spot on Twenty-Second Street. An old carriage house, refurbished very tastefully, expensively. The furniture handcrafted and the carpets bought from the Turks on Thirty-Third Street. He paid somebody to do it, all this decoration, but he prefers not to mention the name when I ask. I think maybe it's the ex, the one I remind him of. Then he buys me a few things. Nothing too extravagant, just some clothes. I'm not some boy who has to be taken care of, you know. I take care of other people. That's what I do. But these gifts, they are particular."

"That sounds terrible," I said.

"Well, they're not me. The clothes. The gifts. I suspect they belong to someone else."

"The ex?"

"I don't mean they belong to him, you understand?"

"Meant for him."

"Exactly. It makes me a little uncomfortable, accepting another man's skin."

"Well, all relationships work that way. You transform, bit by bit."

Marcel nodded. He was listening to his own story, trying hard to bring his fence's tolerance to it. That's an impossible task for almost anyone, but he was giving it a shot.

"What happened?" I asked. "Something has you suspicious."

"Yes," he said. "That's true. You see, he wants me to move upstate. That's the part I haven't mentioned. Terrible, isn't it? He keeps going on about it. He has a house in the Hudson Valley. In Beacon. He keeps talking about it. He keeps mentioning all the antiquing people do in this valley, all the weekend fairs. He says the police will never suspect anything, and I'll have the city agencies off my tail. I can come back anytime I like, take the train, take the car. He has a car, of course. But he only just recently mentioned the house. We were together six weeks. Not a word about a house, then suddenly he mentions it like it's the most natural thing in the world, having this house in the country. I think, well, it may have belonged to the other man, this house. It's a strange idea, isn't it? Why should I care? Perhaps it was always James's and he rents it off season and forgets about it sometimes, doesn't think to mention it to the man he's started seeing."

He was pushing the blueberry skins around his plate and

laughing like it was all a joke. There was sweat at his temples. In ten years I had never seen him sweat like that.

"Let's walk," he said. "You want to walk?"

It was threatening rain outside but not too cool. There was construction on Eighth Avenue and we crossed over to Ninth and headed north through Chelsea. There was construction over there, too, but it wasn't so bad. They were only filling in potholes. The warm, damp air seemed to do Marcel some good but around Nineteenth Street something about him changed. Hands in his pockets, a glance over his shoulder, all the classic furtive gestures he had worked out of his system a long time ago when he was first moving stolen goods and learning how to do it without looking guilty, but which had apparently returned to him in recent times, or only just now. I didn't mention the gestures, but I felt uneasy walking next to him. Each block I had to fight the urge to turn the corner and run. Probably Marcel was feeling something quite similar.

"There's this thing," Marcel said. "It keeps occurring to me. An idea. An absurdity. What if he killed this man? The boyfriend. This ex, whoever he is. It's crazy, I know. But what if he did? People kill one another, it happens—crimes of passion, revenge, quarrels. They finally come to it."

"It's just a weekend house, Marcel."

"It's not only that. I don't know what it is. . . . Forget it, will you? Do me that favor, please?"

Between Twentieth and Twenty-First, on the west side of Ninth, we stopped at one of the card tables. There were always card tables on that block. The one we stopped at was packed with books, old paperbacks. The kind of philosophers you debated in the common rooms of undergraduate dorms, Nietzsche, Kierkegaard, Foucault. Behind the table was the vendor, a man with a stooped back and a broad smile that seemed neither friendly nor threatening. It was just a smile.

Marcel bought a volume of Foucault and said that I should buy something, too, so I did. I picked out a dog-eared copy of Gramsci that was marked on the inside flap for four dollars. I thought maybe we were going to get something out of the vendor behind the table, the stooped old man selling books from a card table on Ninth Avenue, that he was a friend or an associate of Marcel, somebody who knew about stolen books or crooked boyfriends, and a dollar paperback was the toll you had to pay in order to ask him for information. But Marcel only thanked the man and observed my choice, the book I had finally decided to buy, Gramsci's *Prison Notebooks*.

"You're not a Communist," he said. "I don't think so, although somehow I've never asked."

"For my card?"

He shook his head. "Your politics. Isn't that strange? All these years."

We walked a little farther, turned on Twenty-Sixth Street, and circled back into Chelsea through the public housing campus. The sun was threatening to come out any moment.

"Last week," Marcel said, "I did something odd. Not like me at all. I was sitting at my table with a coffee, just back where you and I were sitting, looking at the paintings, something tasteless, a painting of a dog. I don't remember the idea ever coming to me, but suddenly I was in Grand Central. I must have walked. It's not too far, only what, thirty blocks? And without giving the thing any more thought, I got on a train. The Hudson Line. It's a nice train, up the river, all green once you get out of the city and the river is there beside you, the Palisades. The train stops somewhere, I get out. I'm in Beacon. Quite suddenly, I'm there. A small town. A dull town, with its main street. I have lunch somewhere. I'm not really thinking, you see? After lunch, I have ice cream. I don't like ice cream—not the kind you have here in America, it has too much sugar. But it's a warm day, almost too warm for the season, and I order this thing, this absurdity, mint chocolate chip."

We were standing on Twenty-Second Street. Marcel had stopped under a tree and was looking down the block toward some houses. By that time, I felt certain one of the houses was his. The boyfriend's, that is. It was an attractive block, very much the style in the neighborhood, like something out of *The Age of Innocence*, the kind of place the Countess Olenska would have moved to when she was in disgrace from society. I was thinking about books still. You can never really escape them in some neighborhoods, especially in New York.

"It sounds like you had a nice day in the country," I said.

He shrugged. He was still trying to listen to his own story, an impossible task.

"I went over to the river," he said, "with my ice cream. It's not far, the water. The day is warm, but the ice cream isn't melting in my hand. I stand by the river—looking out, watching the currents. There are no boats going by, no kay-aks or canoes, nobody out enjoying themselves, it's too early in the season for that sort of thing, so I'm alone. Then I'm taking off my clothes. Not really thinking about it, just tak-ing them off, the clothes James gifted me. The other man's clothes. I fold them into a neat pile, place them on a bench, and I go into the river, dive in. The water is terribly cold. So cold that it feels like being punched in the stomach. Your breath is gone in an instant and you wonder whether it will come back. Mountain water, you understand? And I haven't been swimming since I was a boy. I hate to swim. I only think of drowning."

"You didn't drown, though."

"But there was a moment. How long was I in the water? It couldn't have been a minute. Far less than that, most likely. Thirty seconds altogether. But there was a moment, a distinct one in my memory, when I was thinking of the bottom and how nice it would be to sit there forever."

A breeze swept across Twenty-Second Street. A river breeze off the Hudson. It was easy to forget that the Hudson River ran all the way down into the city, that it came from the mountains.

"What did you do?" I asked.

"I climb out. I do my best to dry off. There's a sweater in the pile of clothes. It's not so good as a towel but it will do. Then I get dressed and take the next train home. I catch a cold."

He went on looking at the carriage house with its broad doors.

He wanted something from me. I didn't know what or I would have given it to him.

"I'll find out who moves stolen books," he said. "I'll put out queries."

"Forget it," I said. "It really doesn't matter. I don't think it'll help at this point."

"It's an easy thing to find out," he said. "I'd like to ask you a favor in return."

"What is it?"

"You could run a background check on James, couldn't you?"

"You don't want that. Nobody ever wants that. They only think that they do."

"People have asked you for this before?"

"In so many words. It's unnatural, having that information at the outset of a relationship."

"You'd rather find out later, when it's too late?"

"You don't believe that, do you? That it's going to be too late?"

He considered the question carefully before answering. "No," he said, "I don't."

We kept walking back toward the Golden Hound and finally the sun started shining.

When we reached the doorway, he paused to light a cigarette, but decided against it. The busboys were on the other side of the glass, watching us. They seemed jealous, or else they were just curious. It was another slow morning at the coffee shop.

"Thank you," Marcel said. "I don't know what I was thinking before. Forget my request."

"All right," I said.

"I'll look into your book thefts. There can't be many people who traffic in them."

"Really, you don't have to. It won't help. I was just thinking the thing through."

He nodded carefully, like there was a deep understanding between us, and left.

8.

It was another afternoon not too long after and I was with Ulises at Chivito's, a place on Metropolitan Avenue that had been an auto body garage until the taqueria came in. On the sidewalk there were tables with umbrellas overhead. Metropolitan Avenue was just about the last place anyone would want to sit on a terrace of any kind, but it was a sunny day and after a long run I was in the habit of meeting up with Ulises there. The waiters knew him and had come to know me, too, and they always brought a shot of Venezuelan rum with whatever we ordered.

Off in the distance, you could see the Midtown skyline, ghostly like a mountain range. There were flyers on the telephone poles next to the tables warning us that soon all those ghostly vistas would be gone. Who paid for the flyers, I wondered? A community-action group? They hadn't printed an email address or even a phone number on there—only the warning. The city had rezoned the North Brooklyn waterfront from Williamsburg to Greenpoint. Neighborhoods were always being rezoned in New York. Buildings were going up.

Kids were getting off the buses at Port Authority and in Chinatown and they needed somewhere to live. People were making
money downtown trading other people's money and they also
needed homes, and some of them wanted to stay in the city
and would pay for the views. They didn't care whether they
were blocking your view or the sunlight, and most likely they
never would care. There were plenty of things they should have
cared about but didn't and that one wasn't even very high on
the list. It was more complicated than that, but I didn't feel like
working it through, not that day. We had other things to talk
about, Ulises and I, and the subjects we were avoiding, and
both of them took up space. Supposedly Xiomara had passed
through town for a few days and slept on Ulises's couch. The
Paris show was over. It was the success she had been hoping
for and deserved. She was moving to Buenos Aires, I heard.

He and I hadn't spoken in a long time either about Anna
and Newton Reddick or the case I had bungled. He was the
one who sent the woman to my apartment, after all, or at least
she had given me his name like a shibboleth before handing
over the ten thousand dollars in cash and laying out the particulars of a job that should have prompted me to ask a series
of pointed questions but hadn't. Ulises couldn't remember her
face, although he accepted some portion of the blame, craved
it, really—he liked being involved—and wanted to help make
things right. We had talked about that once or twice. He
thought he met her at a party, but couldn't remember which
one. He went to a lot of parties, about as many as you would
expect a Venezuelan poet would go to. One night bled into
another and there was really no hope of distinguishing names

or faces, especially if she was some kind of actress, which was his theory. Still, he felt bad about the part he had played in getting me into that mess, a small part but an instigating agent all the same. For all I knew he made a lot of inquiries, putting out feelers in all the poet and artist circles around town, letting people know to be on the lookout for a young woman who sometimes passed herself off as a famous author in need of legal guidance. If he did, nothing much came of it. I told him that was fine, it didn't matter. I was a lawyer. Lawyers are agents, proxies, and if I hadn't wanted to get shanghaied now and again I would have gone into a different line of work. Ulises never seemed too convinced by that explanation, but he pretended to understand. Still, he felt bad about the night we had gone to Peter Luger and ordered steaks, the night we had been talking about Borges and gauchos and divorces.

On that day at Chivito's, one of the first truly warm days of the year, Ulises was the one who found the newspaper and started reading from it. It was the *Times*, not the *Daily News* or the *Post* or one of the rags they handed out on the subway, which you were always finding in odd places around town, blowing in the wind or getting dragged around on the soles of people's shoes. He was reading aloud from the travel section, talking about the places they were telling people to go, Bangkok and Medellín and the Canadian Arctic. He thought I should take a vacation, it would do me some good. In an absentminded way I was agreeing with him about that, though in fact we'd had that very conversation before, and he had tried to persuade me to go to Cape Cod in the summer. He swore he could get me a job teaching at the Fine Arts

Center in Provincetown, where he had a job himself. He
taught poetry workshops there in August. I could teach all
the artists about copyrights and freedom of expression and
not talking to police, he said.

I told him I didn't want to go anywhere. I liked New York
in the summer. I liked it when the city cleared out and I
didn't mind the tourists: they meant well enough and never
went anywhere I wanted to go. Besides, if I taught everyone
in Provincetown about protecting their intellectual property
rights and the integrity of their work, what would happen to
my practice in New York?

It was a sunny day. The first signs of summer in the wind.
We were just killing time.

He slid the paper across the table. "Wasn't that the guy?"

He was pointing at a small item below the fold, no picture,
only two or three inches of column space, maybe a hundred
words. My eyes weren't sharp enough to read it clearly, and I
thought we were looking at the travel section still. Maybe we
were. Maybe that was where the *Times* kept that kind of material in those days, a joke some miserable editor had decided
to play.

"It's the roll call," Ulises said, seeing that I was struggling.
"The silent goddess."

He was pointing at the death notices, below the obituaries.

"That's our Newton Reddick," he said. "He died."

The way he phrased it was almost touching. Our Newton
Reddick.

"Beloved husband and bookman" is how the notice described him. "Beloved husband and bookman, Newton Red-

dick, 63." It didn't say how or when he died, only that he was gone and before that he had collected and sold books to some acclaim and been married to a woman named Anna. There wasn't going to be a memorial service. There was nowhere to send flowers.

It had been a while and I had done a good job of putting him out of mind and of getting rid of that sinking feeling that used to wash through my belly whenever I got to wondering what exactly I had done to him, to Newton Reddick, a sad old bookman who married well for ten years and evidently had his enemies but had never done me any harm, although I did him some.

I put the paper down and asked our waiter for another beer and a shot.

"You're out of the woods," Ulises said. "That case was bothering you, right?"

"I thought he might sue me."

"Can he still?"

"Not the way I was thinking."

"Then you're out of the woods. That's why they invented the expression, believe me."

Ulises was smiling a little ruefully, nothing too tasteless. He always knew how to act. Once when we were sitting at a table on the sidewalk, not at Chivito's but another place, a woman walking by had a seizure and he was the one who ran over and caught her before she fell, then held on to her while she was shaking. He rode in the ambulance with her, too, and she was fine. He had a kind of native poise about him, or maybe it was class.

"It's not that simple," I told him.

"Life is complicated," he said. "Death is simple."

The waiter brought the beer and the shot and I read the item again. There was nothing more to it.

"He was old," Ulises said. "For her, I mean. Not for dying. For that, he was young."

I let him puzzle out the math for a minute as he wondered aloud about the morality and the implausibility of the pairing, which he thought was pretty high on the latter count, though he didn't think much of the former—that was their business, they were consenting adults and he wasn't a puritan, just the opposite in matters of love, romantic, erotic, or any of the other kinds.

"You know, I always thought I could write obituaries," he said. "They should hire poets. What the fuck else are we good for? I wouldn't say no to a steady check either. It would be a public service, right? Shit, chamo, that could be my vocation. I always wanted one of those."

I didn't answer him. The word must have had a minute to bounce around his mind.

"Seriously," he said, "you could use a vacation. Get out of town. Go to the beach."

"I don't want to go anywhere," I said. "I like New York."

"In the summer?"

"Sure, why not?"

"Fuck, chamo, if you don't know already, you never will."

I paid for the drinks and told him I had to get going. I would see him soon, maybe.

9.

I went back home and took out my files. I've never been one for exhaustive record keeping, much as the New York State Bar Association might have liked me to be. I'd spent too many years digging through other people's paperwork to think there was anything very useful about having a lot of evidence lying around. The only thing I kept on the Reddick case was an invoice I'd manufactured after the fact for the payments from the woman who was pretending to be Anna Reddick and a letter from the Bar Association's attorney verification branch, which I had called and queried in the most discreet fashion I could think of in order to learn that Rebholz and Kahn, the law firm the fake Anna Reddick had connected me to, was also fake, or at least unregistered with the State of New York. There was no great point in studying this scanty paperwork, which I'd kept in the bottom drawer of the rolltop desk, but it made me feel better seeing how faint the trail was and reminding myself again that if anyone had wanted to sue me, there would be some kind of

documentation, there always was. It would have been delivered to me, and I would have kept it there in the desk.

I opened the window and climbed over the sill onto the
fire escape. The drop from the bottom rung to the cement
patio below was fifteen or twenty feet and the ladder was long
gone. If there was ever a fire, you could only hope for the best.
Normally it was a good place to do some thinking, but just
then there were too many pigeons around. There were thirty
or forty of them flying over the street and making a great
racket. It was pretty chaotic up there. Some were perched on
the wires. Willie, our building super, was on the roof trying
to hurry them home to the coop where he took care of them
and doted on them like children he loved but could also be
impatient and even angry with depending on the situation. He
was up there hollering and whistling. He saw me out on the
fire escape and asked if I had seen the hawk.

"No," I said. "Not today. I don't think so."

There was a hawk over Williamsburg that month. It was
new to the neighborhood, or maybe it had extended its ter-
ritory or made some other kind of migration. I didn't know
anything about hawks. Willie said the hawk was out that day
and he was goddamn hungry and we had all better be careful because he was a murderer—there was no doubting it,
you knew that for certain.

Willie looked after five or six other buildings in the neighborhood and kept pigeon coops on our roof and on another
one on Jackson Street. I shielded my eyes and checked the
sky, which was that fine, lucid blue you get for a few weeks
in spring after the rains. After a few minutes, I saw it.

"There," I said. "He's over Ainslie."

"Coño," Willie said. "That means he's hunting."

"How do you know?"

He just knew. It wasn't something you could explain, not easily, not to a novice.

The hawk was pretty soon overhead, but it didn't go after any of the pigeons, not straightaway. It was making a loop about a mile in circumference, coasting between Grand Street and McCarren Park. The loop was getting smaller, it seemed to me, the circle tightening. Maybe I was just feeling Willie's unease. He was pretty worried about those pigeons. There were still some stragglers unaccounted for and the hawk was coming back in our direction. It was a beautiful bird and Willie was right, it looked like a killer, with that lethal calm. Its bottom feathers were speckled and you could see the pure wheat sheen of its skull and of its beak.

Willie hadn't seen a hawk in that part of Brooklyn for years. Not since the last blackout, which was almost three years past. It sounded like for Willie that was a long stretch of peace. I remembered seeing him on our street holding a bat, going between his buildings to make sure things were okay. He had lived through the blackout in 1976 and knew that things could get bad, though it turned out fine that particular summer, in 2003. People mostly enjoyed themselves for a few hours and drank with their friends. If the heat was too bad inside of their apartments, they found somewhere else to go, or they went onto the rooftops. A few people dragged cots onto the sidewalks and tried to get some sleep there, but not too many. The power wasn't off for all that long, although it was still fairly hard on the elderly and the infirm. August in the city is never easy, electricity or no electricity.

"Coño," Willie said again. "I can't see anything against that sun."

I counted twelve pigeons still out there, still vulnerable. They were perched on tree branches and the telephone wires and on the roof of the building across the street, which always got some sun late in the afternoons that time of year. Willie was getting more and more agitated. He had whistles that were meant for the different birds and he was wearing out his lips trying to get their attention. It was shaping up to be a grisly scene but there was nothing to do about it, nothing that he or I could do. In the end, it would be up to the hawk to decide what it wanted.

"I can't keep this up," Willie said. His voice was cracking.

"Keep what up?" I asked, then realized he wasn't speaking to me. He was speaking to the pigeons. He had no wife and no kids. His mother was on Leonard Street, and he had the birds.

A half hour passed like that and the hawk still hadn't made its move, but it was up there.

That night I rolled a joint, drew a bath, and turned on the local access channel loud enough so that I could hear what was playing from inside the bathroom. The movie was *Rear Window*, one of my favorites. It was somewhere near the beginning, when Jimmy Stewart is talking to his magazine editor and they're recounting all the wild stories he's covered over the years, appearances notwithstanding. I was just slipping into the hot water when the knocking started at my

door. I held still in the dark and gave whoever it was a minute or so to abandon hope. It could have been anyone. A
client, my landlord, neighbors. Finally, I dried off and went
out to answer it.

It was Anna Reddick, the real Anna Reddick, A. M. Byrne.
The writer, the widow.

"I couldn't find your number," she said. "I remembered
where you lived."

Maybe another kind of lawyer would have known what
to do or what to say. I invited her in. She was wearing torn
jeans and her hair tied up. She looked younger than I remembered. It was strange seeing her again, not only because I had
been reading in the *Times* about her husband's death that afternoon and wondering why he or she or both of them hadn't
decided to sue me, but also because when that concern first
presented itself several months earlier, I checked her books
out of the library and spent several nights reading her first
and best-known novel, *Unbuttoning After Supper*. They weren't
sleepless nights, exactly, but they weren't tranquil ones either.

The book made an awfully strong impression. It was about
a young woman, a wife, who leaves her husband for no reason and goes traveling. Maybe she has a reason. I suppose that
was what kept you reading, to find out whether she had. But
if there was any kind of secret involved, it was well hidden.
I admired the book a great deal. I couldn't remember ever
having admired a book so much. That was the novel that won
her the National Book Award and fame in her twenties and
probably a lot of other things I had no idea about and never
would. After that I read her other novels too. They were

strange books that defied any attempt at coherent recollection or summary. Odd, staccato books full of people with contradictory motives and destructive wishes.

"I'm sorry to barge in on you like this," she said.

"There's nothing to apologize for."

"Of course there is. It's late. Christ, I don't know what time it is. Ten? Eleven?"

It was almost twelve. I didn't tell her that. There weren't any clocks on the walls.

I took her coat and found her something to drink. She wanted a whiskey. There was something she wanted to tell, to say to me, and evidently it required whiskey. She drank the first glass quietly, without sitting and without speaking, just looking out the kitchen window, which faced the playground, the same one where she had been waiting to ambush me that day in winter, a season that felt like it had happened a long time before—years, decades.

In that time, I must have turned the TV off or the volume down. You couldn't hear it anymore. The last thing I'd heard was the nurse coming to check on Jimmy Stewart and to give him advice, the kind of good homespun advice you always think you want to hear but never do.

Anna was still near the window. My bookshelves were right there. She ran a finger along the spines but didn't take anything out this time and didn't comment on any of the authors.

"You know about my husband?" she asked.

"I read it in the paper. I'm sorry."

"So am I," she said. "Not everybody believes it, but I'm goddamn sorry."

After that, it was a matter of keeping quiet. The silence was just about bearable and then she began to fill it, speaking slowly and never putting down her glass, which was empty by then.

"Newton left the house just before Christmas," she said. "I wasn't living with him then. I have my apartment. He was in the brownstone, where I saw you. I went there one day and his things were gone and I never saw him again. I had tried telling him I didn't care about the damn books, that fucking mess with the pamphlets. He could have sold my library twice over and I wouldn't have reported him to that fucking newspaper. I wouldn't have hired another lawyer. I didn't want the ones I had. I just wanted to file the goddamn paperwork. But I couldn't reach him, not for weeks. He didn't leave word where he was going, he just went. He was like that sometimes. He'd go off hunting some book. He'd be in a church basement in Newport for a month and come up with black lung like a coal miner from the dust. Or he'd go on a bender, here in the city. He'd walk around drinking too much and telling everyone how sorry he was. Nobody ever knew why he was sorry. I didn't. Somebody must have, the bartenders or his friends at the Poquelin. I barely knew the man, if you want the truth. I figured he would come home eventually, tail between his legs, or with a duffle bag full of books, and we'd say we were sorry and go back to our divorce. Then a few weeks ago there was a call from the coroner's office. Christ, that's a call you're never prepared for. The coroner telling you where he is. And then his box. It came in the mail, fucking terrible. I hadn't heard from him in all that time, and then a box."

She drew a shape in the air in front of her. It wasn't a square or a box, but something else.

"What was in there?" I asked, not sure I was following the story, not sure I wanted to know.

"Books," she said. "What else? Books, notes, more books. That's all he was in the end."

It was a suicide, evidently. She didn't speak that particular word or any of the other common euphemisms, but you can tell from what a person doesn't say when it's a suicide. That had been my experience. I poured her another drink and myself a double to catch up. She seemed distracted. She kept peering out that kitchen window, often enough that finally I went over to look myself. There was nothing out there, just the Russian and Ukrainian men at the edge of the playground, drinking and talking and sleeping. That time of year, they didn't have to build fires any longer. I thought about the first time I had seen her, sitting on my stoop, staring at nothing. New York is full of people sitting on stoops and park benches, and you never know what might happen to them, or to you.

"I'd like to hire you," she said.

"It can't be all that bad."

"I've been looking at that ridiculous box for weeks. I can't make any sense of it."

"What makes you think I'd be able to?"

"Maybe you won't. But he was searching for something.

All those weeks, months, bouncing around shitty hotels and bars, spending the last of his money. He died with nothing. It had something to do with the books, only I can't figure what. Whatever it is, it might be the same thing you were caught up in, indirectly. Somebody set you both up. He never recovered, I think."

"You want a private investigator," I told her, trying very hard to be reasonable.

"We don't hire investigators," she said. "We hire lawyers."

I was going to ask her who she meant by "we," but it was clear enough. The wealthy have always placed a great deal of faith in the attorney-client privilege. Discretion can be a kind of religion if you let it go too far. She was watching me closely, the way you might watch for a train.

"Will you take the job?" she asked. "I'd be grateful if you would. I'm goddamn tired of it." She had her checkbook out. "How much did they pay you?"

"Who?"

"The woman who was pretending to be me. The people who hired you."

If I had been able to blush, probably I would have.

"Fifteen thousand dollars," I said. "It was in two installments."

She wrote down double that amount on the check and ripped it from the book.

"I haven't written a damn thing worth saving in months," she said. "It's keeping me up. I'm not myself when I'm not writing. I don't know who I am but it's not myself. Goddamn uncanny."

"Maybe you should take a trip," I said. "Get out of town."

She looked confused, like I'd suggested a rocket ship to the moon.

"Where would I go?"

"Anywhere. You could go to the Canadian Arctic. Or Paris. Everybody writes in Paris."

"That's absurd," she said. "Everything in Paris is exactly like it is here."

She finished her whiskey in a gulp and reached for her coat. It was a knee-length coat and made of wool, too heavy for the good warm weather that was finally coming in.

"I'm glad you're going to help," she said. "You're not so bad as I thought."

After she left I turned the TV back on. *Rear Window* was still going, or maybe they were playing it again—sometimes they did that, showed the same movie back-to-back on a summer night. The water in the tub was cold and I couldn't bring myself to draw another, so I drained it and went into the living room to watch the rest of the movie. They had filmed it on the Paramount lot in Hollywood. Their version of New York, of Greenwich Village, looked about as real as a high school production of *Oklahoma!*, but it didn't matter: there was something authentic about the backyard Jimmy Stewart was peering into from his window. It's unnatural, having all those people living so close together. Of course their worlds were going to collide. That's what I kept thinking about as I watched the movie and held on to the check Anna Reddick had written for me.

Part II

LIFE ON
THE MISSISSIPPI

10.

On Tuesday a messenger showed up with a banker's box that had belonged to Newton Reddick and was delivered to his widow after his death. I hadn't deposited Anna's check just yet. It was perched on the rolltop desk in my living room, hurling a lot of insults at me as I paced around and tried to forget about it. The honorable thing would have been volunteering to help her for free. She was at the end of her rope, and I had helped get her there. The smart thing would have been to tear up the check and walk away from the case. Probably it was too late for that. My curiosity had been piqued. My curiosity was always going off on its own and getting piqued. It caused me all kinds of problems, professional and otherwise. I opened the box and looked through what was there: two notepads, some books, a few pamphlets, a canceled check, and some chits that were either for dry cleaning or the men's dorms where he was sleeping toward the end. A life, stripped to the studs. I couldn't decide whether it was an impressive display of asceticism, or just about the saddest thing I'd ever seen.

I had never handled a suicide before, not in any formal capacity. Once when I was still at the firm, a partner I knew shot himself at his desk. His office was on the forty-fifth floor and you could hear the shot clearly from thirty-seven. This was in one of the towers on Third Avenue, the ones that cast shadows across the East Side and in the afternoon look like gravestones. The man's name was Palmer. He had a corner office decorated with a lot of products sold by companies that were his clients. I got a call to help sort through his papers while the coroner took care of the body. I did it without complaint, sorted through just about every file that didn't have blood or brains on it and a few that did. Afterward what stayed with me was how he arranged his desk so neatly before taking out the gun. There was a note explaining where to find the will and why he was doing it at the office, for the insurance—that way his kids would get some money out of it.

I figured a suicide was like any other case. Stare at it long enough and you'd see it, the reasons would come into focus, the precedents would come to mind, the papers would practically file themselves, except in those years you still had to wrap everything in oversize blue paper sheets before going to the clerk's office. Maybe in other states the sheets were a different color, but in New York they were blue and you had to send away for them from a special paper company. I had a fresh supply in the bottom drawer of the rolltop desk. It didn't mean anything, it was just paper stock, but having some of it around always made you feel like you were halfway there.

For lunch I had cold chicken. It was a superstition, a frankly ridiculous gesture I went through at the beginning of every case because once, in law school, I had taken a seminar with a professor who had been involved as a young man in the prosecution at Nuremberg. He had mentioned that during the trials, Justice Jackson was in the habit of roasting chicken and bringing in cold leftovers for his associate counsel the day before a new witness was called to the stand. That statement, so odd and peculiar and probably apocryphal, made a strong impression on me somehow, an impression that hardened over time into routine. I didn't have any chicken at home, so I went to a place down the street where they sold it with a Peruvian rub, served hot or cold, with rice or on white bread, plantains on the side, for four dollars. They had been serving it that way since I got to New York and the price never changed, though sometimes they gave you only one plantain and other times five or six or more.

After lunch I called the medical examiner's office and got a copy of the Newton Reddick findings. Dying is a complicated business in New York City. There are lots of small agencies involved, for starters, and the patois is intricate and all but impenetrable to outsiders, of which I was one, a novice with a few phone numbers and a voice that sounded respectable enough to pass for the attorney of record, which wasn't saying much. The examiners just wanted to keep everyone placated, since they had already burned Reddick's body. After two weeks passed and a corpse was unclaimed, they had every right to make a disposal and might have arranged with a funeral home to bury him in the potter's field on Hart

Island, but they shouldn't have cremated him. There were rules. I knew that much and let the ME's investigator know that I did and he agreed to email me what he had in his file. It wasn't a great deal, just the death certificate and a few notes about the personal effects. The cause of death was listed as cerebral hypoxia, which is what happens when you hang yourself. At the time there was enough alcohol in his blood to kill him, too, but it hadn't, not quite. I asked the ME's man about the police report, how to find it. He said there wasn't one, the police had never been called.

"Why not?" I asked.

"Hotel policy," he said. "Charming, huh?"

I thought about that, how Newton Reddick had ended up in the sort of place that calls itself a hotel and has a house policy for nonviolent hangings. It was way the hell out on Atlantic Avenue, past the cemeteries, past the turnoff for the airport. Fifty rooms, twin beds, showers in the hall. A long way from the Upper West Side, about as far as you could go within city limits. Still, it might have been worse. He might have died outside, and at least the ME had put a name to the body, although how they managed to identify it, nobody could tell me.

"Maybe they got him on dental records," the investigator said. You could hear that he wasn't sure and never would be—he only wanted to get off the phone and finish his day working with the bodies that hadn't been burned prematurely, the ones that had checked out conveniently at home or with a license in the pocket, not a false name in a hotel registry.

Richard Carstone was the name Reddick had used to sign in at the hotel. He signed it carelessly, as though it were his own. Big, looping letters and chicken scratch. Carstone sounded familiar, so I ran a search. It was the name of one of the wards in *Bleak House*. Dickens. Another book. A joke, or something that popped into his head in the moment, when he was signing in.

I dug through his box again, the one he'd left behind, to see if anything mentioned *Bleak House*. There was a copy of Henry James's *The Ambassadors* and the second volume of six from *The Illustrated Poets of America* series, published in 1885, but no Dickens. The rest weren't books, exactly. They were trial pamphlets, the same kind I had tried buying from him that night at the Poquelin Society. The paper was desiccating, and I was careful turning the pages for fear they'd fall apart in my fingers. They ranged in age, the newest being well over a century old, printed in Ohio. The title on that one was *The Arrest, Trial, Conviction, and Terrible End of Josiah Ewing, Notorious Horse Thief and Murderer*. There were sections missing, or else the publisher had decided to go to print before arriving at the terrible end. Ewing was convicted, but there was nothing in there about his sentencing or the execution. The other pamphlets were similar. Old and grisly. I read them cover to cover looking for some kind of message or maybe a symbol or an annotation Anna Reddick had missed. I didn't know what I was looking for exactly.

A suicide note would have been helpful. I shook down a few pages, but nothing fell out.

Seven pamphlets altogether. None in very good condition,

but they made for provocative reading. I could understand how they might drive you a little mad. Suicide was another matter, but anyone could go a little mad. Reading those accounts of trials, of early America in its glory, you started to get the impression that killing was an everyday affair, something friends and neighbors did to pass the time. The whole country was built on casual violence and squirrelly mitigations, claims of insanity before they had formalized the concept as a defense, references to blood temperature, and strange provocations that involved working animals and unmended fences. It was a crazy country from the start. That was the feeling you got reading the pamphlets.

Reddick was an expert in the field, or what passed for an expert. It was all vague and seemed to hang on old relationships and unspoken agreements and knowledge that was more than esoteric: it was like a game they were playing and nobody outside a few of them knew the rules, which could be changed on the fly. I spent a few hours calling around to the members of the Poquelin Society. The club's name came from Molière, the French playwright, whose real name was Jean-Baptiste Poquelin. Another pseudonym. Molière was a book collector, apparently. There used to be private libraries all over New York, I was told. Nearly all of them had folded and now there was the Poquelin, on Forty-Seventh Street. It gathered together all the strays and dust from the other clubs and dropped them into that seven-story bunker next to the Diamond District. The members gathered in the evenings for the occasional literary debate. Other nights they just played poker. The old men I spoke to were cagey. Some pretended not to know who Reddick was, or that he was dead—then later, after talking for a while and telling me about their own collections, they said they wanted to buy his books and made me very specific, well-informed offers. His legal collection, or what was believed to be left of it, was pretty well-known. When he was younger, he had gone around to courthouses and libraries and church basements in order to put together a bibliography of early American pamphlets. Another collector, a retired FBI agent, beat him to it and published the scholarship first, but Reddick's work floated around for years and helped establish him in the business. His clients were of a high quality. The kinds of families who had home libraries and streets named after them downtown. Nobody I spoke to from the Poquelin seemed to know much about his wife or about their marriage. It was like they never thought to ask or didn't consider it an important part of the man's life. If it couldn't be printed, bound, and collected in limited editions, it didn't exist, or that was the feeling I got chatting with those old men, who could have carried on talking in circles all night if I had let them, giving me shifty answers and always coming back around to the question of whether I was in a position to sell them Reddick's books, whether I knew what I had, and what I wanted for them.

It wasn't a bad case, really. Not as bad as I feared when I agreed to take it on, which I must have that night when Anna came by my apartment, though I didn't remember saying I would, not exactly. It felt good to be busy again. At the start of a case there are always things to learn, research, phone numbers to try. I called the New-York Historical Society, where Reddick had done some consulting a few years before. The reference librarian they connected me to didn't know anything about him—she had never heard the name—but when I mentioned the trial pamphlets she perked right up and told me a story. It was a long story that hung together pretty loosely. It was about the autobiography of an old outlaw, a road agent who had been chased for a long time by the same marshal, and when he was finally caught, while he was waiting in jail to be executed, he had written a confession and arranged for it to be printed. In his will, later on, there was an instruction that his skin be made into leather and the leather used to bind the book. That was something they could do back then, the librarian said. There were hide makers who would work with any material and bookbinders who were no different than the hide makers. In fact, they were in league together. So, the man's confession was wrapped in his own skin, and the book was presented to the marshal who tracked and caught him. There was a great deal more to the story, but I couldn't remember all the details. Some of them were probably embellishments the librarian had invented herself, little flourishes born of passion or boredom or inspiration in the moment while we were talking on the phone, after I had asked her my questions about Newton Reddick. She said that I should come by the library sometime. They were an underappreciated, underutilized resource, the reference desks. The librarians there knew all kinds of useful things. I didn't doubt that, and I told her that I would drop by and look her up.

"Be careful," she said, toward the end of the call. "These books can be dangerous."

"What do you mean?" I asked.

She laughed and said she was just fooling around. It was a joke, a thing librarians said.

That night, after all the phone calls, I dreamed about horse thieves and a posse of old men who were going out riding after them. I was part of the posse and all we had to go riding on were donkeys and mules, but we were going to do it anyway and that was where the dream ended, with all of us standing around the animals trying to figure out how to saddle them appropriately.

I told Ulises about the dream, the librarian, the Poquelin. He asked whether I could bill that time, the time I had been dreaming, since technically I was working, letting my mind adjust to the rhythms and tendencies of the case, and wasn't that something lawyers did, billed the time they spent thinking? He was right, it was. At the firms you couldn't look out the window without charging it to a client, but it wasn't like that anymore. For starters, I was working on a flat rate.

"Don't sell yourself short," Ulises said. "The money is nothing to her. She'd rather hand it over to you than have to think about it. Shit, chamo, you'd be doing her a favor, running the tab."

That was how all artists were, in Ulises's opinion, especially the successful ones. Money weighed on them, the same

as a hundred other things did, only with the money they
could get rid of it easily. By giving it away, spending it on
drugs, houses, women, men, travel, extravagant pens, legal
services, you name it. He was enjoying himself, talking about
the case and Anna. He thought pretty highly of her. You
could hear it in his voice. He wouldn't have joked about her
that way otherwise. He would have changed the subject or
talked about her work, only the work he described would
have been something imaginary, not really hers but something he had grabbed out of thin air, and he would have had
a critical theory already prepared to analyze it with. He could
spend hours that way, and you would only figure out later on
that he was full of shit. He thought that I should keep track
of the expenses and get her to reimburse them later.

"You don't take on many mysteries," he said. "You should
drag this one out if you can."

11.

On Saturday night some people I knew were married at the Cloisters. A pair of lawyers. It wasn't an extravagant or a particularly lavish wedding but there's something uniquely hopeful about a roomful of attorneys dancing, and afterward I decided to walk home, or to try, to make it as far as I could before my shoes gave out or the wine wore off. Besides that, it was a good, warm night. The dance floor had been warm, too, and crowded with all those damp lawyer bodies flailing around, sweating on one another, everyone thinking about the toasts and the ways they might have improved them if they had only been asked, and about the people they would try to go home with. The wedding ended pretty early: at nine o'clock. The Parks Department was strict about the venue and the hours.

For the first couple of hours I had some company, Robert Hariri, a man I'd clerked with who had gone on to become a prosecutor. He was in the gang violence division of the U.S. Attorney's Office for the Southern District, not a group I came into contact with too often, so our interactions were relatively pure. There was nothing I wanted from him and he hardly ever thought about me, not since I left the judge, left the firm, all of it. He was telling me about his regrets and complaining about the sentencing guidelines, which meant he always had to push for harsh punishments for street kids who didn't need that kind of lesson, the world had never done them any favors. We stopped into a bodega and bought sand-wiches, three of them, all for Robert. He was good and stoned and had a vague idea there was going to be an after-party at a bar on the Upper West Side, so that's the direction we went, straight through Inwood and the edge of Harlem and past Columbia. He got into a taxi somewhere around Ninety-Sixth Street after he couldn't find the bar or get any-one on the phone to tell him where it was. I said I would keep on walking. Maybe I'd drop into the museum and see the dioramas. That was the kind of thing he expected me to say. I was an eccentric, in his view. That was the role I'd been playing all night, the eccentric washout, somebody the other lawyers could look at with envy or pity depending on how they were feeling about themselves just then and whether the sentencing guidelines had made them do anything unsavory. Anyway, I had danced a great deal and had the music in my head still, the good saccharine eighties music lawyers and a lot of other people play at weddings. I was glad to be rid of Robert and his problems and looking forward to the rest of the walk. New York was vast and unruly, but you could walk clear across it if you had the time.

That was when I checked my phone. It was a small flip phone that I sometimes forgot about for days on end. It was always dropping calls. I had bought it from the back door of a bodega on the corner of Graham and Conselyea along with a packet of calling cards that gave you pretty modest minutes unless you were calling Yemen, in which case your time lasted forever. I had four new messages, all from unknown callers. I sat down on the stoop of a brownstone to listen to them. It wasn't the Reddicks' brownstone, but it might as well have been. They were all made from that same rock from the same quarries in Pennsylvania, the stuff that looked like it could survive any kind of calamity, natural or man-made, legal or otherwise. The neighborhood was full of them and that was part of its charm, that illusion of stability. Across the street, in another building, on the second floor, there was a man in the window, trying on bathrobes. A middle-aged man. He must have had ten different models to try on, all in different materials and patterns, and he had a mirror set up near the window. He was after something very particular. A look, a style. There was music playing behind him that sounded like it was coming from a gramophone. You never know what people get up to in their privacy and when you find out, sometimes it's marvelous.

I was watching him and trying to figure out my phone and finally I did. The messages were from Anna. In the first one, she asked only if I could call her back. There was something she wanted to discuss about the case. In the next, she said she had found something of Newton's. The third call had come in much later, around nine o'clock, when I was leaving the wedding venue, setting out on that ridiculous walk. It sounded like the recording had started in the middle of a thought she was having and the thought was about *Lord Jim*, of all things, the Conrad novel. She was saying something about the trial, the one the novel is structured around at the start, when Jim is going to be convicted of neglecting his duties all because he jumped off that ship and left the pilgrims to drown. The officers had encouraged him to get into the lifeboat, forced him really, but none of the older men stuck around for the trial, they all fled the jurisdiction—not one of them had that sickly sense of honor that required you to stay and reckon with yourself, only Jim had, and why was that? What happened to them? That was where the recording cut off. In that last message, her voice was quieter, and it sounded like she was out somewhere. You could barely hear her. She said that she was carrying what she had found, the thing she wanted to give me. She was being dragged out by some friends but on the off chance I ever actually checked my messages and if I was free that night, if I was going to be in Manhattan, I could come find her and she would give it to me. She thought I ought to have it.

"330 Amsterdam Ave," she said. "I'll be there until, Christ, I don't know when. Hurry up."

I saved the messages, or tried to. With that phone I could never tell what was happening.

The address was ten blocks away, not too far. A bar on a busy commercial stretch of Amsterdam. It had rained earlier in the evening but now all the bars and restaurants had their windows open. She was sitting in a booth in the window with some people, a group of them drinking, six of them, with their glasses left on the table, the glasses of everything they had drunk earlier. I could hear the music that was playing inside. It was the same kind of music that had been playing at the wedding, the songs I'd been singing to myself all during that long walk down from the Cloisters with the prosecutor at my side, carrying on with his regrets and his supposed compunctions about having to lock up all those hard-luck teenagers.

Anna saw me and waved. It was always strange seeing clients out in the wild, no matter what kind of work you were doing for them. You forgot their lives were carrying on without you and without their legal issues. They needed a drink, to let loose like anyone else, though when you were working, it sometimes felt like they were contained within the pages of your case files.

"Come in, have a drink," she said. Her hands were cupped around her mouth. She was shouting. She looked different than she had in my apartment. There weren't any shadows around her eyes. I don't know what I was expecting. Her message had said to hurry but I realized now she was only drunk and feeling good and when you were feeling that way you wanted new people to come along, you didn't care why or whether they were strangers or your lawyer.

Inside the bar it was like the wedding venue, but without any of the hopefulness, just a load of uptown people grimly drinking and pressing together to see what might stick and wondering whether they'd be able to find taxis afterward. Anna broke away from the people she was with and met me near the door. It was that kind of crowd: you had to help people through. Halfway back to the booth she said, "Let's leave them, I don't want to make all the introductions, okay?"

I told her that was fine. I was sorry to intrude. It was late. And a weekend.

"They're all writers," she said. "I don't know why I let them drag me out. It's terrible here."

"Aren't they your friends?"

"I don't know. I guess they must be. Christ, what an idea."

It was too crowded to move, so we stayed where we were, by the door, and she waved to her friends, or the people she was with. Apparently they had shown up at her house thinking they had been invited for dinner or a party and she couldn't convince them it was a mistake. Maybe she had invited them. She really couldn't remember doing it, but it was possible. Finally, she agreed to join them for a drink instead and this was where they had wanted to go, of all places. She mentioned again not having the energy to make introductions, then started telling me about them anyway. One of them wrote nonfiction, she said, the kind your uncle reads on the toilet but also wins prizes and money. Another, a man dressed in a T-shirt that was about two sizes too small for him and looked like something he had hung on to since junior high, wrote earnest and morbid westerns, like Cormac McCarthy's, only these ones were bad. One of his books had been made into a movie and that had convinced him that what he was doing was right and now he owned a lot of guns, vintage firearms he kept in a house upstate somewhere.

"You should keep him in mind as a client," she said. "Someday he's going to shoot someone. Or himself. He thinks he's Hemingway, when he's not playing cowboys and Mc-Carthys."

There were others in the group, but she had less to say about them. I tried figuring out whether I had read their books, then gave up and asked what it was she wanted to see me about. What did she find? She looked at me like I was crazy, like there was nothing conceivable, nothing in the world she could want to show me just then. I held up my phone to remind her of the messages she had left. She only laughed, like it was part of a joke somebody had been playing, some mutual acquaintance who was always trying to throw the two of us together in unexpected and inconvenient ways. Neither of us spoke for a while after that. I realized she must have been staying at the brownstone, on Seventy-Fifth Street. That surprised me—a part of me was expecting the windows to be boarded and the furniture under sheets.

"It's a book," she said, finally. "I'm sorry. I shouldn't tease you. I'm terrible when I'm bored."

"What do you mean?"

"I found a book. Another one of Newton's. It's nothing, probably. Just an old paperback that was under the mattress. Up near the pillow. Newton did that sometimes with things he was reading, tucked them away like he was a squirrel. *Lord Jim.* I only thought it was interesting because I found it, and because I remembered that you had the same copy in your apartment. I noticed it that first night. I think I even quoted something from it. Christ, what a pompous ass I am."

She had the book with her. It was a pocket edition and that was where she'd kept it.

"Here," she said. "For the evidence locker. I'm sorry, I should've sent it by messenger."

I flipped through the pages. There were no notes, no dog-ears, only a slight curve to the pages from being pressed into the back pocket of her jeans. I felt compelled to read the first paragraph. There wasn't much light in the bar but I managed to make it out, mostly.

"You're drunk," she said. "Where the hell have you been all night in that suit?"

I told her about the wedding, the music, the lawyers, the dancing. I thought she was going to say something about her husband, or about the case she had hired me for, or something else about the book she had found, *Lord Jim*. Instead, she wanted to know about the music that was playing at the wedding, so I told her, in detail, practically reciting the set list.

"I met her once," she said. She had to lean in very close to my ear for me to hear her without her shouting. It sounded like the kind of story you didn't want to shout. By "her," she meant Whitney Houston, whose song had just started playing in the bar, and whose music had been playing at the wedding, the same as every other nuptial in the country, maybe in the world.

"How did that happen?" I asked.

"At the Met Gala," she said. "Years ago, four or five. Do you know what the Met Gala is?"

I didn't, and she said that was wonderful, I should try to keep it that way, thank god.

"She was dressed in this white suit," she said. "I don't know who the hell made it for her, but it had sequins, rhinestones, maybe, and it was the most perfectly tailored thing I've ever seen in my life. She was gorgeous. Everything about her. We talked about the food. Shrimp. She said she didn't eat shrimp or any other maritime invertebrates. It had something to do with her throat. Christ, I remember thinking if I could write just one page the way she sang it, I'd die, I'd end it."

"Why?"

She laughed. She couldn't hear me. Or she didn't care to answer. It was awfully loud in the bar. "Let's dance to it," she said. "It's too depressing to think about otherwise. I'll lose courage. I'll start thinking about her and when I get home I'll put the song on and never dare write again."

"They can't dance in here," I told her. "They don't have a cabaret license."

"Who can't?" she asked. "A what?"

It seemed just then a very reasonable question, and I felt the case, the one she'd brought me, the context of who I was with and why we knew each other, creeping back into the front of my mind. There was one good way I knew of to suppress a feeling like that. Two good ways, and I had already had my fill of the wine, so I told her sure, let's dance, fuck it, I didn't care about their liquor license. There wasn't any room where we were standing, but then somebody moved aside. They played another Whitney Houston song then, the one that everybody knew. It started in with those synthesized drumbeats that let you know something from the eighties was coming.

"Jesus Christ Almighty," Anna said. "Now we have to, come on, we'll die otherwise."

She was just about the worst dancer I had ever seen, worse than the lawyers even. Those long limbs of hers were all moving to different rhythms, on their own time, utterly alienated from one another, but somehow it looked like art to me, something graceful and finished. There was about three feet of space between us. An arm's length, like the space they rope off at a museum to keep you from touching the paintings even though that's what everybody is compelled to do.

"I used to love weddings," she said.

She came in closer and put her arms around my neck, still moving too fast for the song, almost like a dervish, and her eyes were closed and she was singing some of the lines from the song but not others and when she was quiet she would bite her lip. An elbow dug into my back from behind. Somebody shouted into my ear. The crowd wanted to be rid of us, to expel us like a strange organ. We were uptown, there wasn't room, it wasn't that kind of bar, and the music was for ambience or irony or something else, not something you were supposed to dance to, not wildly, with your eyes closed and lips bit. I noticed one of the bartenders pointing toward us. He was communicating with a man at the door, the bouncer, telling him to do his job. The bouncer couldn't tell who he was pointing at. It was too crowded. The angle from the door was obscured.

That was around when I started to black out. There was another bouncer, one I didn't see. He came from behind and wrapped a fat, effective arm around my neck. When I was limp and compliant but not yet unconscious, he started dragging me somewhere. After that I was out for a period of time and in my nose was the smell of sawdust. When I came around, it took me a few seconds to figure out where I'd been taken. It was a storeroom. Anna was there, too, looking a little put out. My head was throbbing, just above the right temple.

"Jesus," she said, "you were right, they're not fucking around here about the dancing."

The man who had knocked me out was there too. "I tried telling you," he said. "I'm sorry." He was sitting on some kind of wooden barrel that had been turned upside down. He was bending and unbending his elbow, working out a strain, or soreness.

"It's all right," I said.

"I tried telling you, you wouldn't listen. You're not gonna sue me, are you? Fuck, I knew it."

"No, I'm not going to sue you."

"He is a lawyer," Anna said.

The bouncer ran his hand through his hair. He was very worried about things. "Fuck me," he said.

I rubbed my finger across my forehead and found the welt.

"He bumped you," Anna said. "Are you okay? It doesn't look bad to me, but I'm no lawyer."

"Fuck me," the bouncer said again. "Are you okay, buddy? I bumped you through the door."

"Like a bride," Anna said.

She was bent over, inspecting the cut. Her fingernail grazed it.

"You'll be fine," she said. "You have dry skin is why it cracked so easy. Let's get out of here."

"You're sure you're all right?" the bouncer asked. "Jesus, buddy, it was happening fast."

Yes, I told him, I knew, I understood. Things were moving fast.

He opened a back door for us and apologized again and I told him it was fine, I was fine.

Outside, the fresh air felt good after the stuffy storeroom. It was getting late, maybe one o'clock in the morning. We walked down Amsterdam and turned onto Broadway. I couldn't feel the cut on my forehead anymore, and the throbbing had eased up. Anna started telling me something about her husband. We only had so many things to talk about. We barely knew each other and had already talked about music and weddings and her friends, the writers she had left back at the bar. She said that when she was younger, when she first met Newton, she believed he had a secret. He gave you that impression, like he was after something. She thought that was how all relationships began: one of you thinks that the other is hiding something worth finding out about.

"What did you think it was?" I asked.

She shrugged. "I was just starting out then. I thought everyone had secrets. That's why I wanted to write. I was going to expose them. I liked that Newton had chosen this ridiculous, arcane profession to dedicate himself to. I was only interested in ridiculous people in my twenties."

"And now?"

She thought about it for a moment.

We were somewhere near Lincoln Center. You could hear the water from the fountains.

"Now, I don't want to expose anyone," she said. "I don't want to write at all. It's just a compulsion. A tic I share with a lot of other self-indulgent people who want to be looked at. If I could give it all up tomorrow I would. I'd go and do something useful. Christ, anything would be better."

"Do you mean that?"

"I don't know. I like to talk. I wish writing were like talking but they've almost nothing in common. Maybe they do for other people. That's another thing I've learned to stop doing, speaking for other people, pretending I know a god-damn thing. Writers have to pretend sometimes, but the good, decent ones figure out how to cut that out and instead they only ask a lot of questions."

"Lawyers too."

She stopped and looked at me seriously. "I'll bet that's true."

We were in Columbus Circle by then. We had walked the loop and were back along the edge of the park. It always gave you an eerie feeling, being around the park at night. During the day you could pretend it was a tame and cultivated place but at night it was a different story and sometimes you would have to cut across it and would get lost and forget which way was north.

"I don't know if I would have divorced him," she said. "I've been wondering about that lately. We were separated, but that's not the same thing, is it? Legally it's a precursor, but in life it doesn't feel like anything at all. That's why people do it, for the illusion of possibility, of options."

"You were pretty close," I said.

"You've seen the filings?"

I nodded. It was what she'd asked me to do. That was the job. It still felt like an intrusion.

"Well," she said, "he beat me to the punch. You've got to give him that, don't you?"

She was quiet after that, thinking about the divorce, maybe, or about something else.

She hailed a cab heading north and said good night through the window as it was leaving. I tried three different subway entrances and finally found one with turnstiles that were working. The trains were running local, and it wasn't until I got back to Brooklyn that I remembered my original plan for the night, that I'd set out to walk home from the Cloisters, twelve miles or more. The late movie that night was *Three Days of the Condor*. I had forgotten how much ground Robert Redford's character covers in that movie. For the first forty-five minutes or so he's just out in the city, killing time, making pay-phone calls, and turning his jacket collar against the wind.

12.

On Monday morning I took the banker's box with all those books and pamphlets down to Mother's, the bar around the corner. They kept the place dark and cool and hardly anyone went there during the day. The owner opened early and served coffee from the bar until noon and didn't mind if you brought doughnuts along with you. I laid out the *Times* real estate section on the zinc of the bar and spread the pamphlets on top. They were worth thousands apiece, or maybe nothing. I had spent a good part of the weekend on the research. I really didn't know what to make of them. Reddick's personal account was drained between June and December of the previous year. The rest was tied up by the separation agreement. There were no checks written in his name and no receipts for his spending, just cash withdrawals in irregular increments, always less than two thousand but sometimes coming in quick succession, a thousand or so every day for a week, then the account was zeroed out just before Christmas, around the same time he left the brownstone, soon after I had defamed him. Where he got money after that was anybody's guess. Anyway, he had his books.

Just before noon Ulises came by the bar and took a shift looking over what was there. He had offered me his services as a paralegal once or twice in the past but I never took him up on it. The truth is, if I had, I think he would have hated himself. He came from a good family back in Venezuela. Doctors and engineers, lawyers and landed gentry, weekends on the *finca*, birthdays at the country club. He had worked very hard to leave all that behind and to become a raggedy poet living in a loft on the Lower East Side, a neighborhood he had dreamed about for years in Caracas, reading his poetry and listening to old records on vinyl. He had a rotating cast of roommates in the loft, three or four or five of them at a time, all artists of one sort or another, or pretending to be. It would have killed him just a little bit to become a lawyer, or even a paralegal.

I wondered sometimes if I was getting the truth about his life in Venezuela. He claimed nobody knew the truth about him except for me, but that was the sort of thing poets told you. They built trust and established rapport like trained interrogators and the next thing you knew you were reading their chapbooks. But Ulises's stories more or less hung together. He had been kidnapped once, not long before he left Caracas for New York. It was the kidnapping season, he said. A winter, or possibly it was spring, when oil prices were low and everybody you knew, rich or poor or in between, was liable to get snatched. He had been driving to university. Traffic was always bad and he was stopped at a light when a man on a motorcycle pulled up to his window and demanded a watch or some jewelry. He didn't have a watch, he never wore one, not even in New York and especially not back then in Caracas. The motorcyclist followed him to the campus and an hour or so later, when he came out of class, there was a second motorcyclist there and also a sedan, a beat-up old Renault. They put a gun on him and told him to get into the trunk, then held on to him for three days. He didn't remember much about the three days—they had him drugged, which was fine by him. Mescaline, he thought, though he couldn't be sure—he had never tried it before or since. Somehow an agreement was reached with his family and he was set free. They drove him back to campus and dropped him on the sidewalk with his pants soiled and his mouth incredibly dry and mysterious cuts on both hands. For a few months afterward he would go looking for the place where they had kept him, driving around and searching for landmarks or a familiar edifice, but it was hopeless. Everything, all the buildings, looked gray and alike, though Caracas was a city of greens and you were always hearing people talk about parakeets in the tree canopies and about the lush Ávila hillsides. The next summer he moved to New York. I never knew how much of the story was true, but it seemed true enough. He told me about it once when he was extraordinarily drunk and we had been talking about García Lorca, a subject he took seriously. Anyway, you couldn't just write off his opinions, not when it came to conspiracy.

And he did have an opinion, a theory, about the pamphlets we were reading, the ones Newton Reddick had been collecting toward the end of his life, possibly draining his bank account in order to buy them, or else he had bought them a long time before and they were the last things he hung on to. Ulises's theory was that they were all written by the same author. None of the books listed an author, only the legal cases or the names of the murderers and victims that the pamphlets were about, and sometimes also the publisher. Barclay Brothers had released a few of them. The rest were from different companies, different years, different cities, spread out across the country.

"What makes you think that?" I asked Ulises.

He launched into a long explanation that had to do with certain pieces of syntax and phrases that were repeated. Most were legal phrases. The author, the reporter, whoever was writing the thing, had likely heard the phrases in court and written them down dutifully, but I didn't say that to Ulises, because he was on a roll and it was always good to see him worked up about something like that.

He said that life works in patterns, and half the time the answer was in a book, the thing you were looking for. Who has the time or talent to come up with original material? People are always lifting schemes and plans from the movies and from books lying around their apartments. All around, every day, the same plots were playing out between us, over and over, the same plots we had watched or read about. They imprinted on us and became part of our psyches or personas.

That's when he hit on it, the first breakthrough, or what I thought of as a breakthrough. I asked him what plot I was stuck in and he thought about it while running his finger along the zinc and leaving a streak of condensation there. Then he said it was *Chinatown*.

"What do you mean?" I still wasn't following his train of thought too precisely.

"Think about it," he said. "It's *Chinatown*, all of it up to this point, don't you think?"

The people who had set me up, he said, were using *Chinatown* as a guide, the 1974 movie, directed by Roman Polanski, written by Robert Towne, starring Jack Nicholson and Faye Dunaway, nominated for an Oscar for Best Picture, a category it was never going to win, not when Francis Ford Coppola had two movies in the running, including the eventual winner, *The Godfather Part II*.

I knew what *Chinatown* was, I told him, what I didn't understand is what he was saying I was caught in, so he explained all the parallels. A young woman, an impostor, hires a private investigator, that was me, to implicate her supposed husband, but it turns out the whole thing was a fake, a ruse, which the private eye went along with because he was greedy or vain and needing publicity, needing a break and too proud or lazy to do all his background work first.

"Jesus," I said.

"No point in sugarcoating it," Ulises said. He was patting me on the back with one hand and with the other topping off our coffees, which had gone cold. The bartender just left the burner on the bar and the pot on the burner and told you to help yourself. There was nobody else in the bar at that hour. It was just the two of us and our box full of old books and trial pamphlets.

"They got you pretty good," Ulises said.

We talked through the rest, but he was right. They had worked me off a script, more or less, and I had played along, more than willingly. I had even gone to the Sotheby's book auction and fanned my tail feathers around. Ulises thought I was being too hard on myself. It could have happened to anyone. We all get caught up in other people's schemes, every day, hundreds of them, hopes and dreams. By the time we recognize one they've moved on to another.

"That's why it's good to have a poet on staff," he said. "We're sharp with patterns and syntax."

"What am I supposed to do now?" I asked.

Another shrug. The answers didn't matter that much to him. He wasn't being paid for answers. He wasn't being paid at all. The whole thing was pro bono. He only wanted to help.

"By the time you figure it out," he said, "you're caught up in the next one. That's how it usually goes. Maybe you should lean into it and play the detective. You're already pretty banged up."

He was pointing to his forehead, meaning my forehead, the welt, the cut above my eye. I told him how it had happened. The bar on the Upper West Side, the dancing. Somehow he hadn't asked me about it before, when he first came in and saw me sitting there at the bar. We had that kind of friendship. It was a quiet understanding.

"Go talk to people," he said. "Shake things up. That's what they always tell detectives to do."

I thought it over and didn't say anything. It was a lot to

take in, all of it. Ulises went on drinking his coffee and leafing through the pamphlets. He was in his element. There was
no place he'd rather be than reading in a bar with lousy
lighting and good air-conditioning. You had to hand it to
him, he always knew what he wanted out of life.

That night, I went to the Brooklyn Public Library—the
main branch at Grand Army Plaza, where they kept a massive
collection of videocassettes and DVDs—and took out a copy
of *Chinatown*. It was better than I remembered, quieter, lit in
interesting ways, and not too much seemed to happen.

13.

I figured Ulises was right about shaking things up, he usually was, and anyway I wanted to get out of the house and away from Reddick's box. I wanted to talk to people in the flesh rather than hearing their disembodied voices over the telephone telling me about corpses and half-baked investigations and the books they were willing to buy if I were in a position to sell. On a flier I decided to head over to Brooklyn Heights. Reddick was one of those mad scribblers who made notes wherever he went. I wasn't much at deciphering his script but I recognized the napkins he was writing on, the ones he dropped into his notebooks now and again and packed into that box. They belonged to Aaronson's by the promenade. It was the cheapest good bagel you could find anywhere in the city and that was more or less what they put on the napkin, "Simply the Best," with a ring under the slogan. They were good napkins for writing on, thick enough to handle all that cream cheese. Reddick had made ample use of them during his last few months alive.

The G was running in two parts across Brooklyn, so it

took me an hour to get over there. I should have walked. Walking was almost always better than taking the train, especially in summer, in the morning, before it got too hot. At Aaronson's, I bought myself an everything with scallion cream cheese and asked a few questions, innocuous and searching, a casual fishing expedition on a Tuesday in the bagel shop. The guys behind the counter weren't the sort who liked to reminisce about old customers, even though it was a slow morning and hardly anyone was there except regulars, all stirring their coffees, waiting for something to happen, or waiting to die. Finally, one of the bussers overheard me and took pity. Maybe she thought it was a lost grandfather situation. Whatever the motivation, she came over to where I was sitting and said she thought she knew him, the guy I was asking for. A skinny goat, always making notes, writing, carrying on to himself in that way old men do.

I told her that sounded like him, Newton Reddick.

"That sounds like half my regulars," she said. "You wouldn't believe the tips." She jingled her apron, which was filled with loose change. "He was with the judge. At least I think so. Used to see them together."

"The judge?"

She walked me outside and pointed down Cranberry Street, toward the waterfront. It was a quiet neighborhood, an isolated pocket of Brooklyn where people knew one another's home addresses. It was hard sometimes to remember there were still places like that and old men going to them every morning, or nearly every morning, ordering their dollar bagels. She told me they used to come in together, the guy I was looking for and Judge Maguire. I asked her if that was Maguire from the Southern District and she shrugged and said it was Maguire who orders a buttered bagel and a coffee to walk with and leaves a decent tip, unlike most of them. That last part she said loudly, so that everyone in the shop could hear her as she held the door open.

"Thanks," I said. "You've been helpful."

She smiled.

I walked down Cranberry, found the right building number, and knocked. It was a town house that had seen better days but was still august in its own stubborn way, perched on a corner that wrapped around onto the promenade. About a hundred yards over was the house on Willow Street where Truman Capote wrote *Breakfast at Tiffany's*. How I knew that, I couldn't have told you. Those things get passed down sometimes and just as often as not they turn out to be lies propagated by graduate students and art organizations. A young woman answered the door and looked me up and down without speaking. I asked if this was Judge Maguire's house and she carried on saying nothing, regarding me in that cool, disinterested way, and I gave her a story, mostly true, about how I was one of Judge Sheehan's old law clerks and there was something I needed to discuss with Judge Maguire, if he had a minute to spare and didn't mind people dropping by. She left me out on the stoop still wondering if I had the right address. A few minutes later the door opened and there was Maguire himself, a little bent, with that cascade of red hair the lawyers used to joke about and admire.

I told him I was representing the widow of Newton Reddick.

He raised a red eyebrow. "The widow of?"

"I'm sorry if that's a surprise, Judge. I'm working on limited information here."

He nodded knowingly and said I had better come in, then.

Inside the house was run-down but with a base level of refinement that couldn't be suppressed by time or dust. It was a vast place, and I presumed there were stupendous views of the city out the west-facing windows, but the curtains were drawn and the lights dimmed. Maguire had seen all of the city he cared to. He had been on the bench thirty years. Before that, I remembered, he had something to do with horse racing. That was an odd career trajectory and he had liked to remind people of it by decorating his chambers with racing regalia. Sometimes he would have jockeys hanging around when he invited the other judges and their clerks for cocktails at the end of a day.

There was no racing regalia in his home, though, only books.

The shelves looked handmade and were packed from end to end, near to bursting.

I told him what I knew about Reddick and his death, which wasn't much. He said Reddick had stayed with him for a few nights earlier in the year. I made a note of the possible dates. That was when Reddick first left the brownstone, before his accounts were fully drained, before the men's dorms and seedy hotels. He was still doing research then, chasing up old books, nursing hangovers, working through the memories of things he had lost and was losing still.

He was on a tear, according to the judge. "I've seen benders and I've seen death marches. His was somewhere in between, not an easy thing to watch."

"What was it about?" I asked.

"Guilt," he said. "Same as ever. Comes down to guilt or innocence, and none of us is ever glad."

The woman who had opened the door brought coffee and shots of whiskey on a tray to where we were sitting in the half-dark living room. The judge didn't introduce her, and I decided not to ask. She might have been a niece or a goddaughter visiting for the summer or somebody from the track. The judge poured his whiskey into the coffee, and I did the same with mine.

"I wasn't a great friend or confidant of Newton," he said.

"What were you?"

"A port in a storm. I knew him from the book trade. You're familiar with his dealings?"

I told the judge I was. I'd seen the pamphlets and had tried to make sense of them.

"Yes," he said. "From the outside it looks pretty sordid. They call them murder books."

He coughed a laugh through the coffee and looked me over. Whenever he raised those red eyebrows you knew he was coming to a ruling. That I remembered from my days at the courthouse. He used to keep the prosecutors, defense attorneys, and even the bailiffs trembling.

"Sheehan always had interesting law clerks," he said. "How's she doing?"

"Private practice. She's saving up for a real retirement."

"Good for her. She can buy a big house of her own and take in boarders. A life of duty."

"How exactly did Reddick end up on your doorstep?"

"He'd done his best to pull himself together before turning up," the judge said. "Dressed carefully, like always. He was holding on to what appeared to be some valuable pamphlets and the old green-eyed monster took hold of me. I'll admit my first thought was, 'Why not invite him in? In his state he might sell me something grand for bubkes.' I have my weaknesses."

"And did he? Sell you something grand?"

"Just the opposite. He took potshots at what I already had. It was a long afternoon."

"What kind of potshots?"

"Stumbling ones. Babbling. Not the caliber of argument I'm accustomed to. He was making serious claims. He believed I was in possession of books with questionable bona fides. He was raving, frankly. I got the sense he was out of a home. An instinct I have from the bench, the track, when a man is sleeping in the stables, when he's gotten himself arrested for a cot and three squares. I invited Newton to sleep it off. We'd talk about it in the morning, his theory, his project. We did discuss it, several times and from different approaches. We would have a solid breakfast, some coffee, walk the neighborhood, and talk things through. He never did convince me."

I got the impression there was more the judge wanted to say, so I blew on my coffee, which had long since gone cold. The whole house was kept very cold, like a meat locker with curtains. While I was waiting for him to speak, I had a brief memory. The Irish judges used to go to Forlini's on Baxter Street when they didn't want to drink in chambers. It was an old Italian restaurant and lounge where gangsters went to drink in the booths next to prosecutors and next to them the judges. The gangsters were gone by the time I came around, but the judges still went there and the law clerks would sometimes have to get them home when they were drunk. The memory I had was of Judge Maguire calling himself a hansom cab when he couldn't get ahold of his clerks after he'd pissed himself. He was standing out on the curb with his pants soaked through. I offered to take him myself, or to get him a taxi. I was there for Judge Sheehan. Instead he called up one of his old jockey pals who was driving a hansom carriage and persuaded him to bring it down from Central Park to get him. It was no wonder he'd been kind to Reddick, I thought. A man like that knew all about favors, and about being high and low and how to play it.

Finally, the judge spoke. He said Reddick was doing more than chasing up errata. He was looking to make purchases. He wanted to buy the books that he was challenging. That's where his money went. Every last cent he could scrounge, whatever he could get his hands on, loans from friends, the proceeds of his own library, his collection. He was using it all to acquire.

"At first, I took it for a scam," the judge said. "Then a guilt trip. Then I really didn't know what it was."

I was beginning to get a picture: The judge in his retirement, his boredom, curious enough when a near stranger comes around possibly looking to hustle him that he invites the man into his home and waits for the play. And of Newton Reddick, not a hustling bone in his body, drunk, possibly despondent, his marriage coming to an end, going around to a lot of collectors' homes telling them they may have purchased counterfeit books, and could he buy them, please?

"Newton was honest," the judge said. "That's hard to come by in the book trade."

"Then why suspect him?"

He thought it over a moment. "Constitutional meanness," he said, "hardened by years of public service. That and the impracticality. If there's one thing I learned on the bench, it's that personal profit is the great driving force of mankind's actions. The ability to calculate it varies widely, but ultimately you can see them doing the math, figuring their ledgers. These weren't Gucci sunglasses. A counterfeit book would be difficult to produce, and what's the point of it all? Newton was in the business. He knew all that. He'd authenticated some of these books himself."

"Maybe that's why he felt so strongly about it," I said.

The judge sighed. He was looking at his bookcase. Probably he was tired of people coming into his home, drinking his coffee, exercising his modest hospitality, and telling him about all the elaborate ways in which he'd been hoodwinked.

"I like my illusions," he said. "They've stood me fine."

"Would it be possible for me to get a look at the books? The ones Newton wanted to buy."

One red eyebrow raised up and lifted a smile from the corner of his mouth like it was on a string. "They're gone," he said. "I sold them blind, after Newton left. Somebody else's problem."

He remembered the titles, though, and wrote them down for me. *The Mysterious Murder of Pretty Rose Ambler and the Startling Confession of Jack Krants* was one. The other was *A Report of the Trial of Reverend Ephraim K. Avery, the Methodist Minister*, published in 1833.

He didn't know who the new owners were. It was all done quietly through middlemen.

"One more thing," I said. I was wondering whether he knew Anna.

There were about a dozen other things I might have asked, but that was the one I chose.

There must have been something in my tone, the way I asked the question. He smiled in what seemed to me a deeply cynical way, a smile that contained within it all those decades of experience and instinct from the track and from the bench and from pissing himself outside Italian restaurants in downtown Manhattan, a Manhattan that was practically lost by the time I showed up, but which he had known intimately. He said he knew of her in passing, hardly at all.

"Newton had some luck in his life," he said, "and knew it could be fleeting. Anna was a very lucky stroke, better than he could have hoped, and not to be trusted for that reason.

He took apart a portion of his life for that woman, god only knows why, maybe she asked him to, but I doubt that. I wasn't his confidant, as I said. Only a sympathetic ear. But he must have had some friends."

We both thought that over for a while. The house was quiet and seemed to be thinking too.

"Now if you don't mind," he said, "the afternoon is getting on, and I've got to have my nap."

I thought I might have to lift him out of the chair, we had been sitting so long, but at the mention of his nap he hopped to his feet looking nimble, and the woman who opened the door appeared in the room again. She had changed into gym shorts and a sports bra but didn't appear to have exercised, or else she had, but the house was kept so cool that nobody ever sweat in there, they just carried on with their lives insulated from the heat, the light, from the city and its speculation.

On my way out, the judge asked if I wanted some advice. I told him I did.

"You've got an interesting practice," he said. "Don't piss it away at the racetrack."

The door closed. I was back out on Cranberry Street, the sunshine like an explosion.

14.

It took half a day, a pot of lousy coffee, a joint, and some digging through the yellow pages online, but eventually I came up with the name of the bookseller who had confronted me at the Sotheby's fine books, prints, and Americana auction, way back at Christmas, when it had all seemed pretty funny and I was just out walking around the city, killing time, enjoying myself. John Stone. He was Reddick's friend, his defender, ready to brawl but then not quite. He had a shop in the borderland between the Meatpacking District and the West Village, it turned out. A good address on the corner of Jane and Greenwich, a tony stretch of the city that had belonged to streetwalkers not long ago but now was home to rows of gleaming condo buildings and lots of restaurants that were scrambling to offer brunch to the people who had arrived in town after watching early seasons of *Sex and the City*.

I took the L train to Eighth Avenue and walked the rest. The sun was driving people indoors and had them huddling under warehouse awnings. Stone's Books had a new sign out front, green with gold letters, only just painted. John Stone was prospering, or appeared to be. You never really know. I've learned from experience never to presume a person is free of obligations.

I stood outside awhile and drank a coffee from a bodega and waited for Stone to come back from his lunch break. He was the only one minding the store from the looks of it. It seemed strange that in New York of all places a shop could close for lunch, but I figured that was why people went into the book business, in order to live by the old customs and illusions. There was a little sign in the window that said, "Back in a Jiff," which meant thirty-five minutes, give or take.

Coming around the corner, Stone was about how I remembered him from the auction. Forty to forty-five, hair graying around the temples, with an ineffectual air that traveled one step ahead of him and advertised his disappointments to the world. He had a paper bag under his arm. I followed him into the shop, not too close on his heels. He didn't recognize me at first and said hello awkwardly and put his lunch down on the counter. He would be with me in a minute, he said. If I needed anything, that is—otherwise I should feel free to browse, only please don't climb the ladders. There were ladders bolted to the shelves—wooden ladders and overstuffed shelves, just the way you want a used and rare bookshop to look, like he had sent away for it in a kit. The inventory was mostly fiction. He had a section in the back dedicated to crime and mystery novels, and on the wall there was a cutout comic strip that had something to do with Arthur Conan Doyle. I didn't understand the joke, or else there was no joke, it was only a drawing.

After a few minutes and some work on his sandwich, Stone recognized me.

"You're the lawyer," he said.

I thought his blood might start to boil again but it didn't. If anything, he was chastened.

"I was picking up lunch," he said. "That's why I was gone. I wasn't expecting anyone."

I told him it was all right, I wasn't in a rush, I should have called first.

"You're here about Newton," he said. "You heard. Of course you did."

He hesitated a moment, then took a bite from his sandwich big enough to fell an ox.

While he chewed I went back to looking at mystery novels. It seemed like the polite thing to do, rather than watching him pack his feelings into his lunch. I told him I liked the sign, the one he had hung out front: it was handsome and caught the afternoon light coming off the river.

"It's taken me years to build this shop," he said, "this collection, this business."

I knocked on one of the ladders, good solid wood for all I knew, and nodded.

I got the feeling he was about to tell me a story. A lawyer is the last person I would tell my memories and troubles to. That's what bartenders and parole officers are for. You were better off talking to a bus driver or the cat in a bodega, nearly anyone but a lawyer who comes around at four o'clock in the afternoon asking questions about your dead friend's affairs, but there's no convincing people of it. In any case he did tell me his story, from an edition of Emerson's *Essays*, printed in Boston in 1841, the first good book he ever laid eyes on, all the way to Stone's Books on the corner of Jane and Greenwich, a shop he opened with guidance from Newton Reddick just three years before. In another five to seven years, if his projections held true, he might even turn a profit. "The nobility of this work," he said, "is what I learned from Newton. He was a true mentor."

I said I'd been hired by Mrs. Reddick to handle some matters for the estate. I was carrying two of Reddick's pamphlets around in an old Redweld folder, and I took them out and laid them across the counter. Stone had a strong reaction to seeing them. I thought for a moment his lunch might be in danger, but then he steadied himself and began turning over the pages and nodding grimly like it wasn't the first time he had seen such horrors but with any luck it might be the last. Yes, he told me, these were Newton's pamphlets, one of his areas of expertise, that is, arcana pertaining to murder and judicial proceedings in early America. You could hear the disappointment in his voice, or if it wasn't disappointment, then maybe it was trepidation. I told him about what I'd learned from Judge Maguire, or what I'd gleaned, what I thought I knew.

"Yes," he said, "Newton was after counterfeits. He'd authenticated these and others himself, about a decade ago."

"Why did he do that?" I asked.

He looked at me like the question was simple, or like I knew more than I was letting on. He said that it was a family matter, and for a moment I thought he might shut down again or go back to his sandwich, but then he decided better of it, or maybe remembered that I was there representing the family, in a backward way, and could use a bit of enlightening, or he was bored.

"They were Liam Moore's books," he said, "and Newton had signed off on them so that Moore could take a tax write-off." It was unpleasant business but not unheard of in the world of art, antiques, collectibles, he explained, and Newton wanted badly to go in and catalog Moore's wife's books, the Van Alstyne collection, so he agreed to do it, compromised himself that once, with great reluctance and regret, a pivotal mistake. Only later on did he find out the books were in circulation again, poisoning a lot of good collections with counterfeits among the legitimates.

"Liam Moore," I said, "as in Anna's father? Newton's father-in-law?"

"An unkind animal," Stone said. "I hope somebody nails him one day."

"Ten years ago," I said, "is when Anna and Newton met, when they got together."

Stone nodded gravely. "When Newton was there to catalog the books," he said, "Anna was there, too, nobody else in the house, just the two of them. Her mother had passed. Her father was, well . . ." There was a long pause. It threatened momentarily to overwhelm the shop with insinuation. "It wasn't part of their deal," Stone continued. "She wasn't, Anna. I don't think it ever occurred to Moore that leaving his twenty-five-year-old daughter alone with a man like Newton Reddick was any kind of risk, if that's how you want to phrase it. Anna and Newton bonded in a way somebody like Moore couldn't understand. Moore didn't care about books. They were collectibles, assets, a passing interest, something to buy and sell the way you would the fixtures. He didn't know how they could bond people together across years and class and everything else."

"And that's what happened?" I asked. "Anna and Newton bonded over books?"

"I don't know," he said. "I wasn't there. I was his friend, that's all. I know he was devastated when she broke it off. He never thought she would. He thought he'd eventually just die and leave her in peace. It wasn't a very happy marriage. I'm sure you've figured all that out by now."

It seemed an understatement to me, a kind one to undercut all that gossip and implication.

We spoke awhile longer in those roundabout, less-than-honest ways, and every now and again I would fall silent and Stone would tell me another story about something terrible or honorable Newton had done and the books he had traded over the years and the wife he had gained, though never fully—she wasn't that kind of person, someone you could count on, and Newton had never fooled himself into thinking she was, only he believed in her, in her writing. He believed in her as an artist. "That was more than her father ever did," Stone said. "I'd like to show you something."

He scurried up one of his ladders and came down with a copy of *Unbuttoning After Supper*, the first and most renowned of A. M. Byrne's novels. It was an attractive book, with an elegant cover and those edges that have the rough look about them like they were just cut, or like an animal was gnawing at them. Stone said it was a fine first edition, that I should take a look at the inscription. On the first page it said, "To my father, the builder, all the love I have, Anna."

I recognized her handwriting from the note she had written me that day in winter. "Fuck off. Yours, A. M. Byrne." She had a way with notes and dedications, there was no disputing it.

"This was Liam Moore's copy?" I asked.

Stone nodded. "A presentation and an association copy. Given to the author's father."

"But now you have it."

"Moore gave it away, sold it for a few dollars. His daughter's novel. I found it on a dollar shelf at some book fair and bought it up so that Newton wouldn't see it there. Newton had a great sensitivity about him, not like those two, father and daughter. If you want to know what happened to Newton, I'd suggest you go looking in that direction. Moore, he's something else."

I didn't answer straightaway and Stone seemed to think I hadn't understood.

"He's a fucking asshole," he said.

I was leafing through the book still, *Unbuttoning After Supper*. It was a nicer copy than the paperback I'd taken out of the library. The weight of it somehow felt very good in my hands.

"How much do you want for it?" I asked.

Stone stammered briefly, like he couldn't imagine parting with it, not for anything, then gathered his confidence and named a price. Fifty dollars. I counted out the money and thanked him for his time, for the information, the book, everything. He packed it into a cotton tote bag.

Out on the street, I glanced over my shoulder and saw him through the window, scurrying up his ladder to fill in the hole where Anna's book had been. He looked pleased with himself, with the sale, or maybe it was just the sudden climb that had him flush. I'd been in the store talking with him for an hour and nobody else had come inside or even stopped to window-shop.

I went to Buvette on Grove Street and ordered a glass of house red so that I would have a reason to sit at the bar. I stored the Redweld beneath my feet and took out my notepad. The woman working the bar got a peek at what I was writing and doodling there and asked if it was really all that bad. I've always filled up pages like I might need the rest for kindling. I told her it was, it might be, I didn't know, that's what the notebook was for. When my glass was half empty, she topped it off to the brim. They were getting ready for the dinner service and from the kitchen you could smell garlic simmering in butter and hear the cooks chatting loudly. It was a small place with heavy curtains in the windows. They made a grilled octopus with celery and olives that was a kind of love letter. I jotted a few more notes about Reddick and his counterfeit book chase, about his relationship to Liam Moore, another piece that lined up with *Chinatown*, and about the thing that was bothering me: why Reddick had taken the blow to his reputation so meekly, so willingly. They'd called him a thief—I had—and he went around town drinking and raving like a penitent, looking for counterfeit books, paying for old sins that nobody truly cared about anymore. Then he ended up dead. It didn't make sense, or at least I couldn't make sense of it, and the restaurant was starting to fill up and they needed the barstools.

15.

Another day, another afternoon. I wasn't keeping close track. It was summer and the days were long and almost anything could feel like work if you wanted it to, and if you didn't, that was all right too. Dumbo was a neighborhood I avoided whenever possible though the truth is, it was lovely, with cobblestone streets and the bridges overhead and the light slanting through the old warehouses, the same way it slants through certain ruined cities in Europe, with a picturesque bend conducive to photographs and wedding proposals, although if you had any business there it only got in your eyes and made navigating the streets more difficult. I almost never did have business there, but it was where Jala Gardezy kept an office and where she liked to drink, at the El Royale. From the outside it looked like just another warehouse. Inside they had fixed it up in the style of Versailles, but with the brick exposed. A private elevator with an operator took you to the sixth floor, where the old rain-jacket factory had been removed and in its place were a lot of marble tables and designer chairs and attractive people dressed in fashionable shades of black.

Jala had beat me there and was waiting on a three-piece chaise longue with her feet kicked up.

"It's good to see you," she said. "You know I love doing favors. What happened to your face?"

The swelling was down and the cut was healing, but in that jagged, multicolored way that sometimes gives people the wrong impression or makes them think you're neglecting yourself. I had bought Neosporin for it and some butterfly bandages, but the bandages never seemed to stay put.

"I went dancing," I said. "Wrong place, it was my own fault, a stupid mistake. How's Mike?"

"He's well," she said. "Sends his love. Work'll kill him someday, but it hasn't yet."

They had been engaged going on three years. Mike had a great abundance of love and I wished she would finally marry him, though it was none of my business whether she did, which is what she seemed to be implying with a subtle gesture, a hand raised to her face, angled so that her chin was perched between thumb and forefinger, a pretty tableau I might have enjoyed some other time but just then was advising me to move on to other subjects, and to make it worthwhile.

"What will you drink?" she asked.

"Whatever you're having," I said.

"That doesn't sound too promising. You've had a blow to your confidence."

She ordered two whiskeys that tasted like they had been

pulled out of a forest fire and mentioned having seen one of my exes in Paris. In fact, Jala had gone to Xiomara's show, the Young Voices of Latin America exhibition. She may have even bought something there, for herself or perhaps on behalf of a client, but she had the grace not to mention what, or how much she paid, or whether Xiomara had asked about me. We carried on in that oblique way for a few minutes until the whiskey started to impose its natural softening effect and I slid a little farther back into my chair, which wasn't a chaise longue, exactly, but had its own special kind of gravity and appeal, like everything did at the El Royale. At heart it was just another bar, but you had to be with a member to drink there and the back walls had been blown out and floor-to-ceiling windows put in with views of the downtown skyline and the bridges. There was a deck out back and a pool that people sat near but never swam in. Occasionally someone would take off their shoes and cool their feet.

Jala was one drink ahead, but liquor never seemed to affect her much one way or the other. It was just an ornament she kept around and something she enjoyed privately even when she was with a crowd of people. We had dated during law school and for a year or so afterward in that spare, serious way students have. We even practiced together at Beauvois, but neither of us was going to stay there very long—that wasn't the idea. She could have comfortably made partner, the smartest lawyer in our class, the shrewdest, the hardest worker, the most adored by partners and clients, who would always take her out and insist on drinking a lot of liquor that never affected her but made them into fools. She quit around the same time I did. I had business cards made with our names on them, a firm of our own, a shingle hung in Brooklyn, and we had a good laugh over them before she told me about the job at the insurance company, the job she was taking.

"Save the cards," she'd told me, "we'll use them on Halloween, it'll be hilarious."

I told her I would, I was glad she got the joke, wasn't it funny? The insurance job suited her. Ballard Savoy. She had been angling for a position there ever since we were in law school. It wasn't just any insurance company. They were the premier outfit in the world among those few specializing in art, its protection, ownership, and now and again, in dire circumstances, the recovery of a priceless painting. Jala was always kind and threw me business when she could, though mostly I preferred to work in lowlier quarters with clients Ulises sent my way. Jala's bosses were Swiss. She operated the New York branch fairly independently, but still, somewhere up the line you had to answer to the Swiss, with their secrets and the ancient grievances nobody can explain.

"So what do you need to know?" she asked.

The look in her eye seemed to promise everything. Answers, access, all of it. That was what working behind the curtain did for you, or it was just the shine of her native intelligence. She was wearing her hair shoulder length now. She had always worn it long during law school. The day she told me she had met somebody else, that it was serious, that whatever was happening between us needed to end, she had it long still but she wore it up that day and it looked to me a strange and beautiful gift, that last glimpse at her neck, something to haunt your nights for a while, but then later on it would seem like a clue and you would have some fun remembering it.

"Liam Moore," I said. "He keeps popping up in a case."

"That's what the email said. I gave him a rundown. Small-time. What do you want on him?"

"How small-time is he?"

"Smaller than he thinks. A real estate portfolio, residential. Scooped up some buildings in Brooklyn when the white people got scared back when. Tenement halls and railroad stacks. Married into society but never got any money out of it. The family didn't trust him and walled it off but paid for him to be accepted by a few clubs, make some donations, get his name on a few boards so he might look a little less dingy. He made some money of his own, but not too much, in the grand scheme."

"And what about now?"

She smiled over the rim of her glass.

"This is the interesting part," she said. "Now he's developing the waterfront."

"Jesus, the waterfront? In Williamsburg?"

She nodded. "The biggest residential project going," she said. "Quite a leap for him, and a little unclear what precipitated it except he had something to do with brokering the rezoning. If I were forced to guess, if you put a gun to me and asked, I'd say he was somebody's bagman. Don't try telling him that, though. The guy has pretensions, airs, thinks he's much bigger than that. For my purposes, he's perfect.

We'll put his feet to the fire and make him buy a hundred policies he's too stupid to know he doesn't need. But what about you, what do you want him for?"

I told her a little about the case, some pieces of it from the margins. There was a part of me that was reluctant to share too much, not because I was worried about the attorney-client privilege or breaking it. That never really mattered between friends. Two people with an understanding, you could always bend your way around the ethical principles and concerns. But there was a part of me that knew Jala could have pieced it together quickly, not just Moore's part in it, but everything that had come before, and it might have killed me to witness her do it right there.

"So your guy was collecting counterfeits," she said. "Interesting. Some people do that."

"Do what?"

"They like fake art. It's a very particular kind of collector who does. Forged French masters, there's a whole market for them, mostly in Mitteleuropa. They get off on the crime. Transgressive collecting. They'll talk your fucking ear off about their transgressions if you let them."

"I don't think that's what was going on here. He'd authenticated the books, supposedly."

"He did," she said. "I know because I saw the paperwork. For the Moore Museum, in 1994. That was what Moore called his little toy, by the way, the private museum he started for all his books and his lousy paintings. It's all there in the dossier. That was a shrewd piece of business from Liam, you have to admit it. Hardly anyone knew about private museums then, what they could do."

"What can they do?"

"Eliminate tax liability, if you know how, and if you've got yourself an agreeable expert. One of the many ways the wealthy have to make sure they won't have to pony up. Imagine if they directed a little of that creativity and legal firepower toward something useful. We'd drown in their noblesse oblige. We'd never hear the end of it. Instead, they lock it all away in museums."

"What kind of expert do you need for it to work?"

"The kind like Newton Reddick," she said. "With one of those, you can get down to tax zero."

"But real estate deals do that anyway. Developers never pay anything to the government."

"Sure, but this was more flexible, and more glamorous than writing off cement mixers and taking losses all the time. Gives it a sheen of philanthropy and lets you call yourself society. Get your claws in a nice, respectable scholar like Newton Reddick and you can write your own bill, give the Treasury some pocket change, and pretend the rest is sitting dormant in all the artifacts you've collected over the years, which of course you've supposedly made available to the public."

She tapped her heel against the Redweld that was on the table between us. I opened the dossier and read a bit about Moore's tax history, and how Newton Reddick was involved, which was fairly minor, but fraudulent nonetheless, enough to torture a pure soul, if that's what he was.

"Read it through again later," she said. "What I want to know now is about A. M. Byrne."

I hadn't mentioned her in the email or in my rundown of the case.

"I'm a good lawyer," Jala said. "I figured out how she was connected. Didn't you?"

"Not at the start."

"Well, you can't win them all, right? So, is she brilliant? Does she make your head spin? You know the only time I was ever late on a law review article was when I was reading her book, that first one of hers, the big one. Like a live wire down off the grid and plugged into my heart."

I said she was, she did, I had been reading the book, too, and knew what she meant.

"Oh, no," Jala said, "she's done a number on you, hasn't she?"

"I'm just confused, is all."

"Well, that's nothing to be ashamed of. Let's have another drink, all right?"

We went onto the deck and talked some more about Anna and her books, about what was written there and what wasn't. Then we talked about the old days, at Columbia and Beauvois, and how it felt to get that first glimpse into the machinery of the city and how it really worked, who mattered, how a conference table was arranged and a board meeting manipulated and a neighborhood rezoned for residential development, luxury pricing on all of it. I had only ever gotten those few glimpses and what I saw was ugly but still it had the interest of any piece of intricate machinery, like a watch or a car engine when it's been taken apart, or a body's insides. Jala had gone further and understood more. She wanted to tell me about it, but it wasn't the sort of thing you could tell someone. That's how we got on the subject in the first place, from Anna's books, talking about things that couldn't be explained, how you had to experience them and even then it was probably hopeless unless the right person came along and dedicated herself to it before everything else, before herself and her happiness.

"Jesus," Jala said, "that book, it's incredible."

The views were something out on the deck. You could see both flanks of Manhattan, the bridges, the shapes of the boroughs at the edges where they met water. Beside us, two women who had been fighting when we first stepped outside had made up and now they were dancing slowly. They were pretty young, the two women. Twenty-five, or maybe a little bit older but not much. It was that age where you fight and make up and it's all an experiment and afterward, sometimes, you dance. There wasn't any music playing outside. None that I could hear.

Jala laughed. "That's why they keep building things," she said. "Young people are always going to move to New York. People in their twenties from all over the goddamn world, they want to meet one another. They want to drink and fight and get laid and pick up coffee and the paper on the way to work. They want roof decks and balconies and they'll take fire escapes to start, same as we did. That Williamsburg project, it's going to make someone a lot of money."

"What do you think they were fighting over?" I asked.

I meant the two women, the dancers. They were whispering something, pressed close.

"That's all you can think about up here, huh? You'll never make it in real estate, I guess."

"No, I guess not."

"Do you remember that note you had up in your office? I think about it when I'm here."

"À nous deux maintenant. A line from Balzac. It's down to the two of us now."

"I know what it's from," she said. "*Goriot*. I read, too, remember? Just not to my detriment."

That made me laugh. Both of us did.

"I'm thinking of leaving," she said. "Moving, going to L.A."

"Jesus, why?"

"Why not? It's a good city. It's where the art is going, the money, everything. It's where the sun goes after it sets, did you know that? Ballard wants an office. Lots to insure in California. Lots of people with more money than guile and they're scared of earthquakes, fire, and people."

"What about Mike?"

"I'll bring him along, too, if he's nice."

She was still gazing across the water at the buildings, which to my eyes looked grand as ever. You knew it was filthy below, but the skyscrapers were like fungus, beautiful extravagant mushrooms growing out of the filth. That was what I wanted to tell her, but I knew she was seeing it differently. She had begun to think about Los Angeles, to dream about the West and a different kind of light the way New

Yorkers sometimes do, especially in winter, then again in summer, and there's nothing you can do for them, they just have to go and see it for themselves. Sometimes the light is in Paris and sometimes it's in Los Angeles. No matter where it is people have to go find it and when they're gone the streets at home feel different and quiet. Your whole life in New York was made up of street corners and stoops and buzzers outside doors. One day you buzzed and there was nobody upstairs to let you in, and that was an answer. It all tied back to real estate, maybe. That's what I was thinking about, and Jala saw it differently.

The women who were dancing went back inside holding hands, a secret between them.

"Look at the planning commission on the Williamsburg project," Jala said. "If there was space for somebody small-time to wedge into the deal, it was there. That's where I would've tried. Or you could forget about it all. Let the old men play games. Leave them their city. Move to L.A."

"I'll think about it."

"No you won't. But come visit sometime. You can stay in the pool house."

She looped her arm through mine and I could feel her smiling. The sun was going down.

16.

An early punch-out and some sleep might have done me good, but when I got back to the apartment I noticed a voice message on my phone. It was from Anna, asking to see me. She was sorry for the urgency but wanted to speak to me as soon as possible and if it wasn't too great an inconvenience, would I consider meeting her that night? She would be at the Aldous Crumley bookstore until ten or so. There was a note of apology in her voice, or maybe I was imagining things and thinking almost anything in the world was preferable to taking the L back into Manhattan for a bookstore party.

"Please," she said to close the message, "if you get this, come, will you?"

It was a warm night and the sidewalks in SoHo were crowded with gallerists getting off work and with young people standing outside bars trying to take up smoking. Aldous Crumley was a somewhat meandering operation on Spring Street and they kept the lights on all night so that anyone who was thinking of robbing the place could see that it was only books inside. The party space was below street level, in the basement. It was hot down there, the same as it always was, and there was the usual crowd of publishing people, grad students, and the lunatics who show up at readings planning to ask the authors questions about the Warren Commission. I had been one of those lunatics not long before, or a different sort of lunatic, I guess. It takes all kinds. When I first left the law firm, the world of arts and letters had seemed very exciting to me, the way it seems to almost anyone who has seen certain movies and read certain books and has fallen off the turnip truck that passes by New York. I had thought I might try to write a book of my own and one day they would be throwing a party for me in the basement of a bookstore. That had felt like a fine and worthwhile goal. That had been some time ago, and in the intervening period I remembered the need to make a living. The truth is, I never really forgot it. I'm plagued by a certain brutal kind of practicality that occasionally masquerades as competence and always keeps me on the path of making a living, whether I like it or not, no matter how many mistakes I might be inclined to make along the way. The basement was full of people holding plastic cups and talking about who they recognized. I wondered how many of them were suffering from the same condition as I was. Not too many, I decided.

Anna was there to give a reading. She was the headliner, so to speak. The two women who had been asked to read before her seemed pretty earnest. One of them I recognized from a poetry collective Ulises had belonged to, before he lost some illusions and figured out how to apply for grants. I felt sorry for the women. They were trying very hard but

then Anna read, and if it were me I would have given up
hope, abandoned my plans, and come up with a different
profession, a different dream. They didn't take it that way,
though, and I supposed that was what being an artist is all
about. They were watching attentively while Anna read from
a few sheets of paper that shook in her hands though she
didn't seem nervous. It was quiet in the bookstore while she
read and everyone was watching her closely. It wasn't a performance, not a visual performance anyway; it was just a
reading. The story she read was about a woman building a
house in the woods, figuring out how to get the timber and
the tools out to the location in the middle of nowhere. It was
a fragment, really. She read for six or seven minutes and nobody spoke or moved or breathed after she was done. Anna
stood in front of the microphone looking lost and pleased.
Finally, somebody remembered to clap, and the rest of us did
too. The woman in charge thanked Anna, then thanked us
all for being so brave. This was an important night, she said.
They were raising money for a literary journal, apparently. It
was a charity event.

I waited for Anna by the bar. It seemed like just about
everyone in attendance at Aldous Crumley that night wanted
to speak to her, or to be seen speaking to her. It took her
nearly twenty minutes to get across the room. At the bar, she
ordered vodka and asked for an extra glass with ice, which
the bartender gave her and she ran across the back of her neck.

That was when she noticed me. I felt caught, like a Peep-
ing Tom. I'd been watching her all that time. There was a
gloss of sweat across her brow and streaks down her cheeks

and jaw. You could see that she was still feeling a little lost, that talking to all those people had done nothing to moor her and probably had just the opposite effect, one face after another, saying hello, asking how she was, trying to say something clever and oblique about the story she had read.

"I didn't think you'd be here so soon," she said.

"I got your message. It's been a busy week."

"That's what I wanted to talk with you about."

She dug two ice cubes out of the spare glass and pressed them onto her skin.

"Your cut," she said, "it's getting better. Green's the good color for a wound, right?"

I lifted my finger but stopped short of touching it. It was easy to forget about except that people kept talking about it and asking me questions. That was the problem with a face wound.

"Listen," she said, "let's go outside, okay? It's too fucking hot in here. I can't think."

"All right."

"Don't look anyone in the eye. It'll only encourage them. Don't look down either."

Outside it was hot too. Summer had come in earnest. She fanned herself with the pages she had been reading before and the ice melted down her shoulders and she asked me if I was uncomfortable.

I told her I liked the heat fine. "It helps me sleep. It used to. I like summer in New York."

"So do I," she said. "Everyone thinks you're supposed to want to get out, but why?" She lit a cigarette from a full pack.

She didn't offer and I didn't want one. "Look, I haven't been myself lately. I've been impulsive."

"You're not usually?"

"No, the fact is, I'm not. That used to bother me. I would try to do a lot of reckless things to believe I was somebody else but then I grew up and got to know myself a little better and stopped trying to pretend I was a goddamn fairy or a wood nymph or something juvenile. You do that for too long and you'll never make anything of yourself but a sorry fucking cliché."

Somebody waved to her, somebody coming out of the store. She waved back and smiled but didn't look them in the eye and didn't let her eyes move down to the sidewalk either. I had a feeling she was coming around to something in particular and kept quiet. There was a bus stop down the block and a man went running toward it like there was a bus there that was about to leave, a bus that was on the verge of closing its doors and going without him, but there wasn't. There was nothing at the stop and when the man reached the pole, he wrapped his arm around it. Anna was watching him with great interest and seemed to know just what it was about.

"I shouldn't have gotten you involved with this," she said. "It was unnecessary."

"I was involved before you came along."

"You didn't mean to be. You were tricked. It could have happened to anyone."

I doubted that but didn't say so. When it came down to it, I had a lot of pride, like everyone else. On second thought, I asked for the cigarette that she hadn't offered. I held it without lighting the thing. I needed something to do with my hands but didn't want to smoke it.

"What did you think of it in there?" she asked.

"The party?"

"The goddamn story."

She was looking away, down the dark end of Spring toward Bowery, past a bus stop.

"It was beautiful," I said.

"I want to write something," she said. "Something new. A crime novel or a thriller. A book where things happen and people aren't just talking all the time and then going off into the woods."

"You can't do that," I said. "You shouldn't, I mean."

"No," she said. "Probably not. I hardly know any criminals."

After stubbing out her cigarette, she said I should consider myself relieved.

"Relieved of what?"

"Duty. That's what I'm trying to tell you. I shouldn't have hired you. It was an impulse."

"I'm making progress," I said. "Real progress, I think, I don't know yet. I will soon."

"I wish you wouldn't. I wish the whole fucking thing would just go away."

I didn't understand where it was coming from. I thought maybe I should tell her about the counterfeit books and about the *Chinatown* script and all the vague unconvincing notions I was starting to develop about her husband's final days and weeks. While I was at it, I could also ask why she hadn't told me her father had been in business with Newton before she'd met him, that quite possibly she was a part of something between them, a grudge or a sour memory. Hadn't that seemed significant to her? Hadn't she thought that information would be useful at the outset?

I didn't ask her any of that. I only told her that I hadn't cashed her check just yet. The retainer. I wouldn't, if that was what she wanted.

"Cash the damn thing," she said. "Don't be a fool. It's only money."

Before I had a chance to dwell too long on that idea, her friends came out from the bookstore. There were three of them: two women in black dresses and a tall man with sunglasses balanced on his head standing between the two women, propping them up like a tentpole. I recognized one of the women from the bar on the Upper West Side where you weren't supposed to dance. She was a writer, one of them who had been sitting in the booth beside Anna. Sometimes the city was like that, full of people you recognized but didn't know. Other days you would run into a lot of old friends but have nothing to say to them, nothing had happened, and you would only stand on the street corner making conversation about how hot it was getting on the subway platforms or restaurants you were planning on going to, but never would.

"We're going somewhere," Anna said. "I don't remember where. Max's, maybe."

I didn't answer. I was still thinking over what had happened, what she'd said, firing me.

"You're welcome to come," she said. "You should. Why the hell not?"

A taxi pulled over to the curb. A moment before, its off-duty light had been on. Without really thinking about it I got in. The driver didn't want to take five people but finally somebody convinced him it was better than idling against the curb. It had been a long while since I'd packed into a cab that way. The tall man was in the front seat talking with the driver, asking him where he was from and pursuing the line even though the driver didn't want to make conversation. He didn't want anything to do with us, he only wanted the meter to run and the ride to be over. There were four of us on the backseat. The women were all wearing perfume and talking about people who had been at the party and about somebody who hadn't been, somebody named Allison or Kathy. It sounded like they were speaking in code. I rolled down the window and leaned my head out like a dog. In fact, as we were turning on Bowery someone on the sidewalk said, "Would you look at that? I don't know that breed," meaning me, with my head out the window.

When I leaned back in, Anna introduced me. She did it pretty graciously, if late.

"He was doing me a favor," she said.

She was on the other side of the seat, looking out the other window onto Bowery.

The woman sitting next to me said she recognized me. "You're a lawyer, aren't you?"

She said I had represented somebody she knew. A friend,

a guy she was seeing, a painter from Holland. He had been house-sitting for a gallery owner who was in Amsterdam managing a club for the summer, or an exhibition that was being held at a club, she didn't know the exact arrangement. The gallery owner was there in Holland and the painter was in New York, in the apartment, which was in the Meatpacking District. He was a very regimented man, she said. He had been in the army. He woke up every morning and did five hundred push-ups and one thousand sit-ups before he even considered mixing paints. Only he was prone to neck pain and sleeping in a stranger's bed wasn't helping and he couldn't get any of the work done before his push-ups and sit-ups, so on days when he was stiff from the night before, he would have to lie on the floor for hours and hours, managing only a single push-up or sit-up every ten minutes or more. If he didn't reach his number for the day, he wouldn't allow himself to paint.

"Can you imagine," she asked, "being so maniacal about a routine that it starts consuming you, like a serpent eating its own tail?"

It sounded like the man had left a strong impression on her. Like she missed him.

I tried remembering who he was, this client of mine, a Dutch painter with back problems. "What was he arrested for?" I asked.

"It was the apartment," she said. "It wasn't his. Aren't you the lawyer?"

Anna laughed. I didn't think she was listening to us. She was looking out the window still. The cab let us out at a bar

at the bottom of Clinton Street in Chinatown. It wasn't anywhere I recognized. There were always new places coming
into neighborhoods like that and old places changing names
or management or some other thing. I didn't think I had ever
been to that bar. The others went inside. Anna asked if I
would stay outside and smoke another cigarette with her.

"You don't have to stay if you don't want to," she said.

I asked if there was something embarrassing inside. Was it
a banker bar?

"You've already seen the most embarrassing things I do,"
she said. "I hire lawyers to look into my husband's death, I
dance poorly, and I stay home writing stories about construction projects."

"Then you read them at parties."

"That's right," she said. "I read them at fucking parties."

"I thought it was beautiful."

"You already said that. But it doesn't matter what anyone
else thinks. That's the rub."

She was looking past me again. Across the street was a
hand-pulled noddle shop. The cook had rolled the dough and
was working it into noodles, which required slamming it on
his prep table over and over again, a thump that echoed out
of the shop and across the street to where we were standing.
Hearing the sound, my mouth began to water, although I
wasn't really hungry.

"Look," she said, "Newton was my support system. In a
fucked-up way, but he was. I would leave him and go running off somewhere for three, six months, however long it
took. While I was away I'd see a lot of people and do a lot

of shitty things and get no work done at all. Then I'd come back home and he would take care of things, of me, us. That's when I would write. It sounds vapid, I'm sure. Fucking toxic, maybe, but it worked for us until it didn't, then I decided to get the hell out. That's what happens, isn't it? Things end, someone has to end it."

"Every marriage is different," I said.

"Have you ever been married?"

"No."

She nodded gravely and didn't laugh or answer or ask me anything else.

Just then another group of people came from the corner of Clinton Street. There were five or six of them and they appeared to be having a good time. They were looking for the bar, which wasn't marked with a sign, and one of them asked me if that was the place. I told him it was, it must be. After they'd gone, Anna seemed different. Whatever mood had struck her, it passed.

She was all done confessing. She was done smoking too.

"Look," she said, "I appreciate everything you've done. I'm sorry to take up your time."

"So that's it?"

"As far as I'm concerned, yes. I hope you'll cash that check. And thank you."

She leaned in to kiss my cheek but stopped short. It was only a gesture people make.

17.

That night, at two or three in the morning, I got a call. I was already in bed and had to dig around in the sheets to find the phone. It was Anna. She sounded drunk or stoned, or both.

"Weren't you asleep?" she asked, then didn't wait for me to answer.

Wherever she was, it sounded very quiet, then a moment would go by and there would be a great clamor in the background, but only for a moment, like she was in one of those old-fashioned phone booths you still sometimes found in restaurants, especially restaurants in Midtown and Italian places around Brooklyn, the kind that only took reservations and never had any openings except on Saturday night, exactly the time when you figured they would be most crowded. Nowhere in Brooklyn took reservations then except the Italian restaurants and they were the same kinds of places where you found the old telephones.

"I'm writing something new," Anna continued, still sounding slightly out of body, or else she was just tired. "It shouldn't work," she said, "but it does. I always get this way when I'm starting something. Uncanny, disoriented. It's a battle between confidence and despair. That's how it is for me, anyhow. I'm sure Martin Amis just opens up his robe and pisses out another novel. Jesus, maybe I am a little insecure. I never talk about other writers, not British ones. And I start making jokes all the time. Performing this silly little routine like I'm in the Catskills working the goddamn summer resort circuit. All these elaborate, drawn-out setups that don't have any punch lines."

I got out of bed and fixed some coffee while she was talking. When it was done brewing I poured it over ice and watched the cubes melt and spoil the coffee, which wasn't any good in the first place. It was from a brick of espresso they sold for two dollars at the bodega. When you added it to ice and milk that was also very cold it could be comforting on a hot night.

"What's the story about?" I asked. I meant to ask her what she thought she was doing, why she was calling. She'd fired me.

"A woman who kills her husband," she said. "She's a painter."

"Why does she kill him?"

"To see whether she can paint."

"Can't she do that while he's around?"

"That's what she has to find out. I've only just started. It's not worked out yet."

I told her I was glad. It sounded like a good project. She must be happy to be writing again. There was a long pause on the other end of the line. I thought she might have hung up, until I heard a noise. It sounded like dishes being thrown into an industrial steam washer, or else I was just imagining things, letting my mind get carried away thinking about new places and jobs.

"I'm trying to work out how she does it," she said. "I'm stuck. I thought you might talk it through with me. If you wouldn't mind. I shouldn't have called, probably. Are you alone there?"

"That's all right," I said. "I've never killed anyone before. I'm no expert."

"Neither have I. This story, I've started it, it's good, I like it, I think about it all the time. But there's supposed to be this death, and what I can't get my head around is her actually doing it. What does it matter, I keep wondering, whether she kills him or he has a heart attack or he swallows a bottle of cyanide? However he ends it, they're still killing each other. You're the lawyer, am I making any sense? We kill each other sometimes, only it happens very slowly. Nobody notices, and so long as you don't pull the trigger, we pretend it was okay. We're all just walking around all day long wiping our finger-prints off of things. That's what I've been thinking."

I thought about getting some water but didn't want to move. Maybe another lawyer would have known what to say. I gave up and kept quiet. Keeping quiet is half the job, only nobody tells you that at law school. They're always telling you other things, about jurisdictional battles and founding principles, but nothing about what to do when a client calls you up at three in the morning wanting to chat. It's something you have to learn about on your own, although in this case there was no client, no job. She had fired me outside a bookstore. We were two people talking on the telephone and neither of us knew what time it was.

"I'm thinking about killing him on the first page," she said. "Like a crime novel."

"Why do you want to write a crime novel?"

"There's something to be said for that kind of efficiency. It's decisive." She was laughing about it. The idea seemed to really please her.

"If it really doesn't matter," I said, "why not have it done already?"

"You mean off the page?"

"Why not? It's in the past, something she's moved on from already. She's trying to paint."

Another laugh, this one a little deeper, like it was rumbling down the telephone lines from wherever she was calling. It was easy to forget that all of New York was connected in physical ways. Gas lines, telephones, power, cable, sewage. A dozen different utilities crawling under the streets. I didn't know where she was. At her apartment or maybe the brownstone or a restaurant with a phone booth and an owner sitting at the bar watching her, thinking about her and whether she was going to go home or hang around all night, keeping him from locking up.

"Do you want to meet somewhere?" she asked. "Christ, I'm bothering you. I'm sorry."

"Sure, do you want get a drink?"

"What about breakfast? Have you eaten? There's a diner at the bottom of the bridge."

She started describing the diner and what was on the walls. She couldn't remember the name of the place or the corner it was on, but I knew where she meant anyway. It was near the bottom of the Williamsburg Bridge, on the Manhattan side. I didn't know the name of it either.

"I can be there in forty minutes," I said.

"You don't mind? Jesus, that's good of you. You're sure you weren't asleep?"

I threw some water on my face and poured the coffee and ice into a plastic cup. I was thinking I would walk to the diner. It would be light out soon and there would be a stream of Hasids going over the footpath to get to the Lower East Side. I always felt more industrious walking in a group of workers like that. When I was heading out the door, the phone rang again.

It was Anna. "You haven't left yet," she said.

"I was just heading out."

"That's okay. I was just thinking, maybe I could get some sleep. That I should get some."

"Of course."

"I hope I didn't bother you. It's just how I get when I'm starting out something new."

"Uncanny."

"Is that what I said? It sounds a little ridiculous, doesn't it?"

"Good luck with it. Do writers say that? Actors are the superstitious ones, I think."

"I think everyone is. It just depends on what you're talking about."

The pause this time was a half-minute, or maybe longer, and then a click. The line was dead. I decided to walk over to the diner anyway. The coffee had me feeling awake and I wanted to go out and be with the Hasids. There were about a hundred of them up on the bridge at that hour, a few walking alone but most traveling in packs of three of four and talking earnestly with their coattails blowing in the wind. It felt like they were all having the same conversation, only you couldn't know what it was about, not unless they wanted you to know it.

18.

Something strange happened the next week. I did something strange, that is. It was a Tuesday morning and I went to Film Forum, where they were showing an 11:15 matinee of *Memories of Underdevelopment*, the 1968 film by Tomás Gutiérrez Alea, which Ulises had described to me as a Cuban *8 1/2*, a pretty accurate comparison it turned out. There was a man in a suit wandering around Havana, doing a lot of thinking about how he had let things get out of hand, and sometimes he would meet up with a woman. The 11:15 matinees were never crowded, but that day, a Tuesday, four or five days after the party at Aldous Crumley where Anna had fired me, there were only three of us in the line to see the film and the other two people were Deborah Eisenberg and Wallace Shawn. I recognized them both. I had read a few of her books and I had seen him in some goofy comedies and other ones that were less goofy. It didn't seem so odd to find them there. He was wearing a flat cap very deliberately, like somebody was going to recognize him if he wasn't wearing it, or like he was cold, and he only took it off when they let us into the theater a few minutes before the show started. I sat down directly in back of them. It was an empty theater, so I could have sat anywhere. They weren't at the center, they were off to one side, a few rows from the back, with about a hundred empty seats around them. But I felt compelled, like the seats were ticketed or assigned. Straightaway you could see it annoyed him, Wallace Shawn. He was balling up his cap, for starters, and muttering. Eisenberg turned, said hello, and smiled confidently and charmingly, then asked whether I had seen the film before. I told her no, I hadn't, it was my first time, on the recommendation of a friend.

"You're going to love it," she said. "You've come to the right place, there isn't anywhere better than an empty theater like this, is there?"

That only made Wallace Shawn more upset, hearing us acknowledge that it was an empty theater. I don't know how long this went on, the three of us chatting about the movie and the Film Forum generally and about the movies we had seen there in recent months, and the repertories. Back then the screening rooms ran on an incline, and the back half of the theater was a little lower than the front half. It had something to do with the subway tracks nearby, Eisenberg said, and just as she said it, a train rumbled underneath. I thought Wallace Shawn was going to throw an elbow backward at me or call management or maybe leave. I've never seen somebody so angry about having another person sit nearby, not even beside him, but close all the same. Finally, the movie started and we didn't have to talk any longer. When it was done and the house lights were turned on, Shawn said to me that I had

spoiled a perfectly good fucking film, and was I happy, had
I satisfied whatever Neanderthal need was driving me to
mouth-breathe onto his neck for two hours?

That was the extent of it, the whole interaction. I felt
pretty bad about it afterward. Getting fired from a case is
never pleasant but it was no excuse to act like a jerk. I spent
the rest of that afternoon and evening putting files in order
and planning my next move. I needed new work, something
I could keep busy with instead of going to the movies and
annoying the people I recognized. I got a good night's sleep,
the first in what seemed like a long time, and in the morning
I made myself a big breakfast with eggs and sausage and filled
a thermos with coffee and put some ice in it and went downstairs. I had a camper chair and sometimes liked to sit out on
the sidewalk to see my neighbors. It was the Italian pocket
of East Williamsburg. A lot of people used to sit around like
that.

Thirty thousand dollars, waiting for me upstairs in the
apartment. I kept thinking about Anna's check but didn't
move to deposit it while the banks were open. I was thinking,
too, about Newton Reddick and the mistakes he had made
and how maybe they weren't mistakes at all, just lapses of
integrity, but that wasn't how he saw things. He had let his
lapses eat him up, even spoil his marriage, though probably
that was spoiled from the outset, for other reasons or no reason at all, just fate. While I was thinking about all that I
flipped through a dog-eared copy of Twain's *Life on the Mis-
sissippi*. I wasn't the one who made the dog-ears. I wouldn't
do that to a book, even a paperback, although there were all

kinds of other things I would do given the opportunity, under the right circumstances. It was another hot morning. The old ladies down the block were fanning themselves and the Williamsburg hawk was circling overhead, looking for pigeons.

That was when Ulises Lima came by and told me that Marcel was missing. Marcel Gonscalves, our friend. I had forgotten Ulises and Marcel even knew each other. I should have known. Ulises seemed to know just about everybody and probably he was drawn in by the fact that Marcel was working as a fence, albeit a genteel one.

"Where did he go?" I asked.

"I don't know where he went," Ulises said. "That's the point, chamo. He's vanished, gone."

It was a serious situation, apparently. Relatively serious. People were worried, anyhow.

According to Ulises, Marcel had been gone almost a week. He wasn't picking up his phone or returning calls or answering emails and he hadn't been to the Golden Hound, either, which was the most unusual part, since Marcel was a man of habits, obsessive you might say, or meticulous if you were feeling generous. His friends at the coffee shop—the regulars and the busboys and the artists trying to get their paintings on the walls—were talking about putting together a search party, Ulises said. They'd already started calling around to clinics and hospitals like it was the old days in the Village, when a person might disappear and then turn up weeks later at the hospital, sick or beaten up, half dead.

"Have they tried James?" I asked.

Ulises said he didn't know, he didn't think so, who was James?

"The boyfriend," I said. "The new guy. Or not that new. They've been together months."

"They don't know about a boyfriend," Ulises said.

That's how it started. We went over to the Golden Hound and spoke to the manager, who was the head of the informal search party that was assembling, and asked him whether they had tried the boyfriend, James. He didn't think there was a boyfriend. He would know, especially if they had met at his coffee shop, if the guy was supposed to be a regular who had hit on Marcel, of all people, and had some luck with it. The busboys would have noticed and mentioned it, that's what busboys do. The manager's name was Frank. He was hauling in a flour delivery while he talked with us. I didn't want to tell the man his business, so I instead I left my card and number and Ulises and I walked up to Twenty-Second Street. That's where the house was, the carriage house that Marcel had been staring at that day when I met with him, the house that had seemed to spook him when he and I were out wandering the neighborhood and talking about stolen books and Gramsci and his trip to Beacon, the trip that ended in the Hudson River. I didn't mention any of that to Ulises. I told him about the carriage house and he agreed that was the place to start.

It was a handsome house with all the trimmings, the kind of place to make you think twice about living in New York because probably you would never have it so good yourself. A woman answered the door. She was fifty or fifty-five,

petite. I asked if James lived there and she just kept on looking at me skeptically, but then Ulises ran a worried hand
through his long poet's hair and spoke to her in Spanish. She
was from Colombia. They were practically compatriots. That's
what he told me later, that Venezuela, Colombia, and Ecuador
had been one country not that long ago and also that
he, Ulises, looked quite a lot like Simón Bolívar, people were
always telling him that. The woman told him yes, a man
named James lived there, James Thurgood, but she wasn't
at liberty to say anything more than that, she was sorry to
disappoint.

Ulises pressed her a little and she said that he was out of
town. He had a house upstate. In Beacon, she thought. She
didn't have the address. She had only been there once, to help
get the place ready for a party. It was near the train station.
She remembered that, because she had walked there from the
station and it had started to rain and she didn't have a jacket
or umbrella.

"There's a 1:10 train on the Hudson Line," Ulises said.
"After that it's a 2:20."

He always knew odd things like that. Train schedules,
showtimes, interest rates.

We got to the train just in time. It was an express and
cleared the city quickly and all the grimy little subcities, too,
and we were out in the country by one thirty, with the river
spreading out and bending this way and that, not like in town
where it was forced into a straight line and mixed with the
waters of the Harlem River and the East River, which wasn't

a river at all, but a tidal strait. Up north, the Hudson was
clean mountain runoff. You could see people in kayaks and
rowboats, leading very pleasant lives in the country. Ulises
slept for about an hour. He could sleep almost anywhere. When
he woke up, he wanted to talk about Anna Reddick, my client,
or former client though he didn't know that part, that I had
been fired, until I told him about it. He wanted to know if I
thought she was a genius. He figured she might be but wasn't
sure and wanted to know my opinion, my legal opinion. I told
him it seemed to me she had an artistic temperament.

"That's bullshit," he said. "Don't let that sway you. This
is important. Think about the work."

I thought about it: the work, her books. "Yes," I said, "she
probably is one."

"Better in that case to give her a wide berth," he said.
"You can only trust the hacks. The real geniuses, they'll cut
you without thinking twice; with the rest of us clerks, you
know where you stand."

The train was just pulling into Beacon then. We were
practically the last ones getting off. The main drag of town
had that half-abandoned feeling, not quite littered with tum-
bleweed but like a place that had been built in a different
time, with different expectations of who would live there and
how many of them, which maybe it had been. I didn't know
much about Beacon. I didn't think I needed to. It was a town
like any other, possibly a little prettier, closer to the city than
some and farther than others. The town hall was a short walk
from the station—just about everything was. By the time we

found the clerk's office it was already closed, along with land records. There was a phone bank in the lobby, near the door. In the white pages I found a listing for "Thurgood, James, 27 South Cedar Street." On the wall was a map of the town's roads. There was a white pages, too, and I flipped through it without explaining why, since we already had the address for James Thurgood. Probably I was embarrassed, though there was no need to be. Ulises knew all about hunches and half-remembered details and the little ideas that gnaw at you when you're hardly paying attention. On the train ride I had re-membered that Beacon was the town where Liam Moore had stored his old book collection, the one he'd had Newton Reddick authenticate all those years before, perpetrating a very mild kind of fraud that benefited one of them and tor-tured the other. It was called the Moore Museum, a nonprofit educational institution. There was no listing. It could have been another Beacon, in another state, but I didn't think so. I had read Jala's dossier pretty carefully in the end. I was looking for patterns or something else.

We walked to Cedar Street, which was on the other side of town. The town was small and you could easily cross it on foot. We went across Main Street, where there were ice-cream parlors and flea markets and finally some people mill-ing around looking like they were waiting for something or somebody to show up, maybe the rest of the townsfolk. Near Main Street the houses were small and packed tight but a few blocks south the plots spread out and had a little privacy. Twenty-Seven South Cedar was a fine, broad split-level with a wraparound porch and a green lawn.

Ulises called it an apple-pie house. He asked if I really thought Marcel was there. We were standing in front of the porch, looking up at the house and its lace curtains.

"Sure, why not," I said, but I knew what he meant, why he'd asked.

A man in his late fifties came to the door, a well-kept man in pressed slacks and a crisp white button-down shirt with the sleeves rolled to the elbow. I got the feeling he was proud of his forearms, a little vain even, though he may have just been cooking or it was warm inside the house and that was why the sleeves were rolled. James Thurgood, a former advertising executive, semiretired, resident of Manhattan and Beacon, New York. He said hello pleasantly. Behind him was Marcel, wearing a T-shirt. I had never seen him dressed down before.

"Jesus," Marcel said when he saw us. "They sent the scouts."

I told him about the search party, the presumed disappearance, Frank at the Golden Hound.

"They think anything above Fifty-Seventh Street is the dark side of the moon," he said.

"You didn't leave word. They thought something happened to you. They were worried."

Marcel shrugged and smiled. "What could happen to me?"

We were invited inside and had a look around the house. It was a sturdy old thing with hardwoods everywhere and some nice furniture and no sign that anyone was being held there against his will, just the contrary. Marcel was the one who gave us the tour. That seemed to please James, who was lingering a few feet behind, watching us discover his home.

He had never met Marcel's friends. He must have mentioned that three or four times before we sat down for a drink. We would stay for dinner, he said—we had to, after coming all that way. At some point between the first drink and the second and the arrival of dinner, James started talking as though we were staying the night. There were guest rooms, he said, three of them. We could catch a train back to the city tomorrow—they left the station every hour, or who knows, maybe we'd be charmed and would want to stay in Beacon longer. He spoke about the town like he was in the chamber of commerce. Marcel didn't notice, or if he did he had made peace with the sales pitch. After all, he'd finally succumbed to it. He seemed to be living there, in James's house.

All through the meal, Marcel didn't mention anything about going back to the city. He was talking about summer and things he wanted to do in the garden. You'd have never guessed from listening to him that he had a thriving business buying and selling stolen goods, a business that was dormant back in the city while he was upstate playing gentleman gardener, or whatever it was he was doing there exactly, enjoying himself. It was an odd dinner. We had grilled fish. There was more than enough for everyone though they couldn't have known we were coming. James did the grilling and presented the fish with some real fanfare. It was seasoned with rosemary and served in a lemon butter sauce beside a garden salad, with white wine to drink. James watched as we ate. I got a strong impression he was waiting for me to ask him something.

"It's brook trout," he said. "I pulled them out myself this morning."

"It's delicious," I said. "Very fresh."

"You can't get any fresher," he said. "The brooks here are wonderful. If you'd like we could go out in the morning. I have extra rods, flies, waders, everything we'll need. And perfect weather."

"They don't want to wake up at that hour," Marcel said. "They're young men."

Marcel was the same age as I was.

"Oh, you'll love it," James said, speaking directly to me, looking me square in the eye.

Marcel must have sensed where the conversation was headed and how long his boyfriend could go on talking about the brook trout. He changed the subject abruptly and announced that I had been working on an odd case. I had been looking for some rare books. Not stolen but almost.

"Actually, he was fired from that case," Ulises said. "Never did find the books either."

"We have some wonderful library sales up here in the summer," James said. "I'm sure you could find some gems if you put your mind to it and were willing to dig. We know all of the flea markets. Beacon has an impressive cultural life. Summer theater, chamber music, the festivals."

"Not those kinds of books," Marcel said. "Some very particular volumes. Strange books."

I understood then that I was being asked to sing for my supper. The attorney-client privilege is all well and good, but when you've been served food people expect you to navigate the ethics and your conscience and tell them something interesting. I thought maybe Marcel was missing his old life, the one he'd been quite happily living only a few weeks or months before. So I told them all about the books, the husband and the false wife and the real one, the case I'd been drawn into and then fired from for reasons I was still trying to discern though probably they were obvious. James was the only one who hadn't heard the story before, or part of it. He didn't seem too interested, in fact. When I was done talking and we had all gone back to drinking the wine, he mentioned something. It was about the Moore Museum.

"Is that Liam Moore?" I asked. "Liam Moore's museum?"

"Right," James said. "He's in real estate in the city. Has a place up here, for his collection."

I didn't think I had said Moore's name. I thought I had been careful not to.

"An insular man," James said. "No real vision of what this town could be. But if you're interested in rare books you might be curious to learn more about his collection. I'm told it's a known library and open to the public. Scholars have been given access. Collectors, too, I imagine. So why Moore wouldn't want an active local arts community, I'm sure I don't know."

"Now you've cranked him up," Marcel said. "You'll have to hear the rest."

It turned out James had approached the Moore Museum the year before. He had been putting together an alliance of local business owners and arts organizations to promote a weeklong celebration in the Hudson Valley. A midsummer festival. Nearly every place he approached agreed to participate. In fact, all of them did, it was that kind of town, except for the Moore Museum. They wouldn't even allow him to use the name in pamphlets. They refused outright, so he went there to speak to somebody and was told by a caretaker that he wasn't welcome.

"Is the Moore place nearby?" I asked.

James didn't seem to hear me.

"I was doing all this for free," he said. "A labor of love, civic pride. That's the thanks I get."

I didn't say anything about knowing the family, and Ulises didn't recognize the name—he wouldn't, I hadn't mentioned it to him either. It was only a coincidence, not even a terribly surprising one, I thought, since the New York arts world is a small one, insular when you get right down to it, and a man who conducts himself like a prick is liable to make enemies and petty rivals wherever he goes, whether he's in the city or hiding his books in the Hudson Valley.

Still, it made me shudder, the connection. It felt like the case had followed me upriver.

After dinner and the cherry pie that was served for dessert, we went onto the porch. There were rocking chairs out there and no screen. The mosquitoes weren't too bad and only seemed interested in Ulises, who kept slapping at his neck and his arms, so often that at a certain point I wondered if he was trying to send me some kind of signal. Maybe he wanted to leave. Probably he did and knew what time there was an express train to the city. I suggested we all take a walk.

"Excellent idea," James said. "One of the joys of life in the country. A walk after dinner."

He poured us each another glass of the white wine, a Chablis that I thought was excellent but may have only been cold and well paired with the brook trout. We walked south on Cedar and made our way into the woods. There were no lights over the street. I got the feeling we were walking toward the brook where the trout were running and James said that we were. Fishkill was the name, and it was just another half mile or so through the trees. He was carrying another bottle of the cold Chablis under his arm. In the country you didn't have to worry about open-container laws or civil misdemeanors. The road was narrowing and the woods were closing in on us.

I asked in an offhand way where the Moore property was and James said we could walk by it if I liked. It was just a quarter mile east, off a dirt path. The dirt path was called Broadway, a joke. Marcel was looking at me like he wished I would drop it. He was pretty drunk. We all were.

"That's it over there," James said, when we were farther down the path. "That's Moore's land." We walked in that direction and James poured Ulises some more wine, then helped himself.

"A real pillar of the arts community," James said sarcastically. "Right here in Beacon."

The land was peppered with maple and oak and some pine in between them. A six-foot-high fence ran along the edge of the property, near the road. It looked like it had been built to keep in cattle, with two-by-fours spanning pillars hammered into the dirt. I hoisted myself up and over. For a moment I thought there might be barbing on top or broken glass the way you find in the city to keep out thieves and pigeons, but there wasn't any. I dropped down on the other side. It felt cooler over there, like the weather or the climate had changed somehow. Ulises climbed the fence, too, but only perched on the top rather than coming along with me.

"I'll be the lookout," he said. "Hurry up, whatever the hell you're doing."

James called out something, but I couldn't hear what he was saying. I was jogging.

The main house was set back a hundred yards from the path. The estate seemed to run through the woods a good distance, maybe twenty acres or more. There was an access road winding through the trees and connecting it to the front gate. I kept to the path and saw what I was looking for. There was a sign nailed to a tree. It said the Moore Museum and had an arrow pointing toward to the side of the house, where there was a cottage that appeared to have been built for a chauffeur or the caretakers or whatever other servants might have been necessary in the years when the family had actually used the house, their country estate. Now it was just an address, another piece of a tax dodge, a tax dodge Newton Reddick had signed off on, years ago.

There were boards on the cottage windows but the front door was unlocked, so I let myself in. The lights worked. There was nothing in there, just old furniture, chairs that had probably lived in the main house once but had been moved out there and forgotten. Twenty, thirty chairs, maybe more—they were stacked and I didn't look too closely. There were no books, not even paperback mysteries or romances on the shelves. Nothing rare or valuable. It felt good to have my suspicions confirmed, though there was no great reason to be surprised. The museum was a joke. It was a cottage in the woods filled with chairs. A tax write-off worth a few million dollars. I turned the lights off and closed the door quietly. Trespassing had brought out my courteous side.

The woods didn't seem so dark or so vast on the way back—they never do. Ulises was still sitting on top of the fence, keeping the lookout, as he'd promised. I couldn't have been gone more than fifteen minutes. Marcel and James had left. Ulises said they were up ahead. He had given them a joint—they were starting to fight and he'd sent them off somewhere to fight privately, with the joint. We turned back toward civilization and caught up with them quickly. Whether they'd been fighting, I didn't know, but it was a quiet walk back to the house, and the joint was nowhere to be found. The bottle of wine was gone too. We were all empty-handed.

James stopped me on his porch, just before the door, and asked if I had taken anything.

You could tell he'd been working up to the question, gathering his nerve. He was whispering. "These people are my neighbors," he said. "It's a respectable town. I'm respected here."

"I didn't take anything," I said. "I just looked around."

"You can't just go hopping fences. This isn't the city."

"I don't hop fences in the city. I'm a lawyer. A respectable lawyer."

I was trying to make a joke but he took me seriously and began to nod.

"You're right," he said. "I'm sorry, you're right. I don't know many of Marcel's friends."

"He's respectable too," I said. "We're all so goddamn respectable it makes you sick."

That time he laughed though the joke had already passed.

"We should get some sleep," he said. "Turn in early, we'll get up at five and go to the brook."

My room was made up with fresh sheets and a towel folded at the foot of the bed. Ulises was down the hall. It was a quiet night in the country. We didn't talk about it in advance but around four in the morning, before the crickets started chirping and before the trout were running, I woke up, got dressed, and left my room carrying my shoes. The floor was ice cold though it was the middle of summer. Ulises was waiting in the hallway. His shoes were on, but he was creeping quietly.

"First train is the 4:10," he whispered. "Vamos, let's get the fuck out of here already."

I didn't bother putting my shoes on until we reached Main Street. It felt good to be out of that house. We cut across some lawns and got our feet good and wet from the morning dew. The whole town was dead and dark and the station was up ahead with the lights on and the whistle blowing somewhere in the distance announcing the arrival of the 4:10, just as Ulises had said. At the station there was a man behind a countertop selling cups of coffee. Ulises bought two of them before the train pulled in.

It was a Thursday morning. On the weekend we wouldn't

have been so lucky and in fact the train was busy, not packed
in tight like the later trains would be but with enough warm
bodies to make you feel comfortable and easy. Ulises asked
me about the night before, going into the Moore property.

"It had something to do with your case," he said. "I saw
that glint in your eye."

"I don't have a glint," I said. "I have intuition, insight,
moments of brilliance and luck."

"You were drunk," Ulises said. "You might still be."

I told him what I knew, or what I suspected, what I was
thinking about and trying in a roundabout way to confirm,
even though I'd been fired from the case.

"We always double back on ourselves and repeat," Ulises
said. "It makes perfect sense."

I didn't ask him what that meant. It was dark outside, but
you could sense the river flowing south toward the city, the
same as the train, everyone moving in the same direction and
the sun due to rise in just under an hour. The coffee Ulises
bought was too hot to drink, but I kept sipping at it and
looking out the window.

19.

I went back to Film Forum a few times over the weekend and to a series of matinees on Monday, Tuesday, and Wednesday. They weren't playing *Memories of Underdevelopment* anymore. Instead it was a repertory of the films of Jean-Pierre Melville, the French director. *Army of Shadows* and one other were showing for the first time in New York. I wasn't looking for Wallace Shawn and Deborah Eisenberg, exactly, but the thought had occurred to me that I owed him, or the both of them, an apology. Probably that would only make him angrier, seeing me again, but you never know. You couldn't control who you were going to run into in New York. Even famous, or semifamous, people had to deal with interactions like that every now and then especially somewhere like the Village, with all those theaters and bookstores and diners. Anyway, I went to the movies a few times and had a vague notion that if I ran into those two again I would either say something or merely give them their space and that would be a kind of apology. All lawyers tend to have a condition. They

suffer from it like a disease, and it has to do with believing
they can fix things, or get to the bottom of them, simply by
talking to a lot of people. That's the sort the profession at-
tracts. I used to think I was immune from it, back when I
started, but had since reconciled myself to the truth. Every
time a screening of *Army of Shadows* let out, people would
linger around outside the theater, on the sidewalk, wanting
to talk to one another, to say something, but they were
strangers, most of them, and couldn't find a way to begin or
get into it.

Later in the week I made an appointment to see Liam
Moore. It wasn't easy to get, but in the end his office told me
to go by the Academy Club on Fifty-Fourth Street. It was a
low-slung, hulking structure sandwiched between the skyscrapers and built from old stone. They fitted me with a blazer
in the lobby and showed me to the member's lounge, where
Moore was waiting, a squat man in a chunky robe that hung
open just above his sternum. He carried a lot of weight across
his chest and seemed pretty pleased with it. If there was any
resemblance between him and his daughter, I couldn't find
it. That's how nature works sometimes, it has a sense of humor. There were two glasses of juice on the table beside him.
He said they had the best mangoes in town, the best anywhere north of San Juan, Puerto Rico, and they should have
them for what the club charged you in fees, but what could
you do, most of the members were grandfathered in, trusts
paid the annuals, and they didn't ask where it went or what
they got for it. His voice was hoarse, like he'd been shouting
or smoking, or both.

I knew a little about the Academy Club. I had been there
a few times when I was still working at the law firm. Clients
would sometimes summon you in the middle of the night
when a case was going poorly. They were rich and simple,
when you got right down to it. They thought of their clubs
like churches and believed the old rules of sanctuary would
be observed and nothing very bad or harmful could be done
to them so long as they stayed within the four walls. Moore
didn't quite fit that crowd. That was what he wanted to
convey. That was what the mango juice was about, why he
was smiling and letting his robe hang open. He asked what
could he do for me. I told him that I was hoping to have a
frank conversation about Newton Reddick, and maybe we
could speak frankly on a few other related subjects while we
were at it.

"By all means," he said. "I'm here to help, young man.
You look like hell, to be honest."

He was pointing at the cut on my forehead, which had
stalled out in the healing process. I told him most of what I
knew, that he, Liam Moore, had collected trial pamphlets a
long time ago and that when he needed a tax write-off he
had the idea of forming a private museum for them and Newton had held his nose, put his conscience on ice, and finally
agreed to authenticate some fake or false or counterfeit books,
so that the donation figures could be inflated. That Newton
was researching those same books, the fakes, toward the end
of his life. I said the timing seemed a little suspicious to me
and I was guessing it had something to do with development
of the Williamsburg waterfront, in Brooklyn.

"You've mentioned a great number of things," Moore said, "that are none of your business."

I wasn't so sure. I told him I'd first been hired by somebody—an impostor. An actress, possibly.

"Yes," Moore said. "She was mine, if that's what you're wondering. That business was between Newton and myself and he understood the message perfectly. You were paid, weren't you? Pretty well in fact. What's your billing rate? What did you get? Do the math for me, would you?"

He didn't seem at all embarrassed about the confession. His robe slipped open further.

"Why were you trying to set him up?" I asked. "Did he have something on you? The books?"

Moore sighed, a great sigh of exhaustion with all the world but especially me. We'd only been speaking for a few minutes. Maybe he wanted me to believe he had something better to do.

"Why would I care about some fucking books?" he said. "Get a library card if you're so interested in them. That's what I could never understand about Newton's so-called profession, his little circle of hell. If they wanted all those books why didn't they just go to the damn library?"

I waited a moment while he worked through whatever ancient grudge was bubbling up.

"It was a tax write-off," he said. "I could've written off the fucking drapes but I chose the books. Newton couldn't forgive me for looking at it that way. It was all decoration, as far as I was concerned. Something to put on a shelf. But just so you don't think I'm a philistine, I have still got some of those books. I sold a few over the years, but I have kept some too. Several."

I told him I knew that, and that I'd been to the Moore Museum. I'd seen his tax filings too.

"You're really out to make a nuisance of yourself, aren't you? What do you get out of it?"

"I don't know," I said. "I'm just asking questions."

"Jesus, get a hobby, would you? The rest of us have work to do."

I asked if that's what he was doing on a Friday at three in his robe. Was that work?

He laughed quietly, to himself, like I wasn't there. I was nothing in his eyes, nobody, a nuisance.

"What do you think of my daughter?" he asked. "Read any of her stuff?"

"Yes," I said, "all of it."

"Ah, you're one of those. A fan, huh? Never been much to my taste. They leave you cold, like her. Can you imagine, a twenty-five-year-old, beautiful, a trust the size of Central Park, and she ties herself to a limp-dick old man? You know what she was doing, right? Building a museum to herself, and who better to work it for her? He was the goddamn attendant asleep in the corner."

I told him I didn't think so. That wasn't it, that wasn't it at all.

"You're probably sleeping with her now," he said. "What's the bar's view on that? Lawyers get funny about that. You can never get a straight answer, is how it works. Always with a caveat."

"She fired me, actually. I'm here on my own."

"That's right, I forgot. You're just asking questions. I'm all for being helpful."

"How did you get the development rights on the waterfront?"

"I bribed a planning commissioner. With books, if you can believe that. Another fucking book nut, so he got a library of eighteenth-century European erotica and a few paintings that fell off the back of a truck. Eight hundred grand's worth, for his trouble and mine. That's how your precious Brooklyn gets rezoned. So that's my piece, and I fought and clawed like fucking hell to get at it."

He smiled a thin-lipped, distant smile and slid back further into his chair. We were sitting in plush leather armchairs and every now and again he would cross or uncross one of his legs. He seemed awfully proud of himself, sitting there. He had fought and clawed and believed it meant something that he had. He had been poor once, when he was young, and now that he wasn't anymore he thought it all had meaning: his rise, his marriage, his bribes and permits, the cotton robe he was wearing and letting slide open to show off his old man's skin, all pocked and flaccid.

"I'm not your villain," he said. "You know that, don't you?"

Maybe I did know that. I wasn't so sure anymore.

The porter came over and cleared away our glasses of juice. Moore had drunk them both.

"Let's go for a stroll," he said. "This room is fucking depressing."

There were nymphs and satyrs painted on the ceiling, frolicking there, a different world.

He led the way and I followed down a dark hall that was lined with oil paintings of sporting scenes, dogs and foxes and horses. It smelled as though somebody had been burning incense. He gestured at a few of the paintings but didn't say anything. I didn't know what it was he wanted me to see in them. Maybe he owned them. Maybe he had lent them to the club. Another tax write-off. I half expected to be knocked out, bopped on the head, and dragged into a darkened room to awaken hours or days later, maybe in another place altogether, somewhere outside the city in a barn or in the cottage of a country estate, somewhere remote and woodsy where people used to play racket sports in the mornings before luncheon. Nothing happened, of course. We kept on walking down the dark hallway. Finally, we passed beneath a stone arch and came to a balcony overlooking a pool. The pool at the Academy Club was famous, or infamous depending on your perspective. I had heard about it many times but had never seen the thing for myself. There was mist rising off the stonework. Through it you could see five or six bodies moving through the water. They were nude. That was what gave the club its infamy. Members were still allowed, or maybe encouraged, to swim naked between noon and seven. It was a bonding ritual of some kind. The atmosphere was dark and reverent but through the chlorine mist, with the help of a few discreetly set lights, you could see the whites of men's backsides just under the water's surface.

"Look at them," Moore said. "People have tried to stop

it, you know. Challenges over the years. From Jews, femi-
nists, the health commissioner. The Catholic Church even
intervened once, a little halfheartedly. Didn't have a leg to
stand on in the fight. The truth is, you can't stop them, the
Brahmans. They love this shit, and they don't care if you
think it's twisted or strange or corrupt. You can't stop it, but
you can join. All you have to do is own something they want.
They'll let you in their little clubs and they'll let you go
swimming. You're a part of it all, then."

"I don't want to be a part of it," I said.

Moore was still looking down into the pool. He was leaning over a stonework rail.

"Ever done a closing?" he asked.

"No. Nobody ever asked me to."

"A lawyer who can close on real estate," he said, "will
never go hungry, not in this city."

"Are you offering me something?"

He shrugged. "You interested? It's a checklist you gotta
run through. Nothing to it."

"No," I said. "I don't want to do any fucking real estate
law."

A few seconds later, he dropped his robe. Underneath he
was naked, no trunks, no underwear, nothing. He was wearing sandals but he got rid of those, too, and made his way
down the stone staircase to the pool. The staircase was steep
but he descended quickly, the way a child might if he got to
the pool and his mother or father let go of his hand and his
friends were waiting in the water for him. He didn't dive in.
There was another staircase into the water, and that one he

took more deliberately, saying hello to some of the other men. They were all naked and very cordial.

Before, it had seemed like there were only six of them but now that the mist was clearing, or my eyes were adjusting, I saw that there was twice that number, maybe more, and some of them were hanging around the pool's edge and in the dark corners, talking to one another in hushed tones like lovers. They were talking about real estate, maybe, or people they knew in common who might be useful to one of them if they could make the connection, or they were talking about something else entirely: women they knew and whether there would be traffic on Madison Avenue later. I used to wonder what they talked about in the star chamber during downtime, in between rulings. Every court has downtime. The judges tell jokes to their clerks, and the attorneys laugh, whether they can hear the jokes or not, to show that they're part of it all.

Moore started swimming laps and I stayed awhile and watched, still not sure what I was doing, why I had come, what he had been telling me, or why I had thought it would be helpful to hear. He was a strong swimmer, graceful even, considering his age and weight. I watched him do five laps, with kick flips on either end, and when I decided he wasn't coming back I found the exit myself. There was nobody at the coat check and the doormen didn't seem too concerned, so I kept the blazer they'd lent me when I first arrived. It had a crest on the lapel, and it fit me fine.

Part III

A PURE WOMAN
FAITHFULLY PRESENTED

20.

I wasn't expecting to see Anna again after writing her a memo. I owed her that much, at least. It was a brief, somewhat orderly memo with subheadings and bullet points and for good measure I gave the thing a case and matter number, the way we used to at the firm. In fact at the firm they would hand out sheets of paper with the day broken down into six-minute increments and all those tranches were expected to be given a case and matter number, even if it was just free time you were spending thinking about nothing, or you were trying to eat your lunch. Later on it was all done by computer. You had a grid of tickers in the corner of your screen and whatever you were doing all day long one of them was running, someone was paying for it. From the outside it could look like an oppressive system, and it was, but there was a logic to it, and like all logical things you could find some comfort there whenever you needed it. Anyway, I drew up the memo explaining everything I had learned about her husband's death and various expenditures and conspiracies and the grudge he held against her father—an old grudge, yes, but it may not have seemed all that old to the two of them. You can never tell what kind of regrets will linger around all those years, and then when you're vulnerable they start to metastasize. Reddick was book-crazy at the end. That was the memo's conclusion, more or less. I cushioned it with all kinds of legalese, which was like slapping a case and matter number on the top of each page, another piece of armor, a veneer of professionalism to soften the blows. I didn't have her email address so I sent it by messenger. A friend of mine, a neighbor, needed the work. When I first moved to the city, Midtown was littered with bike messengers. You couldn't step off the curb without looking both ways for them. Now there were only a few dozen hanging on, making ends meet.

A few more days passed. I wanted to enjoy the weather, to walk around my neighborhood, stopping in anywhere that caught my attention, talking to people at bodegas and play-grounds, sitting in the camper chair outside my apartment and pretending it was a beach, like the old Italians did and with the charred skin to prove it. I walked by the waterfront and saw they had broken ground. There was a line of back-hoes on the curb along Kent Avenue. I followed it to a build-ing with the garage doors thrown open and a pungent smell coming from within. It wasn't a bad smell, only strong. It smelled like earth, like a farm. I couldn't figure out why, but guessed that either the backhoes had come directly from the country somewhere, a farm project, or else the building had been a stable once and had never got rid of the smell. You used to come across stables in strange pockets of the city. The police still needed them, and so did the hansom carriages.

You'd be walking around the edges of Hell's Kitchen and suddenly there was the smell.

Ulises came by one afternoon, or possibly called first, though he rarely did that, preferring instead to drop in unannounced and to leave the same way. He told me he had found the girl.

I didn't know who he was talking about. "What girl?"

"The fake," he said, "the impostor."

It turned out he meant the actress who had been hired to play Anna, the one who had paid me ten thousand dollars in cash under false pretenses and got me chasing after Newton Reddick in the first place. I had almost forgotten that Ulises was the one who sent her by to see me. He said he had run into her again at a bar on the Lower East Side, Glasnost. It was very late and he had taken ketamine but he was sure it was her, so he bought her a drink and they got to talking and she finally admitted to everything, how she had been paid to go see some lawyer. She didn't know what it was all about, she hadn't asked, that was the point of being an actress, you accepted and then disappeared into a role. In addition to being an actress, Ulises said, she was also an aspiring writer. A memoirist or an essayist, she was still deciding, but had applied to some MFA programs. They had gotten along pretty well and had a few drinks and she told him that if he wanted, she would write up her story, her exploits as an actress and provocateur, which is what she called herself, and sell it to him, or to his friend, the lawyer, if it would be useful. Five hundred dollars.

"What does she want five hundred dollars for?" I asked.

"Her confession," Ulises said in earnest.

"That's all right," I told him. "I already have a confession, I don't need another."

"Two hundred," Ulises said. "She's a good writer, chamo, and it'd be her first sale."

I said I'd think about it. I figured he was in love with the woman, or with her writing. I was sitting in the camper chair outside my apartment, taking in the sun, reading a book. It was Anna's book, in fact, *Unbuttoning After Supper*, the copy I had spent fifty dollars on at Stone's bookshop and had meant to be careful with, but in the end there were a few coffee stains on the pages. I had been reading it a lot lately. Ulises sat down beside me on the stoop and didn't ask what I was up to. He could already see what it was and approved in a vague, bighearted way of the despair growing inside me. At some point, maybe while my eyes were resting or while I was concentrating on a sorrowful passage, he left to go talk to somebody across the street who was passing on foot. I was still there in my chair getting sunburned later that afternoon when Anna showed up. The real Anna Reddick, A. M. Byrne. I was embarrassed about the book that I was reading. So was she, and neither of us mentioned it. I closed the cover and slid it under my leg.

"I got your memo," she said. "It wasn't very thorough. It sort of looked that way but wasn't."

"I wanted to close out the case," I said. "You're supposed to write a memo to the client."

"So it's closed. How did you like my father? Did he make any speeches about progress?"

"There was one about swimming. I don't remember the others."

"Well, we better talk it over."

I packed up my chair and books and an empty thermos and we went upstairs, which seemed dark and cool after being out on the sidewalk all afternoon, though the truth is it was hot in there, too, only not so hot as it was outside. I hadn't installed the air conditioner yet. It was a window unit and I always tried to put off installing it as long as possible. Sometimes I made it through the whole summer, though there wasn't any point to the practice—your electricity bill ended up almost as high, running a lot of fans and opening the freezer door.

"It's more than I've written lately," she said when we were upstairs. She was talking about the memo. "You don't seem to care too much about style, though. All that stilted lawyer crap and the bullet points for emphasis. You should try writing clearly. It'll give you the illusion of a craft."

"Do you want something to eat?" I asked. "Or a drink. I could make something."

"I haven't eaten all day," she said. "Would you really mind?"

I opened up the cabinets and the fridge and showed her what there was, which wasn't much. She asked if I knew how to make French toast, or was that too odd a request?

"Sit down," I said. "Get your red pen, if you like. Cut up the memo. It's yours, you bought it."

That wasn't entirely true. Her check was still sitting on the rolltop desk, undeposited. She was dressed in canvas sneakers and jeans with the cuffs rolled and a button-down shirt that hung loose over her hips and her hair was tied up and her face was flush, which gave her the air of somebody who had just run in and lost a race. I was joking about the memo, but she looked around for a pen and found one and made some notes. When she was done, she didn't show them to me. It was only a reflex, maybe, or an urge.

"My god," she said, "that smells good. How much butter did you use?"

"All of it," I said.

We sat down at the table, which was in the kitchen, and ate and talked about work, hers and mine, what I was going to do next, did I have a lot of active cases taking up my time? That last question was meant as a joke, since she had come by at four or five in the afternoon and had found me sitting outside with her novel, willing to go make her French toast.

"What are you going to do?" I asked.

She shrugged. "You mean now that I have your memo? What, should I go to the DA?"

"You could go to somebody. I could help you."

"What's the point? You didn't like my father? He had some strong opinions about you too."

"Like what?"

"He thinks you're trying to take advantage of a widow who hasn't had time to grieve. He thinks you're trying to fuck me, if you want to know, and to be paid two or three times for the service. My father likes to give speeches, like I said. If it's not about progress, it's about somebody getting fucked. That's how he sees things. I don't blame my mother for checking out. Who could stand all those godawful speeches? He never wanted an interlocutor, never mind a wife."

I thought she was going to tell me then what happened to her mother, but she didn't. It wasn't one of those speeches.

She pushed the bread around in syrup. She had already eaten three slices and was moving on to a fourth. It was good, as far as breakfast food goes, but eating it late in the afternoon could put you in a strange mood, I knew from experience.

"If you want to fuck me," she said, "say so. I'm all for mystery but it starts to get tedious."

I wasn't sure how to answer. She didn't seem to be speaking directly to me. It was more like she was addressing the room. I noticed she had taken off her sneakers. They were under her chair, a pair of cheap sneakers with the laces still tied, and she wasn't wearing socks. Her toes were unusually long. She looked like somebody who had gone barefoot all summer.

"Come on then," she said.

It wasn't hard for her to figure out where the bedroom was. It was a railroad apartment. One room led into another and except for the bathroom there were no doors, only passages between rooms where the space got a little narrower and then opened up again and that's how you knew you were somewhere else. The windows were on either end of the apartment. There was good light coming in. It was that time of the year with long afternoons that seemed like they would melt over the sidewalks. She walked ahead, sat on the edge of the bed, and took off her clothes and folded them into a neat pile and put the pile on top of my dresser. Her sneakers were still in the other room, under the kitchen table. She had an athlete's quiet confidence in her body. There was a sheen of sweat down her back and I thought about offering a towel but didn't want to appear rude or ungrateful or worse. There was a fan blowing nearby. We got ourselves tangled up and untangled and then went back to it again, like you would a hobby or a game. The bed, my bed, was something called a full XL, which meant that it wasn't as long as a bed should be and your feet were likely to hang over the end. I always felt bad about that. The bed frame and mattress were there when I moved in and I had never gotten around to replacing them somehow.

That went on for some time, though never so long as you hoped. When we were done, she asked if I liked being a lawyer. There wasn't any sarcasm in her voice. I thought there might be and was surprised not to hear it. There wasn't all that much space between us in the bed and I could feel the warmth off her skin. The fan was oscillating, and the air felt good every time it swung across.

"I like it better now than I used to," I said.

"What was worse before?"

There were a thousand things I might have told her, but I decided on just one.

"I didn't like working for companies."

"You prefer starving artists?"

"Sure. Any time."

"And when they don't pay?"

"Eventually they do. Or I forget about it."

"What a neat system," she said, sounding again like she meant it.

"What I'd really like to do is write," I said.

There was a long, deadly pause and then she began to laugh. "You're joking," she said.

It was a cheap mattress and I could feel it buckling as she laughed.

I told her yes, I was joking. It was a hell of a good joke. We both thought that it was.

"Thank Christ," she said. "You don't know how often I have to have that conversation."

"As pillow talk?"

"All the time. Even when they don't quite say it I'm lying next to them knowing that's what they're thinking about. Their manuscript. They're wondering if they dare bring it up, if now is the right time. They want to tell me all about an idea they have for a novel. A great novel."

"Sounds exhausting."

"It is. But what's the alternative?"

I didn't answer. I didn't know what her options were, or what she needed.

A little while later, I told her I had an idea for a novel.

"It's about a woman whose husband disappears," I said.

"That sounds terrible," she said.

"Does it?"

"Everyone knows you only write about lost women. It's the wife who has to go missing. . . ."

She was going to say something else but her voice trailed off and the mattress was still. I lay there thinking about it, how I couldn't remember reading a book or seeing a movie about a husband who disappeared. They were out there, only I couldn't think of any then.

"What about your book?" I asked. "The new one, the painter and her husband."

"Killing husbands is different," she said. "A man's not missing if he's dead."

It was quiet and the apartment was getting dark. Through the windows you could hear other conversations. The couple downstairs was fighting. You couldn't make out what exactly they were talking about but it had that endless up-and-down, back-and-forth rhythm that fights take on late in the day or very late at night, when it feels like they'll never end and you both start looking around the house for something that could end it for you. There were fights like that all over the city, but they were especially bad in railroad apartments, where there weren't any doors to slam shut. That's no way to live with another person. I wasn't sure Anna was listening to the fight but then she mentioned Newton. She said they never fought, not once in all of those ten years. She wished he had thrown a glass, picked up a goddamn tumbler and hurled it to the wall.

"He was always careful with things," she said. "Sometimes you just want a baggage handler."

She didn't explain what that meant. I had the image in my mind for several minutes.

Later on, I woke to find her dressing. "I have to go," she said.

"All right."

"It's not because you told me the idea for your novel."

"Wasn't it a wonderful idea?"

"It didn't help, but it's not that, really. I just have to go."

I went to the window and saw her leaving out the door. She was driving an old Jeep. It was parked along the curb, next to a fire hydrant, and I thought I saw a ticket on the windshield.

21.

That week a storm blew in off the water and it rained like
hell all over Brooklyn. When it was done there was a carnival in my neighborhood. Not a street fair like the ones you
saw moving around the city all summer, with the same vendors selling grilled corn and beaded necklaces and silk-
screened T-shirts, but a proper carnival with a Ferris wheel
that rose up over the BQE and a Tilt-A-Whirl run by a team
of grim, tired-looking men wearing jean shorts and holding
clipboards. It started around dusk and went past midnight
when the weather held. They had it every year like that. It
was run by a church group. On the fifth night some local
men lifted a statue of a saint while their mothers watched,
then paraded it through Williamsburg for an hour or so with
a brass band out in front of them. Anna showed up on my
stoop again that night and asked if I knew about the carnival,
did I want to go? She had already been and had a fistful of
tickets for rides and games. It was only a few blocks away.
We walked over there together and stayed for an hour or two.
Afterward the streets were empty. It was a Sunday, maybe

eleven or eleven thirty. She asked how many more nights the carnival would go and I told her that was it, it was over. They had lifted the saint, paraded her, and now she would rest for another year.

"I wish I had known that," she said. "I would have done things differently." We were walking underneath the BQE, and there was water splashing over the sides, rain that had built up on the highway from the storm that had come in that week. She was carrying a bottle of grappa wrapped in wicker, a prize she had won playing one of the games. It was a card game I had never seen before. It seemed to me something distinctly Italian, or even more particular than that. She knew how to play and had beat five or six old women who were there competing with her at a folded table set up in the street, in between the rides and the food vendors, where people could watch. It tasted fine, the grappa, but left your throat coarse. We sat in the playground across from my building and shared the bottle there on a bench and she told me about some time she had spent in Italy.

"Fifteen months," she said precisely, like she was consulting a datebook. Five months outside Naples, then Sicily for three months, then over to Venice, where she knew some people who lent her a house. She loved borrowing something like that, something outsize like a house, a life that wasn't hers, something she could use and then slip out of like a skin. Upstairs, after the grappa was done, we went to sleep, and in the morning she was gone. There was a note on my desk that said if I didn't hear from her soon, I should look her up in Venice. It was a joke, I figured, but I didn't know for sure, not at first, and I tried remembering whether she had mentioned an address or the name of the place, the villa she had borrowed from her Venetian friends.

She started coming by more often around then, always in the Jeep, never by subway or taxi or any of the other forms of public or semipublic transport. It was high summer and the city had started to clear out and between the people who were left, you and your neighbors, there was a new kind of camaraderie. She liked the area, East Williamsburg. It wasn't somewhere she had ever been except to see me about our case, which receded quickly enough now that there was a memo in the file. That's always how it is. You think the memo won't change anything, but it does. I bought new sheets, towels, small things to keep around the house.

I had a new project going. I must have told her about it, because one day she asked if it would be okay to come along. It wasn't an interesting case. It wasn't a case at all, it was a favor, with manual labor involved and some paperwork. I asked her why she would want to, and she said she liked logistics, they were like plot, and she had never been any good at plotting but admired writers who were—they had plans and ingenuity to fall back on when everything else went to hell. All she had ever been good at was creating an atmosphere, and lately she had started to question whether that was a skill at all or just a parlor trick or some kind of scam a few people enjoyed.

"I promise to be helpful," she said. "I won't ruin anything with atmosphere, on my word."

The favor, the job, was for Marcel. He needed someone

to oversee the liquidation of his warehouse. That's what he called the space where he kept various goods he was in the middle of unloading. He had left everything where it was when he went to Beacon. Now he didn't know when he was coming back to the city—maybe never, or else in the fall—but when he did come back, if he did, he was going to make changes and start something fresh. He was tired of fencing, just like he'd grown tired of banking and before that law school. He asked if I would help. He would send the buyers, only he needed someone around to organize things and make sure there weren't any police or private detectives or insurance informants coming by trying to pass themselves off as legitimate. Nobody was better positioned to do the work, to make sure the warehouse was cleared and disposed of in an orderly fashion, since after all my name was on the paperwork, and if he got stung it was only a matter of time until they went for the lawyer who helped him form the dummy corporations and Caribbean holding companies.

I told him I'd be happy to do it. Other than night court, I didn't have much going on.

In those first days I was mostly just moving dust around—that's how it felt. I was always prying open crates and lining things against the walls and tearing off plastic wrap and foam and the other materials that Marcel used to conceal what it was he really owned or was selling on consignment. Mainly he was holding on to paintings, small sculptures, antique flatware, china, silver, and some jewelry. The jewelry and gems were kept in large boxes with lots of smaller compartments inside. Everything was labeled but the labels were sometimes deceptive or just wrong. There was some antique furniture, too, but I couldn't move all of it alone and it was lucky that Anna was around and willing to work. She was careful about always lifting with her legs and made sure that I was too. There was a small Shaker desk in the back of the main warehouse, and she got in the habit of using it when we weren't moving anything too heavy and I didn't need her for something special. She would sit there for hours, posture ramrod like a piano student, then other times she was reclined, feet perched on the desktop, looking like she was on the verge of falling asleep. She was writing, longhand, in lined notebooks. She was getting a lot done and hours would go by without her pen ever coming up for air. One day, she asked me not to sell the desk to anyone. She wanted to buy it when we were finished, though not before. It was working for her. She was superstitious about things like that. I called up Marcel and he said that was fine —he didn't remember a Shaker desk, give her a fair price. The warehouse was in Greenpoint, near the ramp onto the Pulaski Bridge, in an old taxi garage. The desk was in what had been the dispatcher's office. There was a radio kit in there, too, but it didn't work. The receiver hung on a cord behind the desk and every now and again Anna would pick it up and try to use it, but nothing ever came out, not even static or dead air. Probably it hadn't been used in decades.

She didn't appear exactly happy to me. You wouldn't have called that happiness. Only she was busy writing all the time and occasionally helping me haul oversize items onto carpet-end dollies. The buyers were people Marcel knew and trusted, or they seemed to be. They spoke about him fondly and mostly said they hoped this was just a phase he was going through, that he'd come back. Anna didn't want to be introduced. She wasn't trying to be rude, only you could tell from across the room that she was focused on something and it was better not to interrupt for introductions or casual conversations about stolen goods and mutual acquaintances. One of the buyers, a small, nervy man who was dressed like Andy Warhol, took out a pistol and waved it around for a minute, then put it away and apologized. It happened on a Tuesday afternoon, not too long before we were finished for the day. He had been upset about something, a price, maybe, or some mix-up with the inventory, or else Marcel had promised him something that I didn't know about or understand. I didn't think Anna had noticed any of it, the incident with the gun. She never seemed to be paying attention to anything outside the world in her notebooks, but then, when the days were finished, when we were alone and talking, I would realize that she was picking up on everything, noticing all the people who came in, recalling things I had missed, details about their clothes or patterns of speech or the way they held themselves and whether they had wanted to get the hell out of there or linger around and smoke and talk about paintings. She was the one who noticed that the man with the gun was dressed like Warhol. She said that he was perfect, just what she had needed to get through a passage that had been giving her problems. Sometimes if you were patient and ready, the world would deliver you things like that. I wanted to know what she was writing but didn't ask her. She was filling notebooks by the day. After hours, we would go somewhere for dinner, or she would drive back into Manhattan for supplies. She left a few things around my apartment, some clothes and books that she was reading. The books were nonfiction, histories of esoteric things and practices and people I had never heard of. When she stayed, in the mornings we would drive over to the warehouse together. She would drop me at the gate and while I was opening up she would get doughnuts from a place on Manhattan Avenue where they brought them out on metal grates and let them cool against the wall.

One day, late in the morning, when all the doughnuts were gone and we were starting to think about lunch, Jala came by the warehouse for a viewing. I was surprised to see her. She said I shouldn't be—of course she knew Marcel, everybody knew him. She and Marcel had an arrangement, a right of first refusal in case anything he was holding was insured by Ballard Savoy. She looked through the paintings, flipping through them in a way that appeared to me both careless and highly attentive, obsessive almost, like the people you saw in record shops in the Village and on Bedford Avenue. None of the paintings seemed to interest her too much, not professionally. On a personal level, she said Marcel had impeccable taste and she didn't see how a fence could be so selective, better than a curator really, but there was the evidence lying all around us, with a half-assed lawyer to guard it. I heard laughter behind me, coming from Anna.

"That's A. M. Byrne," Jala said. "You're holding her hostage. You could get into trouble."

She went back and introduced herself. She was the first

one to do it all week. They talked about the paintings and what would happen to them, where they would end up, how they would get there, who would go looking for them, what they were worth and to whom. Anna was the one asking questions, mostly. They were very specific, considered questions that I couldn't have begun to answer without speculating, or worse, which she must have known, since she hadn't asked me. Jala knew all kinds of things. They talked about artists and the styles and influences that they believed Marcel was susceptible to and Jala explained her theories as to who his clients were, what they paid him, and how he worked. They liked each other, you could tell. There was an understanding between them, and it was like I had quietly disappeared.

Later, Anna asked me what kind of name Gardezy was. She had her notebook open.

"Afghani," I said.

"Did she grow up there?"

"No, in London. Her parents were diplomats."

She crossed out something she had written.

"What about Xiomara," she asked. "Is that Catalan or something?"

"What did she say about Xiomara?"

"Nothing, we were talking about paintings. Art. Sculptures. That sort of thing."

"I didn't come up at all?"

"Honestly, you didn't. I'm sorry, that's not meant to be mean, it's just the truth."

She was sitting up very straight in her chair again, like that piano student.

"Xiomara is Mexican," I said. "The name, I don't know. It could be Catalan."

She nodded, like it was the just the confirmation she needed.

"Thank you," she said. "That's it, for now."

22.

On the rooftop across from the warehouse in Greenpoint
they used to show movies. There were no cinemas in North
Brooklyn then, none that I knew about. People would invite
you onto their roofs, or they would simply start showing
something up there around dusk, projecting it onto a sheet
or ideally something better and more durable, like a wall. If
you saw them from the street and felt comfortable you would
shout up and they would tell you how to get through the
door by using the buzzer or knocking in a certain way or just
letting yourself in. The city showed movies in the parks, too,
but on the rooftops there was a breeze. Anna wanted to go
up to see what was happening. It had been a long day and I
was covered in dust but we went. Brooklyn was new to her.
It all seemed charming and odd, maybe. Summer was a good
time to be stuck there. Upstairs, on the roof, there were
folding chairs set up between the old chimney stacks and
vents. There was also a cooler and a sign that said to leave
cash if you want something.

The movie they were showing was *My Dinner with Andre*. We only stayed for a few minutes. It wasn't something either of us wanted to watch and the breeze was hardly anything, just a sour whisper off the Newtown Creek. On the drive home neither of us said much of anything. It was a distance of just over a mile. The Polish delicatessens along Manhattan Avenue were doing brisk business and in McCarren Park there were lots of people sitting by the fences smoking and passing around bottles in paper bags and some of them were playing music.

That night, around ten, Jala turned up with some people. Another surprise visit. They had just driven in from somewhere, the Hamptons it sounded like, and none of them could explain why they had left the island and come back to the city. It was like a migration, or some other natural phenomenon that you simply had to follow without interrogating the urge. That's how people came and went during the summer, especially a summer as hot as that one. There were five of them. They had filled up Jala's little car, which was an Audi of some kind, a sedan. They were all pretty drunk, except for Jala, who was the one who had collected them and driven them back for the night, for purposes known only to her. She was fun to be around. She and Anna went over to the window and talked awhile, sitting on the ledge, blowing smoke toward the fire escape. They stayed like that for fifteen or twenty minutes. From where I was sitting on the couch, in between those strangers who had come into my home seemingly without cause or explanation, I was enjoying watching the two women as they smoked, talking confidentially, obviously sharing a connection or a secret, which was the same thing when you got right down to it.

Later, after the others had gone, Anna was still sitting on the window ledge.

"I like her," Anna said.

She meant Jala. The cigarettes they had shared were in an ashtray beside her.

"She's read all your books."

"Has she? She didn't mention that."

I waited to see if she wanted to tell me what had been mentioned. It didn't seem like she was going to. It was like we were posing for a painting, like neither of us could move or speak and the air around us was oil that had to dry. A strange thought, but that was what came into mind just then, while I was waiting to see what else she might want to say about their conversation. There was an open bottle of wine next to her and empty glasses but she didn't reach for them and I tried remembering whether it was my wine or something Jala had brought along.

"Apparently my father has a partner," Anna said. "Jala looked into it. His real estate venture."

There was a question in her voice. Maybe wondering how Jala knew anything at all, although probably not. Probably Jala had explained it all with her usual alacrity and that impression she always left with anyone remotely in the posture of a client: of radical competence, of utter reliability, that feeling like you were talking with a genuine, honest-to-god professional, even when it was midnight or later on a Tuesday and you were sitting on a windowsill, smoking.

"A group named Whitehall," she said. "Do you know who that is?"

I must have smiled or laughed or maybe my posture changed.

"What is it?" she asked.

"Nothing, only he won't get a dollar out of it. Nobody does with them."

"That's what Jala said too. She said nobody ever comes out of a deal with the Whitehalls except bloodied or worse. That they're always looking for fronts and faces that can be burned later without a thought. That there's a food chain in New York, and my father is somewhere in the middle and when he tries to go up a rung the Whitehalls have it rigged to snap in half and they're down below waiting to eat everything that falls off. Something like that. It was all so vivid but now I can't remember how it went. She sounded sure, though. She's a very sure person."

"Yes, she is."

"So, it's true? He'll walk away with nothing."

"Worse than that. They'll stick some debt on him on the way out. Or maybe culpability."

"For what?"

"The bribes, if I had to guess. Overages, maybe. Fines, if there are any. Debt, certainly."

"So they're clever people, the Whitehalls?"

"Cleverer than him. Meaner too. They've been rich a long time. So have their lawyers."

"So have we. Except my father hasn't been. I guess marriage doesn't count for anything."

I was smiling again. There wasn't any point in hiding it. Anna smiled, too, and we went back to watching the movie that had been on before Jala and those strangers, her friends, had come by. The movie was a bootleg recording of something called *Must Love Dogs*. Anna had been walking around Manhattan Avenue in Greenpoint earlier and had gone into a bodega where they sold bootlegs, and she had bought six for twenty dollars. Not a particularly good deal, not in a bodega, but that was what she had paid for them. It didn't seem like she had chosen the movies with any special attention. Probably she had just wanted to see what a bootleg would be like. It was like any other movie except grainy, and sometimes the handheld camera they were using would shake. Still, it wasn't a terrible recording. We watched the whole movie and didn't talk anymore about real estate or food chains or the Whitehalls, though I presumed it was what we were both thinking about. Meanwhile John Cusack, Diane Lane, and their dogs were falling in love.

Jala called later on, sometime in the middle of the night. I picked it up on the second ring.

"Is she there?" she asked.

"Yes," I said.

"You should try to hang on to her awhile. That's a hell of an interesting woman."

"It's late, isn't it?"

"I don't know. You didn't mind me talking about the case, did you? With her, I mean."

"No, it's fine."

"I launched right into it. I can't help myself sometimes. You know how I am about work."

"I don't mind. Don't worry about it, okay?"

"Good, I was worried. You're a good lawyer, you know that? I don't tell you often enough."

She sounded like she'd had a lot to drink. Not drunk, exactly, but sentimental.

"All right," I said, "thanks."

She laughed. It sounded like she was calling from somewhere. A party, or a rooftop.

"I have to go now," she said. "I'm glad you picked up the phone."

Anna slept through the call. She could sleep through almost anything, it seemed like.

23.

It wasn't a relationship, only it felt sometimes like we were the last people left in the city. That's why you stick around in the summer, that feeling of abandonment and emptiness, and if there's someone else around to experience either or both with you, all the better. That, and you could find a table at almost any restaurant. The bars were never too crowded either. Even the places that didn't have permits would put a few tables on the sidewalk and offer discounts on just about everything. They would serve wine frozen to a slush, half price before eight, or the bartenders would cook something at home then bring it to sell, something that could be warmed up easily or served cold on a paper plate beside a bag of chips or pickles. Anna always ordered things like that when they were available. She would eat almost anything that was cheap. Food didn't seem to matter to her, only she was always hungry, and it had to do with the writing. She was working just about all the time. I didn't need her help at the warehouse any longer. The largest items were all gone, hauled off by Marcel's buyers. But I didn't want to interrupt her work.

One morning she came in with the doughnuts and a newspaper under her arm. It wasn't like her, walking around with a paper. You didn't need that kind of thing unless you were taking the subway, and she had the Jeep, a black Wrangler with a beige soft-top that was always down. It was the *Times* under her arm, the arts section, and inside it were some event listings. One of the listings announced a touring exhibition of the Moore Museum, a collection of rare books ranging from late seventeenth-century religious texts to early American legal miscellany. Underneath all that there were music listings and whoever had arranged them had some interesting ideas about the people who were left in the city and what they wanted to do with their nights.

"What do you think it means?" Anna asked. "Why now? He's taunting me. Like I'm an idiot."

I told her what little I knew about private collections and tax dodges of that sort. You had to give the public occasional access. That's why there was an empty cottage in Beacon with a mailing address and an obscure location, so that the public could visit but would never want to. There were museums like that all over the state, probably. We had no good way of knowing. Occasionally they went on tour so that it wouldn't look like they were being too private. It was a kind of performance. Shadow and light, smoke and mirrors, like all charities for the arts.

"I want to see them," she said. "The books, his road show. It's tonight. Will you go with me?"

"What for?"

"I don't know, only I think I ought to go. Don't you think that I should?"

I didn't have any advice on the subject. I'd already collected my thoughts in the memo and the memo was filed away somewhere in her apartment, or maybe she had shredded the thing.

"I'll go with you," I said. "It would be better if there were two of us."

The exhibition was at the Poquelin Society, of all places, Newton Reddick's old clubhouse. The scholarly society with a building in Midtown. It was probably worth twenty million, but they weren't selling. Maybe they never would, it would go on like that forever, with the old men coming to check on their books and pamphlets and delivering their footnoted lectures that nobody could really hear, then they would pour drinks. It seemed like years ago that I had been there, decades even. November to August. Who knows how many people had vanished in that time, or died? The city pretended to keep tabs on people, but it was an impossible task. There were too many ways to get out, between the subways, buses, and taxis. Too many streets and on every one of them a row of anonymous buildings and windows with drawn shades.

We drove into town in Anna's Jeep. We nearly killed someone in the Diamond District, one of the men who hung around outside the shops asking if you wanted to buy or sell, depending on how they sized you up, what kind of person they thought you were, and they were never wrong. This particular guy was carrying a coffee and wearing a yarmulke

on his head and a gold cross around his neck. He stepped off
the curb without looking. Anna wasn't paying close attention
either. She had been drinking earlier. She'd had something at
my apartment, another in the warehouse, and we had stopped
at a bar on the way, parking next to a fire hydrant outside the
Old Town on Eighteenth Street. After the near accident was
over, with all the other diamond hawkers watching and serving as witnesses, the man we had almost hit lifted the coffee
cup he was carrying over his head to show everyone that he
had managed not to spill it, an impressive feat. It was a deli
cup, the classic Greek pattern, the kind that leaked no matter
how carefully you held it. One of the other diamond hawkers
gave him the thumbs-up, and he walked away smiling.

"Do you want me to drive?" I asked.

Anna was sweating. She wiped her forehead. It was another hot evening with no breeze anywhere and the top was
down on the Jeep and the diamond hawkers were around us
chattering and sizing up tourists and the office workers who
were passing them by on foot, looking in the windows at the
stones, which were impossible to ignore completely, no matter how hard you tried. We were circling the neighborhood,
looking for parking.

"We're a block away," she said. "I can get around a few
fucking avenues." Just then, she found an open spot.

Outside the building, there were a few old men smoking
and talking. The exhibition was on the third floor. We took
the elevator, one of those old-fashioned cabinets with a brass
folding door. On the walls of the elevator somebody had
pasted a lot of pages out of books. Books that had fallen apart,

I presumed, or been otherwise dismantled. That's what passed for decoration in a place like the Poquelin Society. The pages were all laminated and with the glare of the light against the laminate it was difficult to read anything. One of the pages I could make out was from Thomas Hardy's *Tess of the D'Urbervilles*. I realized I had never seen the book's full title before, which was apparently *Tess of the D'Urbervilles: A Pure Woman Faithfully Presented*. Anna saw it, too, and laughed, and I got a terrible feeling like she was carrying a gun or some other weapon. She wasn't, but sometimes people give you that impression and there's a reason for it, and it would be foolish to pretend there wasn't a reason, or to wish it away. She got out of the elevator and took two or three menacing steps into the room. It wasn't an overly elaborate setup or a stylish room though it had some art on the walls and old rugs thrown around. Whatever usually resided there had been cleared to make room for the display cases. The books were lit from below, like sculptures, and the glass enclosures around them kept you from flipping through the pages. This was the Moore Museum, the summer exhibition. A few dozen books and a catalog at the door. Anna was looking around the room. Looking for her father, it seemed to me.

"I don't think he'll be here," I said.

"Doesn't he have to be?" she asked.

"I don't see why. It's all the same to the IRS."

"That's absurd," she said. "This whole country has gone mad. What's the point of all this?"

I told her I didn't know, that's how it was. With taxes, death, all kinds of things.

She was still glancing around, scanning faces. The old men looked alike in certain ways.

"He'll show up," she said. "He's a goddamn peacock when you give him the chance."

There were some beautiful books on display. A treatise Galileo had supposedly debunked, an essay from the *Federalist Papers*, some Bibles. Off in one of the corners, collected in a lone case, stacked like road maps at a gas station, were the legal pamphlets. The murder books. There were twenty or thirty of them there and you couldn't see the title pages and there was no way of knowing whether they were legitimate or counterfeit or something in between. Probably they were different pamphlets, not the ones Newton Reddick had been concerned about or looking for. All the same, it ran ice down my back seeing them there and seeing that nobody in the room was paying any attention to them. They were an afterthought. There was only a small crowd in attendance. Twelve old men shuffling around the room, looking for hors d'oeuvres. The air-conditioning was running full tilt and I wished I had brought something along, a jacket or a sweater. Anna was studying the books closely, looking for something. She put her hands on the glass cases and, trailing behind her, I noticed she was leaving fingerprints. Her fingers had something on them, possibly ink from the pages of the notebooks she had been writing in earlier that day.

"Do you see something familiar?" I asked. "Anything you recognize? Something of yours?"

"Let's get out of here," she said. "This was a bad idea. I don't want to be here anymore."

We went back onto the street and it was dark. It hadn't felt like we were inside for long, but we must have been, or else we arrived at that hour when all the light disappears suddenly and the city seems to hold still for a moment like it's deciding what to do next, which way to run. Across the street was a bar. There were some tables out front, high-tops, and at one of them was Liam Moore. He was sitting across from a woman. She looked pretty young. Twenty-five or so.

We went over to their table. He and Anna looked at each other without speaking.

Finally, he asked if we had been to the exhibition.

"Yes," Anna said. "Have you?"

"Just to see that it was set up. I don't like being there. Gives me a strange feeling."

"It's death," she said. "That feeling you get from the books."

Moore nodded thoughtfully. "Could be," he said. "I've never considered what it was." He appeared to me to be making a great effort to keep himself suppressed, to be polite. "This is Rebecca," he said. "Rebecca, this is my daughter, Anna, and her attorney."

Rebecca seemed to think it was a joke. It was, I suppose. I wasn't anyone's attorney.

"I thought you might call," Moore said. "I've been waiting to hear from you."

Anna shrugged. "I figured I'd catch you here."

"A response would be considerate. After the trouble I've gone to."

"Was it a lot of trouble? With the exhibition, you've had so much on your mind."

It was quite a tone in her voice. I wouldn't have wanted to be on the other end of it, though it didn't appear to have any effect on Moore. He was used to it, probably. They had a lifetime of grievances behind them and he seemed to think that whatever was happening between them now was just one more to the tally. Maybe it was. I didn't know what was going on, really.

A waitress came out from the bar and asked if she should bring more chairs.

"No," Anna said. "You two have a lovely evening. Rebecca, it's been a pleasure."

I shook her hand, Rebecca's. She must have held it out to me.

The Jeep was parked a block and a half away, pretty close to a fire hydrant, but it hadn't been ticketed yet.

"I could use a drink," Anna said. "And some air. Would you walk a ways with me?"

I told her that was fine, of course I would. She was my ride home.

We turned the corner onto the avenue and got a drink from the first bar that wasn't Irish. They agreed to pour the drinks into cups so that we could take them to go. That wasn't something they normally did but it was a Tuesday night in August, who else was stopping by with money to spend? Madison was cleared out. Even the storefronts were shuttered, except for the occasional luggage shop or dry cleaners. The cups they poured the drinks into were from a deli, the Greek design again, and between the ice melt and the vodka, the paper started to wilt. Anna didn't seem to notice. She was walking uptown quickly and looking around at everything like she was trying to capture a memory. Midtown East wasn't somewhere I visited too often anymore; I didn't know about her. When I had first looked her up on Lexis, when I was worrying about who she was and whether she was going to sue me, I saw an article in the *Daily News* or the *Post* or somewhere like that about how she had been spotted at Café Renard. She was with Salman Rushdie—that was what the article said—and the reporter seemed to think it was brave, going out with him to Café Renard. It must have been when the fatwa was still going, or else there was another kind of bravery involved. Anyway, I didn't know where Café Renard was exactly but I thought it was in the area, or maybe it was farther north. We kept on walking for ten or twelve blocks along Madison, heading north.

"Do you want to talk about what was going on back there?" I asked.

"No," she said. "Do you?"

"I could, if you wanted to."

"Is that supposed to impress me?"

Just then somebody passed between us, a woman with three roller suitcases. She was walking quickly and managing all the bags somehow and Anna stopped and looked at her curiously and watched her going down the block and getting into a cab, which was waiting for her. Seeing the woman made me think again of the man we had almost hit in the

Jeep earlier, the diamond hawker. It was one of those nights when everyone seems memorable.

"What's the longest relationship you've been in?" Anna asked.

She was watching the cab drive away. The avenue was clear. There was no traffic.

I told her about it. There wasn't a great deal to the story, but it was a year of my life.

"That was Xiomara Fuentes?" she asked.

"That was Jala," I said. "Xiomara was shorter than that. Seven months."

It felt like her notebook was out. She looked me up and down, foot to head.

"A year isn't much," she said. "But it's enough to know. It ought to be."

"To know what?" I asked.

"Whether you should leave. That's when alarms start to go off. You never listen to them."

"She left me. They both did. I've never actually broken up with anyone."

"No, I didn't think you had. I could have guessed that about you. That's not what I meant."

"What about you?" I asked.

She didn't respond, and I felt stupid about having asked. I already knew the answer.

When we were done with the deli cups, we went to another place and ordered wine, a bottle of something very cold and served on ice in case it wasn't already cold enough. Anna drank a glass of it quickly and I got that feeling again like when I thought she might be carrying a gun, only this time it was the certainty that there was something she was going to tell me, that she had been building toward it for some time, possibly all night, or only since we had seen her father at the high-top table outside of the bar, sitting there smugly with a younger woman, congratulating himself on the various purchases and bribes and deaths that had brought him to that place.

"He hired an investigator," Anna said. "My father. Weeks ago. Maybe months, I don't know."

"What kind of investigator?" I asked.

"A professional. Somebody named Oweida."

"What did he hire him to do?"

She finished what was left in her glass and poured more and looked at the wine. It was lousy wine, maybe the worst I had ever tasted. The bottle said it came from somewhere in Idaho.

"Newton is still alive," she said. "A ghost, wandering. That's what the report says."

I felt my stomach drop, and a new line of sweat started running down my back.

"What do you mean he's alive? The investigator said that?"

"Supposedly he faked his death," she said. "Over debts, or to get away from me. I really don't know. They sent it to me last week. I read it once and put it away. I don't believe it, not a word of it. My father likes to keep busy with little conspiracies, schemes, and games, and he wouldn't hesitate to get an investigator wrapped up in them. It's his innate cruelty.

He'd burn ants if you gave him a magnifying glass. He'd call it progress and laugh himself silly."

She seemed to me very calm, having said her piece. There was a stack of cocktail napkins in front of her and she took one off the top and found a pen in her pocket and wrote down an address. It was on North Fifteenth Street in Williamsburg, just a little under a mile from where I lived.

"That's where Newton's supposed to be staying," she said. "It's better than a fucking novel."

"But you don't believe it?"

"No. I'm done believing any of them. Have some more, okay? Do that for me."

She poured the rest of the wine into my glass and we sat there with the address on the napkin between us. The bartender asked if we wanted another bottle of the Idaho white but didn't seem too hopeful about it. The place was empty except for a group of old women at one of the tables. They were playing cards and every once in a while one of them would knock sharply on the wood. They were drinking beer and the beer would splash around.

24.

It was another muggy evening, damp almost beyond belief. Greenpoint always felt a little warmer than the rest of the city. A small, melancholy neighborhood lost to time, with street names like Java and India, which made you feel like you were in a Conrad novel, somewhere far away, the air heavy with mosquitoes and regret. It had something to do with the docks, probably, or the old work yards. Marcel's warehouse was all cleared out. The paintings and sculptures and jewelry boxes and artifacts were in other hands and the leftover junk was tossed in the garbage and the floors and walls were blown clean with a power washer rented from a hardware store down the block. It had taken almost three weeks, but everything was gone. I was glad to be free of it though I didn't know what I was going to do next. Maybe nothing, or I'd deposit Anna's check finally. I wanted to look at the report her father had commissioned from that private investigator but had too much pride to ask her for it. It wasn't professional pride—I didn't care about any of that. A real investigator might have bested me in a search a dozen times over and it wouldn't have been any great blow to my self-esteem. All the same I was curious, or more than that. I was thinking about it an awful lot and wondering when she would finally tell me what was going on, what her father was up to, who makes up a thing like that, and when were we going to talk about the address she had written on that cocktail napkin, the address on North Fifteenth, which was just ten blocks or so from where we were in Greenpoint. Finally, while I was locking up the gate that last night and preparing to lose the key forever, Anna said, sighing, that we ought to go take a look.

I understood what she meant without having to be told.

"All right," I said. "What are you going to do if he's there?"

She shook her head. "He won't be. He's dead, but I'd like to see who's using his name."

She laid out a theory for me as we walked from Greenpoint into Williamsburg. There was no particular border between the two neighborhoods, or if there was it had to do with McCarren Park, even on the waterfront, which is where we were walking, past the old mills and factories, some of which had been converted into lofts or communal housing but most of which were empty. Eventually they would be sold off to developers or put to some other obscure use. You can never tell in New York. Anna's theory was that somebody had stolen her husband's name and Social Security number and his license, taken out a string of new credit cards, and was now using the alias to live in Brooklyn, evading debtors or police or somebody, or else just racking up the bills until they became too heavy to bear, then it was on to the next sucker. She laid it out logically, matter-of-factly, like it was nothing but a puzzle that she had managed to put together. While we were walking, she asked me to hold her notebooks.

I said that if her theory was true, she might go to the police. I didn't think they would help, not really, but you can never be sure.

"No," she said. "I just want to go see this crook. I want him to see my fucking face."

We found the address on North Fifteenth. It was one of the old factory buildings made of brick and asbestos, a half block from the water, between Franklin and Wythe. Somebody was coming out the front door, and I caught it before it could close. There were three floors, with two lofts on either side. We knocked on all six doors, but nobody answered. It was a Thursday night around nine, maybe later. We'd been working hard all day and I had lost track of time. The sun had set. The building was a run-down place for roommates who found one another on Craigslist and on the corkboards they still sometimes posted in coffee shops. I thought I had been to a party there once, in one of those lofts, a sweaty cave where they were playing electronic music and projecting black-and-white movies onto the brick walls and you couldn't find a bathroom anywhere. It might have been some other building, I wasn't sure. There were a hundred others just like it in the area. Pretty soon, they would be gone. The rezoning assured all that. If you came back in a year, you wouldn't recognize the area, or you would but the only thing you'd have to talk about would be memories, places where you had gone to dance or to buy weed.

"We can come back," I said. "Somebody will be around later."

"I need a drink," she said. "This was a bad idea. I don't mean to spoil a beautiful night."

She must have been kidding about the night. It was low tide on the East River and there was no escaping from the smell. It was getting late. More people were out on the street. The neighborhood was coming alive. There were a lot of bars around and people standing outside of them smoking and drinking and watching to see where the crowds were headed, toward the trains on Bedford or the clubs that opened in warehouses along the waterfront but never advertised and didn't have any signs, or somewhere else. Everybody seemed so young. It occurred to me that probably I had attended my last warehouse party, that while I lived a mile away, if I ever walked down Berry Street at that hour again I would be just another old man out meandering in the dark.

We went into a bar on the corner of North Eleventh. The windows were closed and there wasn't any air-conditioning, none that I could feel, just a few fans turning slowly overhead and a clientele that didn't care about the heat or was ordering drinks with lots of ice. There was a jukebox somewhere and it was playing the same three Talking Heads songs on a loop. We talked some more about identity theft, which Anna had been researching pretty extensively from the sounds of it, possibly for her novel. I couldn't tell from the way she was describing it—everything blurred together and it wasn't obvious where her worries ended and the novel began. She seemed to know a lot about it, anyway. How card numbers were lifted and then collected in tranches and sold online. How to handle a trace. What you needed to change your name legally without publishing it in the newspaper, an old-fashioned requirement that was still in effect most places but could be avoided if you were clever about it. She kept wiping her forehead with cocktail napkins and leaving them on the bar. It was an old place, or had been decorated to look old. There was a lot of nautical gear hanging on the walls and the bar was made out of teak. She got up from her stool and walked over to the window that faced the street and stood there watching people go by. Finally, I joined her.

"It could be anyone," she said. "Nothing's easier to steal than an identity."

"I ran credit checks," I said.

She nodded. "When last? In June? For a skilled thief, that's a lifetime ago."

Sometime later, a large group passed by the bar. It looked more like a herd than a group. There was something animal about them. You got used to seeing things like that on the streets in New York. Sometimes there was no explanation for it, none that you could decipher, and other times it was because of train delays. It happened all over the city but especially at Bedford Avenue during the summer. There were always delays in the tunnel under the East River. The L would sit down there for twenty minutes or longer sometimes, and when it finally pulled into the station it seemed like everyone who was left in the city was on that train and they wanted to get aboveground. You would have to sharpen your elbows and hope for the best, going up the stairs.

"Christ," Anna said. "Look at them."

The group was headed west, toward the river. She kept watching through the window and something changed as she did. She put her drink down and dug through her pockets for something, money it seemed like. She didn't have any and that caused a momentary panic, like she was trapped, and I told her I had it, it was fine, then searched my pockets for a ten. Everything in the bar cost four dollars. It was a special, a happy hour that ran in summer. She said something else, but I didn't hear what. She was out the door, and I had to hurry to catch her.

Outside, my eyes were still adjusting to the dark. The bar had been dark, too, but it was different outside and the street-lights were dim and plenty of them weren't working at all. Anna slowed down, though she still had a purpose about her, or a destination in mind, and I asked if we were going somewhere, back to Fifteenth Street maybe. Before I was done with the question, we had turned in the opposite direction, heading south. There were still a lot of bodies up ahead of us, that pack from the subway, but not so many as before and as the blocks went by, one by one, more of them curled off and there were just a few desolate shadows left, anonymous like all the other shadows in the city except that I got the feeling we were following one of them. The idea came to me gradually and then with a great certainty. There was a man up there. He had been ahead of us, at exactly the same distance, ever since we walked out of the bar.

"Who is that?" I asked. "Do you recognize him?"

She didn't answer. We kept walking. A traffic signal

changed and we nearly caught up to the man, who was waiting for the light to change though there were no cars around
and everyone else had crossed without needing to be told that
it was all right to try. I got my first decent look at him then.
He was wearing jeans with the cuffs rolled and a dark T-shirt
with a messenger bag slung across his back. The bag looked
heavy and he was listing slightly to the side where its weight
hung down. Finally, the light changed and he started moving
again. I didn't know what an identity thief looked like. It was
like Anna had said before, it could have been anyone. It was
that kind of crime. Still, I felt sure that she knew the man,
that we were stalking him in a very particular way, and that
it was only a matter of time until she decided to do something, to confront him.

We went like that for another five blocks. She was wearing sneakers and moving silently and her eyes never left the
figure ahead of us. On North Fifth we turned again and were
on Wythe. The diner was on our left and Metropolitan up
ahead. On the right was Zebulon, where they brought in big
brass orchestras every other Saturday night and Ulises once
danced with a woman he swore had been married to Fela
Kuti. Beyond all that were the bridge's pillars.

I had never followed anyone before, not like that. It wasn't
an unpleasant feeling, walking through the city that way,
through a neighborhood I knew but was seeing now in a new
context, through the eyes of this stranger who had a destination in mind, somewhere he was going to, and therefore so
did we, only we didn't know where it was.

Finally, he stopped at a lit storefront. It took me a moment to see that it was a coffee shop, a place I knew. It stayed open late and refilled your cup for free and they would sell you beer in a can if you wanted it. There were two long wooden tables inside and once he had his coffee fixed the way he liked it, he settled into an empty seat and took out a hulking laptop. He stared at the screen before starting to type. He typed slowly, with the hunt-and-peck method. That was the first good look I got at his face. There was a guilelessness about him, even then—an openness to the world.

It was Newton Reddick. Alive. Typing with his own two fingers.

A breeze came off the East River. It was like holding smelling salts under your nose.

"Jesus," Anna said. She was watching him through the glass, fogging it slightly with her breath. Her voice came out after the breath, low and coarse. "I'll fucking kill him."

It sounded like she meant it. I didn't know how to respond. He had been dead all those months. It takes your mind a second to catch up with the truth sometimes, and in the moment, that first moment, all I could think was that he looked okay. Younger than the last time I'd seen him, several years younger or maybe a decade, although it was probably just the jeans and the T-shirt creating that illusion. The laptop in front of him cast a glow across his face. A strange but not unflattering light.

Anna went inside. I followed behind her before the door could close. Reddick didn't seem to notice us at first. He was focused on that screen. He looked comfortable and happy, like he was settling into his night and the hours ahead held a number of surprises and small pleasures.

"What the fuck is going on?" Anna asked.

He glanced up, startled. "Anna," he said. "Anna, it's you."

I thought his heart might stop, but he summoned the nerve from somewhere.

"It's very good to see you," he said. "Would you like something? Something to drink?"

I give him credit for courtesy. It was a kind of reflex and it told you something about him. He was scared, ambushed, and of all the ways he might have tried to buy himself some time, to think or react or bolt out the door, he had chosen to offer her something, a drink. He had a pureness, a delicacy about him that couldn't be suppressed, even in times of confrontation and crisis.

"Newton," she said, "you're supposed to be dead. What the hell is this?"

He didn't answer, but nodded gravely, like he understood the confusion.

"Yes," he said. "I'm so sorry. I wanted to tell you. I was waiting, you see."

"I don't, no. Have you lost your fucking mind?"

"Not at all, Anna. Not at all. I owe you an explanation, of course."

He folded his laptop and stood from his chair. His coffee was steaming. He hadn't been able to take a sip, it was too hot, and when he stood up, some spilled over the rim onto the table. Before he could speak, Anna told him to go to hell. She

said it decisively, evenly, like it was a place he had asked for
directions to and she knew just how to send him there. For
his part, Reddick seemed momentarily frozen, unsure whether
to stay and clean the coffee he had spilled or to follow her out
the door. I told him I would take care of the mess. While I
was mopping up the coffee, a woman sitting at the other end
of the table asked me if that was A. M. Byrne, the novelist.

"No," I said, "but she gets that all the time. That's Anna
Reddick."

The woman nodded understandingly and went back to her
work. She had a notebook in front of her and was writing
something there with a fountain pen. Poetry, I thought. She
had a little inkstand next to her coffee and every so often
would dip the pen into it.

I sat down in the chair where Reddick had been and
eventually took a sip from his coffee. I would have guessed
he drank it black, but it was loaded with milk and sugar,
sweet enough that it stung your gums going down, or it did
mine. I wanted to give them some time alone. They were
standing outside the shop, close together, talking sometimes,
then one or both of them would be still. Neither one looked
all that upset. I didn't think anyone was going to be killed,
although that's never an easy thing to be sure of from a distance and through a window.

After a time, Anna knocked on the windowpane, loudly,
three sharp raps. She waved at me to come out.

I packed up Reddick's things—his laptop and messenger
bag—and brought them outside with me.

"Newton's writing a book," Anna said.

I've heard voices more derisive, more poisonous, but not too many. We were on the sidewalk, standing on cigarette butts. There were about a hundred of them on the ground out there. What had passed between them in those moments alone, I couldn't have guessed. It wasn't my business to guess—it never had been though I had tried. Every marriage is opaque, even to the people inside it, and from the outside you haven't got a chance. Anyway, I wasn't sure if they were married still. Maybe the death certificate put an end to that, whether it was true or not. I hardly knew anything about marital law, not in New York or any other place.

"What are you writing?" I asked him.

He was staring down at the cigarette butts on the sidewalk, or at his sneakers, a pair of blue canvas Chucks. It was the uniform in that neighborhood around that time. Even the pigeons wore them. He didn't dare speak. I wouldn't have, either, not with a wife looking at me that way. He reached out and took the bag—his bag—from my shoulder.

"It's a novel," Anna said. "Says he's always wanted to write one. Spent his whole life buying and selling other people's books and wanted to find out if he could write one for himself but didn't know how to do it with me around. Couldn't imagine how he would even begin, is that right? Newton, correct me where I'm off. You wanted to write, and this seemed the best, most reasonable way to do it, yes? You thought maybe you'd even win me back once I read the thing."

He was listening to her carefully. His breathing had slowed.

"I don't know," he said. "I just wanted to try it."

"I've heard of people doing that without faking their deaths," she said.

"Yes, I know."

"But that didn't seem practical to you?"

"We were going to be divorced."

"Yes, that's right. Better to avoid that messiness, I suppose."

"I just mean, it was impossible. You were going to go through with it. You were."

"I don't know, Newton. I don't know what to tell you. Well fucking done."

We stood quietly and then, across the street, a woman in the second story of a row house opened her window and dropped a bag. It landed in a garbage can and she stayed there a moment, leaning on the windowsill looking pleased with herself, then waved to us and went back inside. Anna watched her do it with what appeared to me a deep and sincere admiration.

"That's the way to handle things," she said, to no one in particular.

I introduced myself to Reddick then. I hadn't done it before, though maybe she had told him what I was doing there or possibly he remembered my face. In any case, he didn't seem too surprised. We shook hands and he said he was pleased to see me, some kind of noncommittal phrase like that. His grip was unsteady and his knuckles were swollen. I told myself it was from the typing he had done those last several months, but it might have only been the effects of age.

25.

New York is a good place to hide—it always has been. The judge I clerked for at the Southern District, before she was a judge, had been the lead prosecutor on the Five Families case, the one that finally cracked the New York Mafia in the eighties. She told me once about the informants they used, foot soldiers who were turning on their families, a thing you supposedly didn't do and which meant you were marked for life, destined for a date with the garrote. But the prosecution never lost an informant during that time. It went on for years and they didn't even bother with witness protection, they just moved the guys from one borough to another. Turned out, it was all a myth, the Mafia's legendary ability to track you anywhere like a bloodhound from hell. They couldn't even find you in Astoria. The task force rented a few apartments in different sections of the city and every few months they would shuffle people between them. I was thinking about that, seeing Newton Reddick. He'd been in Brooklyn, in Williamsburg, all that time in a third-floor loft on North Fifteenth. He shared the place with four people—three

Germans and a Canadian, all of them flight attendants. He went to a coffee shop every night to work on his novel, the one he'd been wanting to write for such a long time but hadn't been able to for some ineffable reason, though he had time and money and a wife whose agent probably would have done her the favor of shopping it around. He liked his new life. He liked writing in a coffee shop. A dollar a cup and he never had to feel bad about asking for more. He was going by the name Richard Carstone. It was the same name he had used to sign in at the hotel, the one where he had supposedly died. A seasoned investigator would have thought to follow that lead. Anyway, he had his routine, and it gave him a clean, reliable satisfaction. That's how he described it. A thousand words, then he would go out walking from the Williamsburg Bridge to Greenpoint and back. You could never tell what you were going to see, especially as it got late. He had never known that about himself, that he liked to stay up and outside all hours of the night. You could hear from the way he talked that he had discovered a lot about himself in those last months. That was why you moved to Brooklyn, I figured. He had only been late trying it out.

We were walking around the neighborhood by then, the three of us, talking. It was after midnight. I wanted to leave them but Anna said I should stay, that I needed to, she didn't want to do anything she'd regret later and if she did, she wanted her lawyer around to help. It seemed to me they were both handling the situation with a strange kind of restraint that bordered on the absurd. I kept a few steps behind. When I drifted too far behind, she would turn and ask why I was lagging. I could hear them pretty clearly. They weren't whispering—it wasn't one of those discussions. She asked him a lot of questions about the death, how he faked it, and the paperwork. Her questions were specific and if she had been holding a pen she might have taken notes. He described things with as much detail as possible. Neither one brought up the subject of why. Maybe they had spoken about it earlier, or it was obvious to practically anyone and wasn't something they felt the need to address. Reddick seemed to have a lot of affection for his new neighborhood. He kept pointing out things to her like he had discovered them, the lights of the bridge, the old ferry landing at the end of Grand, a bar he liked on Kent. Somewhere on the waterfront I asked him what it had to do with the development, the rezoning.

He turned on his heels and looked at me seriously. His eyes glistened with concern. I thought about that first night at the Poquelin, how he came over to offer me help. I felt I knew the man, though we had only met that one night, for an hour or so. We were practically strangers.

"What do you mean?" he asked.

"Liam Moore," I said. "The counterfeits, the rezoning, the buildings they're putting up here. They're tearing out the docks and the warehouses and putting up three high-rises with city views. That's just the start. The whole neighborhood will be a condominium lot soon, in a year or two."

"I didn't realize that," he said.

"Moore helped get the permits. He bribed a planning commissioner with some rare books."

His stare turned from bemusement to professional interest. "What kind of books?"

I tried hard to remember what they were, what I'd been told. "Vintage erotica."

He shook his head. "Not mine. He must have gotten them somewhere else."

That made sense just then. It was a city full of books. The possibilities were too vast.

We were walking by one of the construction sites. It had already been walled off and there were a lot of signs on the green plywood fences warning you to be careful and telling you not to post anything there, that there would be fines, and also you should call a number to report violations, though it didn't say what kind of violations, whether they were talking about the no-billings-posted rule or something on the work site. I remembered that a few months ago, it felt like years, Ulises was working on a project for a real estate developer. He was writing poems and they were going to be printed on the sides of construction site fences and on street corners. It sounded pretty ridiculous to me just then, but no more ridiculous than vintage erotica or a coffee shop that refilled your cup all day and night without charging you again or asking you to buy something to eat. The whole place seemed a little crazy to me, but I didn't really mind: it wasn't any of my business. I was a lawyer still. We were meant to be discreet beyond all reason.

"Try to keep up," Anna said. "We're almost there."

I couldn't tell whether she was talking to Newton or to

me, or if I'd misheard her. How many months had she spent looking for him, wondering what had happened? Now she had him. Around us was empty air and dug-out earth but you could almost feel the buildings underfoot, ready to break through the surface like stalks looking for sun, like you could leave them alone with a little water and they would grow on their own, rise up thirty-two stories, and hire a realtor.

She steered us toward the water. We were trespassing, probably, but it didn't matter. There was a narrow corridor between two construction fences. It went all the way down to the shoreline, where the tide was starting to come in and there was some garbage washing up against the rubble of what looked like an old seawall. Out in the distance were the city lights. They skimmed along the surface, and you felt pretty small, comical, standing there at the water's edge.

"A bit farther," Anna said. "I've never been down here on the Brooklyn side. Newton, have you? What am I saying, this is your home now. You've been everywhere, I'm sure. All those walks. That's the key to a good novel, isn't it? Lots of fresh air and a few good walks. Your thoughts circulate the same as blood. Christ, we've got a lot of shop to talk, haven't we?"

Newton seemed to be taking her questions in earnest.

"I don't think I've been here," he said.

"That's good. A raw experience. Something we can share, that's sweet, isn't it?"

There was a jetty out into the river. It wasn't a jetty, exactly, but a string of rocks, slick and exposed by the tide, that led to the skeleton of a dock that looked charred, burned almost to ash, though it was probably the corroding effect of the salt in the East River, and of who knows what else. It was sturdy enough to walk on, though they couldn't have known that. Anna went first and Newton followed her, looking unsure. I kept to the shore. Standing out over the water they didn't seem like such an unlikely pair. It was dark and he was wearing those jeans and his canvas messenger bag. She offered her hand to help him from the rocks onto the dock frame. They stood there with the city in front of them, looming monstrous and lovely, and then, after she had leaned in to say something to him, something I couldn't hear, he took the laptop out of his bag. It must have weighed ten or fifteen pounds. His thin little arms poking out of the T-shirt sleeves could barely hold it up, or anyway that's how it looked to me from the shore.

Using both hands and planting his feet first for the leverage, he threw the laptop into the water. Anna didn't react. He didn't look at her to see whether she would. He was staring at where the computer broke through the surface. There was hardly a splash. There were all sorts of tidal pools and eddies there and they could have swallowed just about anything whole. It seemed to me Reddick's knees buckled momentarily, or maybe I was imagining that, making the moment more dramatic than it was because I was sure that whatever he had on there, whatever he had spent those months writing, it wasn't backed up anywhere. He was an old man and they never thought about that kind of thing. It was gone now, drowning in the East River and irrecoverable.

Anna turned and called back and asked me to come out onto the dock.

"Bring those notebooks," she said.

I was still carrying her notebooks around. Her pens were in my back pocket.

"Why?" I asked.

"Just come out here, for Christ's sake. Come on, are you scared of a little water?"

"Why do you want the notebooks?"

"I'll tell you when you get here. Come on, you won't believe the breeze. Newton, tell him."

Reddick said something, only I couldn't make out what. It was addressed to her, a secret.

"That's right," she said, smiling. "That's absolutely fucking right, isn't it?"

She looked so happy just then. Like he had told her a joke, or she had told one and it was something that had been bouncing back and forth between them for years, something terrible and private. I didn't know what was going on between them, exactly, but that was when I decided to leave. If either of them called out after me, the wind and the sound of the river swallowed it up.

26.

It was around five in the morning, maybe later, and I was at Kellogg's Diner on Metropolitan Avenue, telling Ulises about what had happened. I must have called and asked him to meet me there. I didn't remember calling him but the chances that he would have been passing by the diner at that hour were pretty small. He didn't even live in the neighborhood, though he spent a lot of time there and was usually heading somewhere or other by train, either the G or the L. People were always complaining about the G in those days, but it seemed to work fine for Ulises.

We were sitting in a booth and looking out the window onto Metropolitan and Union. There were five or six trucks out there idling in the dawn, waiting for something, maybe gas or supplies before they got on the highway, and the neon diner sign was reflecting pink and blue off their side panels and in the puddles that filled the potholes along Metropolitan. There were always puddles on that stretch of road, though it hadn't rained in some time. There had only been the damp heat that wouldn't let up. Ulises listened carefully as I told him everything I could remember about the night, from the moment we locked up the warehouse until the moment I left Anna and Newton on the dock, whispering and throwing things into the East River. I still had her notebooks with me. Her pens too.

"Did you read them?" Ulises asked. "I'd be curious what she's writing lately."

"No," I said. "That would be unethical, or something."

"But you took them."

"To preserve them. I'll send them to her by messenger."

"She must not have been too happy about you walking away with her property."

"Probably not. Maybe later on she'll be glad."

"You really think she was going to throw the notebooks in? Destroy all that work?"

It was a fair question.

"I don't know," I said. "I asked her what she wanted them for, but she wouldn't tell me."

Ulises nodded in that solemn, almost ridiculous way he had that told you he was concentrating very hard but not on what you were saying, or else he was hearing you fine but the thing that had his concentration was beyond all under-standing, even his own. He used that nod several times as I went over the details again and tried explaining to him what had happened and why and where Newton Reddick had been all that time and what he claimed to be doing. He had wanted to write a book of his own. It sounded simple, when you said it like that.

When the waitress came around with the check for the

coffees we were drinking, Ulises said we had better order some food. We would think more clearly with a hot breakfast in our stomachs. I ordered French toast and he asked for something called the complete package, which was more or less everything on the menu. He could eat, when you got right down to it. The waitress seemed to like him and brought around two extra plates of crispy bacon.

"Maybe she was going to push him in," Ulises said. "She wanted you to come stand next to her, the only witness, and you're covered by privilege. The perfect murder, that sort of thing. He's already dead, so it would be double jeopardy, wouldn't it, assuming he can't swim and didn't hit his head on the way down? Or maybe he would do the right thing and let himself sink. I read somewhere you can't drown as a matter of pure will, but what do they know about it?"

"Maybe," I said, then tried explaining to him what double jeopardy was, how it worked, why so many people seem to misunderstand the concept. He didn't really care, his mind was racing ahead and he was infatuated with the phrase, not the accuracy of it. That was the trouble talking with him at that hour, five in the morning, at a diner with a neon sign. He'd get caught up with details, or with the sound of a phrase that meant nothing, or that meant something entirely different. I kept thinking about Anna and how it had been having her around those last few weeks. I didn't think I had ever met someone who could sit quietly for such long stretches, hours on end. Probably I never would, and in the future I'd remember her as more restless than she really was.

"Hey, I've got a car," Ulises said, and pointed out the

window at a Chrysler LeBaron, a convertible painted some
kind of earth tone between clay and mud. The top was down
and it was double-parked next to a cop car. There were always
cop cars on Union Avenue. I didn't even know Ulises had a
license. He knew the subway system and the bus lines and
the regional train networks better than anyone I had ever
met. One of his friends had lent him the LeBaron. "I've got
it all month," he said. "Needs to be back for Labor Day. I'm
taking it to the Cape."

"When does the workshop start?" I asked.

He was leaving for Provincetown soon, I figured. He
taught that poetry workshop at the Fine Arts Center every
year there and said they paid him good money to do it, although he couldn't explain why. Apparently there were people who wanted to go to Cape Cod to write and they wanted
Ulises there to guide them, to give them encouragement and
criticism and to have a drink with them in the evening after
all the writing and encouraging was done.

"Not for a few days," he said. "Shit, let's go somewhere.
You need to get out of New York. This case turned your
head around and you gotta go get it back on straight somewhere else, somewhere new. You need a different landscape
in front of you. You need new scents in the air."

"It wasn't New York that did it," I said.

He shrugged. "I'm not saying it was, I'm just saying you
should go somewhere."

We ordered more food and the waitress refilled our coffee
and called Ulises by his name. She said it the way diner waitresses say "darling" or "sugar" when they're talking to you,

only with Ulises it was his name, the one he'd given himself when he arrived in New York from Venezuela.

"I still think it had something to do with the buildings," he said. "Real estate is everything."

"Maybe," I said.

"Don't you think?"

I told him again about how Reddick had reacted to the suggestion. He was in the dark, the same as I was, or doing a convincing job of pretending to be a simple man with his head in a library. Sometimes a conspiracy is just another word for life carrying on without you noticing it. That's what I said, anyway, a thought that occurred to me in the moment. It made Ulises laugh.

"And you're just going to accept that?" he asked.

"No other option," I said. "You can't work the same case forever."

"That's true. You know, you're starting to sound like a poet."

"How's that?"

"You're embracing the ambiguity. It takes some people years to learn that."

I paid for the breakfasts and left an extra twenty on top of the tip to prove that I was still a professional, a lawyer with a bar card and all my student loans paid off, not some snake-bit poet. The waitress pocketed the cash and thanked Ulises for coming in and looked at me a little suspiciously, like it was the first time she was seeing me, like I was a ghost walking into her home. Her name was Anne-Lise. She had it sewn onto her uniform in letters that were like calligraphy.

Outside it was light and the trucks were gone and the cops

who had also been double-parked were nowhere to be found.
It was a bright morning and full of empty summer promise.
I looked west, toward the waterfront. There was a slope on
Metropolitan and you could see all the way to the shoreline.
I doubted Anna and Newton were down there still but they
might have been. Maybe like a pair of seagulls they were
going to wait around all morning for the sun to come and
warm them before they left their perch. I really didn't know,
it was their business now.

Ulises said he didn't have anywhere to be. He was thinking of going for a drive, getting out of the city for a night or
two. He knew some people upstate with a house. He knew
a woman in Rhode Island. There were people all over with
houses and it was summer, wasn't that a beautiful thing? The
LeBaron got lousy mileage and the gearshift sometimes got
stuck between second and third, he said, but there was twenty
dollars in the tank, maybe more. I got into the passenger seat.
It was made of artificial leather and was cracked at the seams.

"All right," I said, "let's go."

Ulises smiled. "Don't fuck with me. If I get on that highway I'm not turning around."

"Good, I won't ask you to."

"I'm serious. We're leaving the city. No bags, no maps, no
plan."

"Perfect."

"We're going right now, no looking back."

"Put it into gear already. You know how to drive, don't
you? That one's the clutch."

The car lurched as he found first gear. It was a beautiful machine, in its own ugly way.

"We need to give her a name," Ulises said. "If we're gonna drive her, she needs a name."

"What do you want to call her?"

"You're the poet, you tell me."

"The hell I am," I said. Then I thought about it for a while. "What about Desdemona?"

"Christ," Ulises said. "That's an awful name for a car."

There were people behind us, honking. We were on the entry ramp going about ten miles an hour. It had been months, maybe years since I'd ridden that way in a car. Not a taxi, just a car. I found the radio and turned it on. Héctor Lavoe and the Fania All-Stars were playing "Mi Gente." The speakers were just about dead and Héctor Lavoe's voice was like a knife, cutting them open.

"Holy shit," Ulises said. "That's the way to leave the city. Turn that up."

He started drumming along on the steering wheel and we picked up speed.

"Que canta, mi gente, que canta, mi gente, que canta, mi gente."

"You know," he said, "I've got a case coming your way. A friend who needs help."

"What kind of help?"

"Visa stamps, passports, that kind of thing. He's a trumpeter from Montreal."

"No divorces, please."

"Nothing like that. He's touring all fall on fake papers, back in December."

"Great, I've got nothing going on until then."

"That's the way to live, chamo. Work them as they come."

We took the BQE through Queens and got on the Triborough Bridge over Randall's Island. The city was in the rearview mirror and it looked pretty small from up there. We talked about where we should go. The first decision, Ulises said, was whether to head inland or keep to the coast. Inland, we would reach the hills eventually and the old resort towns and maybe the air would be thin and cooler there, but along the coast were the beaches and the ocean. He kept talking about how, on the coast, a person could always make a living digging for clams if literature fell through. He could sell what he wanted, eat the rest, and make a clean, honest living all year round, unless there were problems with algae or market prices. I couldn't imagine Ulises in gaiters come winter. I didn't think he'd dug a clam in his whole life, but it didn't matter, it was nice listening to him carry on with that poet's nonsense.

I closed my eyes and in the wind was a trace of salt.

ACKNOWLEDGMENTS

Thanks to:

Jack, Kathy, and Franny Murphy, and the home full of books we share.

Duvall Osteen and the team at Aragi Inc.

Ibrahim Ahmad, Marissa Davis, Bennett Petrone, Alex Cruz-Jimenez, and everyone at Viking who worked on this book.

Leonardo and Gisela Henriquez. Adriana and Ignacio Pardo.

Jonathan Lee, Riad Houry, Dan Sheehan, and Téa Obreht.

Everyone who shared those odd, gone years in New York.

The Center for Fiction for their generosity and support. The Bibliothèque Mazarine, the New-York Historical Society, the Arthur W. Diamond Law Library, Sotheby's, the Blue Stove, the Grey Dog, and other institutions offering opportunities for research, writing, and sustenance.

Debevoise & Plimpton, good sports and above reproach. Shannon Rebholz, Anne-Lise Quach, Elliot Greenfield, Louis Begley, Hon. Barbara S. Jones, and other rabbis along the way.

And most of all, to Carolina Henriquez-Schmitz, my beating heart.